Maybe Now, Maybe Never

Endorsements

Told from alternating points of view of Rachel, Marla, and Suzanne, respectively, the novel effectively offers a look at the tribulations of adults in late middle age ... The honesty and openness with which the author examines familiar experiences has a grace of its own. Watching three very different women find common ground as they pursue second acts for themselves is poignant and compelling. [Posti] presents characters with grit and fortitude.
—*Kirkus Reviews*

Chris Posti does a masterful job of pulling together three high school friends reunited at their forty-year reunion. She develops the three varied personalities and stories laced with healing, introspection, forgiveness, faith, and romance in a common struggle to save their hometown. Developing one character and one storyline is hard enough for a writer, but Chris has done this with three, has done it well—and with some mystery.
—Donna K. Stearns, Biblical fiction author, *The Nazarene's Price*

Life may not be all sunshine and roses, but you'll have a great time following these three awesome women who are determined to handle their unique life situations with wit, compassion, and faith. *Maybe Now, Maybe Never* is a realistic, fun, and faith-friendly story for women of all ages.
—K.L. Gilchrist, Author of contemporary stories for women of faith

Chris Posti has the ability to weave a delightful story of well-developed characters who come together as they deal

with their love for one another and their personal struggles. Highly recommended.
—**Claire O'Sullivan**, author, *Romance Under Wraps, Silk & Slippers, Rules of Engagement*

Different women, different experiences, and different secrets. But their similarities and connections are undeniable. If you look closely, you may even recognize your own friendships on these pages. Chris Posti's *Maybe Now, Maybe Never* is a real page-turner!
—**Robin Luftig**, Author, Ladies of the Fire series

In a small town you'd love to visit, follow three friends as they band together to challenge each other and themselves while finding the joy in life. Chris Posti, in *Maybe Now, Maybe Never* takes us on a journey with wit and tenderness that gets to the heart of friendship.
—**Kristine Delano**, Author and Podcaster

A mix of the wonderfulness found in lasting friendships, the strength found in small towns during times of challenge and crisis, and finding renewed purpose as one drifts from middle age to the senior years. Three women in their late fifties are reunited when one of them marries and the stage is set for challenge, mystery, and romance. Chris Posti takes readers on a fun ride as they get to know these three complex gals.
—**Linda Wood Rondeau**, Author/Speaker, *The Ghosts of Trumball Mansion*

Chris Posti's *Maybe Now, Maybe Never* will keep you turning pages and wondering what could possibly happen to three friends who have been reunited again in their hometown after years of separation. Better than a daytime drama, this well-written story will provide the discovery of

old love, new love, and surprises that will keep you crying and laughing as life for these almost golden aged ladies gets complicated. A little mystery, some family issues, and a cast of intriguing side characters make this a delightful story.
—**Bettie Boswell**, Author of Christian Romance and Children's Books

Maybe Now, Maybe Never

CHRIS POSTI

A Christian Company
ElkLakePublishingInc.com

Copyright Notice

Maybe Now, Maybe Never: Real Life and Romance for the 50+ Woman (Next Act Book 2)
First edition. Copyright © 2024 by Chris Posti. The information contained in this book is the intellectual property of Chris Posti and is governed by United States and International copyright laws. All rights reserved. No part of this publication, either text or image, may be used for any purpose other than personal use. Therefore, reproduction, modification, storage in a retrieval system, or retransmission, in any form or by any means, electronic, mechanical, or otherwise, for reasons other than personal use, except for brief quotations for reviews or articles and promotions, is strictly prohibited without prior written permission by the publisher.

This is a work of fiction. Names, characters, businesses, places, events, locales, and incidents are either the products of the author's imagination or used in a fictitious manner. Any resemblance to actual persons, living or dead, or actual events is purely coincidental.

Cover and Interior Design: Derinda Babcock, Deb Haggerty
Editor(s): Cristel Phelps, Deb Haggerty

PUBLISHED BY: Elk Lake Publishing, Inc., 35 Dogwood Drive, Plymouth, MA 02360, 2024

Library Cataloging Data

Names: Posti, Chris (Chris Posti)
Maybe Now, Maybe Never: Real Life and Romance for the 50+ Woman (Next Act Book 2) / Chris Posti

316p. 23cm × 15cm (9in × 6 in.)
ISBN-13: 9798891341296 (paperback) | 9798891341302 (trade paperback) | 9798891341319 (e-book)
Key Words: romance novels for older women; second chance books; small town romance books; divorce fiction books for women; Christian contemporary romance; novels for women over 50; later in life romance

Library of Congress Control Number: 2024xxxxxx Fiction

Dedication

To my daughter Elizabeth—
You are beautiful inside and out.
I love you.

Acknowledgments

Writing a novel is arduous, rewarding, surprisingly fun—*and* it's a team effort.

I owe a gigantic debt of gratitude to my ACFW "Little Loop" group—Jamie Ogle, Kristine Delano, and Diane Samson. These women are treasures. They shared their talent and knowledge freely. May it return to them, multiplied.

WFWA critique partners Kelly Hitchcock and Eileen Donovan also jumped in with their bi-weekly critiques—such an enormous help during the final editing. A big shout-out to you!

I am so grateful for publisher Deb Haggerty of Elk Lake Publishing and her team of professionals, including graphic designer Derinda Babcock and editor Cristel Phelps.

Many others have supported me throughout this process, including my husband, Dave, and my daughter, Elizabeth, along with her family.

My love and appreciation to each of you!

Most of all, I thank my heavenly Father for blessing me with the ideas and the words in this novel. Apart from him, I can do nothing.

Chapter 1

RACHEL

SATURDAY

Mercy me. Rachel Baran gawked at herself in the ladies' room mirror, shaking her fake shoulder-length hair. Even in the church's bright fluorescent lighting, you couldn't tell it was a wig.

All the way from Port Mariette to Pittsburgh, her neighbor Frank hadn't said a thing about it. Now, could she fool her old high school friends too? Suzanne would be too engrossed in marrying Rob to notice—but what about Marla? She never missed so much as a crooked eyelash. As if Rachel wasn't already emotional enough. She sure didn't need anyone asking about her hair.

She exited the ladies' room and tapped across the tiled foyer in high-heeled sandals. As soon as she entered the sunlit sanctuary, she let out a deep sigh that threatened to convert into a sob.

How the heck could she enjoy Suzanne's wedding when today would have been her and Stan's fortieth anniversary? If he were still alive, this wedding would be a joyous occasion. Instead, every grin she gave would be as phony as her hair.

Way down the center aisle, Frank rose from a pew and moved onto the thin white runner. A smile spread across his clean-shaven face as his gaze trailed over her whole body.

Over the past year, her also-widowed, next-door neighbor Frank had wormed his way into her life. She'd agreed to be his companion—a silly term in her estimation, but she refused to call a grown man her boyfriend. Besides, at this stage of life, no way did she want another husband. No, sirree. Stan had been it. Anyway, when Frank wasn't complaining about his health, he made for pleasant company.

Rachel stopped a few feet in front of him. "What'cha lookin' at, Frank?" With no one else there yet, no need to use her church voice.

"You look pretty enough to be the bride today."

"Aw, thank you." She fake-smiled wide enough to show her teeth, whitened just yesterday. Marla claimed whitening them took ten years off a woman. Rachel wasn't so sure, but at fifty-eight, she'd given it a go. Besides, whiter teeth might distract eyes from her hair.

The wooden pew quivered as Frank plopped beside her and kicked his wet umbrella under the pew in front of them. For the first two weeks of June, the rain had been relentless in southwestern Pennsylvania, and this morning's skyful of dark clouds signaled no end in sight.

"I guess we didn't have to arrive quite this early," Rachel said.

Frank tugged at his tie. "Nothing wrong with arriving an hour early for a wedding. We might've run into traffic or had a hard time finding our way in the rain."

"At least we're not late." The new highway had opened last year, shortening the drive from Port Mariette to Pittsburgh to a mere half-hour. New highway or not, she still felt far removed from Pittsburgh and the rest of the world.

Fine by her.

But she felt distanced from Suzanne and Marla too. And that was not so fine. Back in high school, the three of them were so inseparable their classmates collectively called them *RÉSUMÉ*—short for Rachel, Suzanne, and Marla. Phonetically, the nickname worked, and Rachel treasured the bond it represented.

When last year's high school reunion brought the three of them together for the first time in forty years, they quickly became close again. No one was more surprised by this than Rachel, whose life had turned out nothing like Suzanne's or Marla's.

Suzanne had just lost her airline trainer job, and while staying in Port Mariette for the reunion, she teamed up with her sister to launch a charming art consignment shop on Main Street.

Marla took the opportunity to locate the daughter she'd given up for adoption forty years ago. Grace, it turned out, also happened to be the adopted daughter of Rachel's sister. Quite the surprise, but everyone eventually recovered.

It seemed both her friends might stick around Port Mariette for a while, but soon after the reunion, Suzanne moved from Pittsburgh to California, and Marla flew home to Manhattan. Although they came back to town once in a while, some of the magic had been lost.

For Rachel, though, that old saying still rang true—the more things changed, the more they stayed the same. She alone remained in Port Mariette, just as she had her entire life. Was there something wrong with her for disliking change?

More than a year after Stan's heart attack, she'd finally come to accept the adjustments his passing wrought. Her oldest son Pete had moved back home after a divorce, and together, they created Food 'n Fuel, a successful enhancement of the old gas station Stan had left behind. She'd never considered herself entrepreneurial like Marla, but she eked out a decent living in a Rust Belt town using nothing but her previously taken for granted cooking skills. Even Marla couldn't have done that.

Rachel had forced herself to socialize too. That's how she'd ended up on the St. Cyprian's Academy fortieth reunion committee and reconnected with her classmates. But at the reunion itself, the moment she felt some romantic sparks while dancing with her high school crush Tony Mastriano, she decided she had adapted enough. She picked up her purse and went home.

Now, though, her eyes roamed the spacious church. No kneelers, statues of saints, or candles to burn. Not a whiff of incense or a single pane of stained glass. "Well, Frank," she sighed, "I don't think we're in a Catholic church."

Frank cocked his head. "*Living Water Church*—that sure doesn't sound Catholic. Not Protestant either. What kind of church is this, anyway?"

"Nondenominational. Suzanne used to come here when she lived in her condo across the river."

"A little bare-bones, don't ya think?" Frank swiveled his head around. "I like St. Cyp's a whole lot better. Especially for a wedding." He looked Rachel straight in the eye, waiting for her response.

"Yeah, I'm used to St. Cyprian's too." She squinted. "But that cross dangling over the stage is pretty dramatic. I kinda like it. Maybe just for today, I could stretch out of my comfort zone."

"You? Stretch out of your comfort zone? Good luck with *that*." Frank gave her knee a comforting squeeze.

"Oh, my. I hope I remembered to bring some tissues." Rachel reached into her clutch. "I'm wearing mascara today." Her ploy of wearing extra makeup to distract people from the wig was clearly a tactical error.

"I'll bet Marla will wear lots of mascara," Frank deadpanned. "Maybe even false eyelashes."

Rachel could tell he was joking. "Probably. That woman never cries." Rachel shoved a few tissues in her dress's side pocket. "All set now."

Frank cleared his throat. "Forty-five minutes to go."

"Mm-hmm," she said. "What a shame Rob's son couldn't make it today. I wanted to meet him."

"Oh, I don't think he had any intention of coming to his dad's wedding. Pretty flimsy excuse, if you ask me."

"Kevin has an important job, Suzanne said. All the way in Seattle. He couldn't get away."

Frank waved a dismissive hand. "Aw, gimme a break. I was in Florida enjoying a visit with my son, but I flew back for this. Even put on my suit. And I'm not a member of the family."

The man had a point. Rachel wrapped her hand on his burly forearm. "I appreciate that you came back early."

"Only for you." Frank laid his tanned hand over hers and paused a moment before speaking. "I really missed you when I was away."

"I—I missed you too." She replied in a whisper and blinked a few times. Did I really? She considered her feelings for a moment, then decided she *had* missed him. But how much? And why?

They sat there silently, unmoving.

Then Frank inhaled loudly, as if he needed a double dose of oxygen. He pushed himself up from the pew and moved into the aisle. His eyes darted around the sanctuary.

"Restrooms are in the foyer." Rachel pointed behind them.

But Frank didn't budge. His full face turned a deep shade of pink.

"Frank! Are you okay?" Rachel stretched her arm toward him.

He grabbed the pew's armrest and, perspiring, drifted down on a knee.

"Are you dizzy? Is it chest pain?" *Oh God, don't let him die of a heart attack too!*

Frank's eyes had a pleading look as his mouth opened, but no words came out.

Rachel reached for her cell phone. "I'll call 9-1-1!"

"No, No!" He wiped his forehead with the back of his hand and released a breath. "Look, Rachel, let's not waste the rest of our lives. We're not getting any younger, and you know how I feel about you."

Her throat constricted and her eyes widened. *Don't say it, Frank! Please don't say it!* After Stan died, she'd worked so hard to perfectly reconstruct her life. She couldn't allow Frank to shake it up again—but short of slapping her hand over his mouth, what could she do?

"Rachel, will you—"

The church's rear door banged open, and she spun, relief flooding her at the interruption. "Marla's here!"

Rachel jerked Frank up to his feet. Their eyes met, and she felt a twinge of remorse at the sadness in his. The poor man had no idea that thoughts of her deceased husband had been running through her mind all morning. She touched Frank's arm with her fingertips.

"Oh, Frank." If only she had given him a heads-up about her anniversary date. It may not have changed her reaction, but it might have stopped him from asking.

"Marla's got lousy timing," he muttered, dusting off his pant leg.

Rachel spread her hand across her chest. *No—perfect timing.*

Chapter 2

MARLA

SATURDAY

"Our flight was delayed!" Marla called as she and Warren approached the front pews rolling aluminum carry-ons behind them. With each stride, a large sapphire pendant bounced on Marla's smooth skin. "We had the limo driver bring us straight from the airport." She came to a halt and so did her pendant.

"Glad you made it." Rachel reached out and gave her a long hug. "Frank and I can drive you and Warren wherever you're going after the reception. We came in my Chevy."

"Great." Marla almost said it sarcastically but caught herself in time. Until she picked up her BMW in Port Mariette, Rachel's old fabric-seated Chevy would have to do.

"Warren needs to catch a flight back to New York right after the reception," Marla said, her manicured nails skimming the sleeve of his bespoke suit. "I'll be staying with Grace at my spa."

Pride swelled in Marla, not only because she had managed to initiate a relationship with her daughter, but because they'd labored together to convert Aunt Adele's neglected mansion into a stunning day spa. Not with her own hands, of course. That's what contractors were for. A pity the spa was located in Port Mariette instead of Manhattan. If it were, she'd be swimming in more money than she already was.

Marla glided into the pew behind Rachel and Frank and tossed back her long, straight hair. It spilled down her back, silky as the half-slip the nuns of St. Cyprian's Academy used to mandate underneath the girls' pleated skirts.

She leaned forward and poked her head between Rachel and Frank. "I really wish they'd invited Grace. It's not like they didn't have the space." Marla waved a bejeweled hand. "This is practically a megachurch."

Warren unbuttoned his suit jacket. "How many times are we going to discuss this? Grace is not related to Suzanne or Rob. She's not even their friend. There's no logical reason for her to be invited to a small wedding like this."

"I didn't say it had to be a *logical* reason." Marla pouted her ruby-colored lips. "But after all, Grace *is* my daughter, at least by birth. Besides, I'd like to spend as much time with her as I can while I'm here. Don't you agree they should've invited Grace?" Marla looked forward at Rachel, staring wide-eyed at the snappy exchange.

Warren sighed. "Your logic is so convoluted it's enough to wear down a veteran lawyer like me. And believe me, I'm used to this kind of nitpicking nonsense."

"It's not *nitpicking nonsense*," Marla responded in a loud whisper. "Don't forget, Grace is related to Rachel too, and Suzanne has met Grace a few times this past year. So, it's not like she'd be some stranger showing up." Didn't anyone see her point?

Warren rested his forearm on the back of Rachel and Frank's pew. "You'll have to forgive us. We're both operating on about three hours of sleep."

"Oh." Rachel gave them a wan smile.

Marla scanned the side of Rachel's face. A little pale. Something's up with her. Is she sick? After a pause, Marla continued. "We were up late working out a few lingering legal issues." Last year, she'd made a killing selling her Gemstones Gyms. Then, her divorced parents had passed away, leaving her two large estates to sort through. As if that weren't enough, her aunt had moved into an assisted living facility and turned over her Port Mariette mansion and fifty acres of wooded land to Marla. Suddenly shockingly wealthy, she'd asked Warren to help her establish a foundation. It made for a great tax shelter, plus she got a kick out of funding projects in the backwater town of Port Mariette.

The clanging open of the church door interrupted Marla's thoughts. The mother of the bride, relying on a cane and her younger daughter's arm, moseyed forward. Suzanne's daughter Jill and her husband followed them, their baby nestled in Jill's arms. What a shame Grace never married. By now, Marla could have been a grandmother many times over.

A moment later, Rob's daughter entered, her hair twisted into a careless topknot. Marla whispered in Warren's ear, "She looks like she got about as much sleep as we did."

After a round of hugs and hellos, everyone took their seats and carried on with cheery small talk, Marla's specialty. She'd perfected it over the years while catering to her wealthy gym clientele.

Up front, a young woman in white walked to the keyboard and readied her fingers to play. At the first note, the guests fell silent. A few bars later, Suzanne's tiny granddaughter let out an oversize wail.

Marla stared, her heart aching.

Jill rocked the baby back to sleep, and the melody continued.

Rob appeared from the side of the stage, looking trim and fit in a navy suit and an impossibly white shirt that provided a striking contrast for his tanned face. Alongside him came a short and stocky man sporting a bushy beard and tattoos across his thick hands. The pastor's grin was nearly as wide as Rob's.

After the reunion at St. Cyp's last year had stirred her spirit, Marla, and sometimes Warren, had gone church shopping in Manhattan. After making the rounds at several denominations, they almost committed to one of them, but the press of daily living squeezed that right off their calendars. She'd been surprised to meet such an assortment of preachers, none of whom resembled the stolid priests of St. Cyp's. But she'd gotten used to seeing variety, so neither the beard nor the tattoos on today's preacher fazed her.

The soft music segued into the traditional *Wedding March*. In an instant, everyone's eyes were trained on the back of the church, where both doors had been propped open, revealing a striking bride stretching all five-foot-three-inches of herself into a perfect pose.

As the guests rose from their seats, Marla squeezed Warren's firm arm. "Wow, look at her!"

With every hair of her updo in place, and looking far younger than fifty-eight, Suzanne floated down the aisle in a lacy, formfitting, ivory dress. She smiled and made eye contact as she passed by each awestruck, camera-clicking guest.

That woman sure could command an audience. Not as well as Marla could, but still.

Suzanne reached the end of the bridal runway and settled beside Rob. For a few seconds, neither of them moved as they gazed into one another's eyes.

Rob reached for her hand and caressed it, then brushed it with a tender kiss.

Marla's breath caught. So much love emanating from them, she could almost taste it. She sneaked a sideways glance at Warren. He was stifling a yawn.

Not entirely unexpected, but even so, a bit annoying. Sure, Warren's love notes were sweet, but what woman could live on them alone? There had been a time his power and wealth appealed to her, but that was before she surpassed him on both fronts. For now, at least, their shared history, together with his strong physique and legal wizardry, kept their relationship going.

An excessively long *aww* emanating from Rachel distracted Marla from her analysis of Warren's attributes. The sound segued into soft sobs.

Frank stood still, as if nothing was amiss.

Marla leaned forward to check on her. Maybe she *is* sick. "Are you okay?" Marla whispered, examining the back of Rachel's hair while patting her on the shoulder. Rachel soon quieted.

The pastor waved his tattooed hands, motioning for everyone to sit. Suzanne and Rob made their way to two armchairs on the side of the stage. Along the way, Rob kept his hand on the small of her back and sneaked sideways glances at her, as if he couldn't believe his good luck. Why couldn't Warren be demonstrative like that?

The pastor took a step forward and called out a name. "Ms. Galani." He lifted his bearded chin to motion Marla forward.

She stood, and Warren gaped at her as if she'd turned into a surprise witness for opposing counsel. He was not alone in his confusion, though. Only a few others knew what was up. That's how Marla liked it. Unpredictability was one of her hallmarks.

"Excuse me." She passed in front of Warren's stiffened knees, then dramatically pointed the toe of her stiletto into the aisle. She took one long, intentional step. Having captured the crowd's attention, she moved forward like she owned the church. Today might not be her wedding, but she could still have her moment.

While lifting the mic from its stand, she took some slow, deep breaths. Last time she'd sung in public was nearly a year ago, but she'd been rehearsing like mad, and besides, performing came naturally to her.

She gave the bride a wink then nodded to the keyboard player, who plinked a few introductory notes. Soon Marla's breathy voice filled the church.

> *"The Bible tells us*
> *that a cord of three strands*
> *cannot be broken, oh no, oh no.*
> *A cord of three strands*
> *cannot be broken*
> *when God's together with you two..."*

On the final note, loud applause broke out. Warren clapped so enthusiastically she thought he might break into one of those crass two-finger whistles he used at Yankees games.

Amid the clapping, she returned to her pew, head down. Another missed opportunity. Grace should have been here. How could Marla strengthen the relationship with her daughter if they had nothing in common except for a day spa? She let out a long sigh and hoped the next few days would offer opportunities for them to bond.

The pastor strode to the pulpit and launched into a talk that was both humorous and serious, but mainly provided lots of marital advice. It all sounded like common sense to

Marla, but having never been married, she hadn't had the opportunity to test any of it first-hand. The pastor soared to his conclusion while pointedly looking over the small crowd, as if he intended his next comment not just for the bride and groom, but for everyone present.

"You may think you're close to entering your golden years, but—" he said with great articulation, first looking at the couple and then the guests, while dramatically raising a finger. "—I ask you to remember. God has a plan for your whole life, not just until you reach a certain age. If you're a willing servant, the Lord still has many adventures in store for you."

Adventures? Marla crossed her arms. No, thanks. I've had more than enough of them. Now, all I want is to be bonded with my daughter.

Chapter 3

SUZANNE

SATURDAY

Adventures? Suzanne perked to full attention. Bring 'em on! Meeting Rob in Phoenix, moving from Pittsburgh to be near him in Carmel, switching careers to become an artist, and now, getting married—what might be next? She had no idea.

At the moment, though, her skin tingled as she thought about the *adventure* she and Rob would have tonight in that fancy hotel honeymoon suite.

The pastor interrupted her wandering thoughts as he addressed the guests. "Now, let's take a moment to silently pray for this couple before they say their vows." He motioned for everyone to remain seated.

Rob squeezed Suzanne's hand, so small compared to his. "Almost there, honey." He closed his eyes to pray.

Even in a church, Rob's touch sent a zing through her. While her physical attraction to him was tremendous, his character drew her to him all the more. Here was a man who'd visited his ex-wife at a memory care facility every week until she passed on—just because no one else would, their kids included, and because in his mind, it was the right thing to do. How many guys would do that?

In fact, Rob was so selfless that initially she had doubts about his motives. Over the year they'd dated, though, he'd proved himself to be the man of integrity she'd been yearning for.

He'd never break her heart like her ex-husband, Mike, had.

Or her high school boyfriend, Tony.

Or her father.

She lightly squeezed Rob's hand. Yes, he's the one she'd been searching for. "Love you, babe," Suzanne whispered.

She looked out over the pews and spotted her high school friends, Rachel and Marla. Without those two, Suzanne wouldn't have made it to the altar. This past year, anytime she struggled, they'd offered priceless advice and support. She'd be sure to thank them again at the reception.

Her eyes drifted to her precious granddaughter sleeping in Jill's arms. Despite some skirmishes with Jill and her husband when they first married, Rob's coaching had helped Suzanne navigate those waters.

What a pity Rob didn't have the same great relationship with his own children. His daughter was in line for a promotion if the project she was leading hit its goals. But falling behind schedule gave her anxiety and an excuse to snipe at her dad during their weekly phone calls.

At least, she made it here for the wedding.

Rob's son had simply said he couldn't get away. Rob took it in stride, explaining that Kevin could be obsessive about his work as a software engineer, even to the point of sleeping on a cot in his office for days at a time. Kevin's behavior did seem odd, but having only spent a few hours with him, Suzanne could hardly judge.

Besides, she'd decided to let Rob deal with his own children as he saw fit—proof she'd learned that lesson about giving up control.

Rob squeezed her hand, as if he sensed her mind was elsewhere. She bowed her head and prayed—first for her marriage to Rob and then for an improved relationship between him and his children. From this day forward, they'd be her stepchildren, and whatever problems they brought to the table would now be Suzanne's to share.

The pastor took a step forward and raised his hands to his sides. "Now, the moment you've all been waiting for." He turned to the couple and in a commanding voice said, "Mr. Robert Jackson and Miss Suzanne Fleming, please step over here." Facing the guests, he added, "This couple has written their own vows, which they will now say to one another."

Rob, managing to look both distinguished and excited, read his first, pouring emotion into each syllable and glancing at Suzanne every few words.

When he finished, she said, "That was lovely."

Then it was her turn. She'd planned to recite the vows from memory, but her nerves would not allow it. Instead, she read her words slowly, then at the end, moved by the power of her commitment, she adlibbed an extra line—"I choose to be yours for the rest of my life." No matter what, she was wholly committed to this man. Nothing could sever their tie.

Rob's eyes widened at the unscripted addition, and a loving smile washed across his chiseled features.

She winked at him in return. Throwing in a little surprise was something she'd hoped to do on their wedding day, but adlibbing a line of her vows? She never could have predicted anything like that. Surely the addition was Holy Spirit-inspired.

The pastor's voice boomed with enthusiasm. "You may now kiss the bride."

Applause and a few cheers broke out during the lengthy kiss, which segued into a dip. Suzanne's updo held together throughout it all, but she almost lost her balance. They should have practiced more.

Holding hands, they strode down the aisle, laughing and smiling. To Suzanne, it felt like they were dancing, but she knew that in her four-inch heels, that couldn't possibly be true.

After passing through the double doors, they positioned themselves in the foyer to receive their guests.

Rob wrapped his arm around Suzanne's waist. "I love you, sweetheart."

"I love you too, honey." Bursting with joy, she rose to her tiptoes and touched his lips with a kiss.

Suzanne's mother led the approaching crowd as they inched toward the back of the church. How she'd aged since that latest fall on the stairs. Suzanne's sister was grinning as she coaxed their mother along, but she looked weary too. Caring for their mom as well as running the art consignment shop the sisters co-owned might be harder than Andrea had been telling her.

Rob leaned to whisper in Suzanne's ear. "My phone's been vibrating." He sheepishly pulled it out of his pocket. "Sorry. I really should check it." Rob was not only a psychologist, but a mighty popular one, now that he'd written some books and routinely spoke at conferences. In fact, that's how they met. She was setting up a registration table in a hotel hallway when Rob passed by on his way to give a keynote address down the hall. He invited her to dinner, and on a lark, she took him up on it.

"It could be an emergency with one of my patients." His eyes left hers and drifted toward his phone.

Not exactly what she expected in her receiving line, but definitely part of her new life. "Who is it?"

Rob's brow furrowed as he looked at the phone's screen. "It's Kevin."

Chapter 4

RACHEL

SATURDAY

After dropping off Warren at the airport and Marla at her spa near the edge of Port Mariette, the final leg home should have taken less than five minutes, but to Rachel it seemed like fifty.

First, there was the long silence between her and Frank. Then, he cleared his throat.

Rachel held her breath. Would he finish his marriage proposal—or talk about something else? Throughout the wedding and then the luncheon reception, she'd thought of little else but how to respond to Frank's interrupted question.

He cleared his throat a second time. "Nice wedding."

"Uh-huh." She answered quickly, relieved the silence had ended.

"I guess we're not going to have one of our own." His hands gripping the wheel, Frank's eyes jumped from the road to Rachel.

"Oh, Frank." She thought of touching his arm but held back. "I'm sorry. It's just that I'm—I'm not myself today."

"What's that supposed to mean?" he said with an edge in his voice.

Her shoulders drooped. "If Stan were still alive today, this would've been our fortieth wedding anniversary." She turned to look at Frank. "Maybe I should have mentioned it to you."

"Oh." The edge had disappeared. "Gee, I'm sorry. My timing was even worse than I thought."

"Well, you kinda caught me off guard."

"I thought that in a church, right before a wedding, you might've felt in the mood to say yes." He paused. "Are you saying that if you'd been expecting it, your answer might have been different?"

She considered how to reply. "I—I—" What could she say? Although she appreciated Frank's company, she recognized the chasm between wanting to spend the rest of her days with him—and once in a while needing him to open a pickle jar. As it stood now, she was not willing to commit to more than the pickle jar.

"No need to answer," he muttered. "Message received." He stopped at a red light and tapped his thumbs on the steering wheel. "Stupid lights."

Last year, when the State constructed the new highway, Port Mariette got northbound and southbound exits, along with the town's first traffic signals—one at each end of Main Street. For a town nearing economic collapse after the steel and coal industries had deserted it, the highway was an answer to prayer. Even so, changes like new traffic lights came hard to the town's thirty-three hundred residents.

Rachel ignored his irritation. "Any chance you'd still like to be companions?" Hoping to smooth things over, she spoke in a gentle tone. That had often worked with Stan. Maybe it would work with Frank too. "I'd like to continue that way. But maybe you feel different about it now."

Silence again, for a long minute. Frank turned into Rachel's driveway, parked the car, and handed her the keys. "I'll think about it." He shoved himself out of the driver's seat and shuffled to his house next door.

Rachel remained in the car, hands on her lap as she digested the day. She certainly hadn't expected a marriage proposal right before her friend's wedding ceremony. Even Frank should have known better than to steal Rob and Suzanne's thunder.

But maybe she should have seen it coming. He'd made such a fuss about getting to the church early, and on the way there, he was sweating in spite of the air conditioning being set on high. During those weeks with his son in Florida, he called her every night, ending their conversation with "Sleep tight, my dear delight, don't let the bed bugs bite."

Such an incurable romantic, that Frank. She rolled her eyes. *Why didn't I see that proposal coming?*

After a shake of her head, she got out of her car and plodded up the porch steps. What a long day, and it was only half over. She took the housekey from under the welcome mat and unlocked the front door.

Cinders, at least, was happy to see her. At fourteen, it took more than Rachel's arrival to make him jump, yet he made up for it with excited panting. He followed her through the living room into the kitchen, his nails clicking on the worn linoleum. As soon as she opened the back door he pranced outside and headed toward his favorite shrub.

She caught sight of a note on the table from her son Pete—*Out with Lindsey*. Good. Pete needed some female companionship, and this Lindsey seemed like a nice woman. Definitely young enough to produce a child for him, which was Rachel's number one qualifier for any woman Pete might date. Having another grandchild would be a joy, but more important than that, Rachel wanted her oldest son to have at least one child of his own before it was too late. His first wife had tricked him out of that, but if Pete were smart, he'd remarry and start a family pronto. Heck, Rachel had married Stan when she was eighteen and birthed their boys one after another. By big city standards, maybe she was a little young for all that, but in Port Mariette, no one waited until their thirties. At least not back then.

She plopped onto the nearest seat at the kitchen table and rested her forehead on her palms. What about Frank? What would happen with him? Would he still come over to let her dog out when she was at work? Would they have dinner at Dom's Restaurant on Fridays? And how about their weekly Canasta games? Playing cards with Frank was a simple but fun diversion—talk, laugh, have a beer—the only drawback was she was convinced he cheated. He'd always get up to grab a beer, then swing behind her before sitting down again. The rest of that hand, he seemed to know exactly what to discard.

Now, she might never know, but even if he had been cheating, did it really matter? After today, their relationship was probably over anyway.

She sighed. What had she ever done to deserve a lonely old age?

Her mother, still healthy in her eighties, would insist fifty-eight was not old, but like Stan always used to say, life is like a roll of toilet paper—the closer you get to the end, the faster it goes. This past year, the pace had been overwhelming. She knew plenty of people in Port Mariette who'd died in their sixties. No wonder. The steel and coal companies had pumped their lungs full of asbestos and coal tar. Maybe her end was near too.

Marla and Suzanne would probably outlive her. Those two looked ten years younger than she did, and neither of them struggled with their weight. Rachel had tried to keep off the pounds she'd lost before the reunion, but with being surrounded by food at her commercial kitchen, every day was a battle often lost.

On top of that, both Marla and Suzanne had been pampered with facials and massages all their lives. Criminy, those two practically lived in a gym. Who else had time for that? Rachel certainly didn't. Never had, never would.

Life could be so unfair. Now, Suzanne was married to Rob, and Marla was in a relationship with Warren. Both men were handsome, wealthy, polished professionals.

Rachel? She had Frank.

Or maybe not.

A distant thunderclap sent Cinders scratching at the door to be let in.

"C'mon in, big fella." She opened the door and scanned the sky. "Looks like another storm's moving in."

Her cell phone rang—Frank's ringtone. She picked it up right away. "Hi. What's up?"

"Thunderstorm's on the way. Make sure all your windows are closed."

"Thanks, Frank." Was he sending her a signal? "That's sweet of you to remind me." She clenched her fingers, then released them as she dropped herself onto the sofa. "Wanna come over for a game of Canasta sometime this week? I'll bake some of those raisin cookies you love."

Chapter 5

MARLA

SATURDAY

Two seconds after Marla entered the spa, she kicked off her stilettos. Grace was at the reception desk on a business call, so Marla quelled her desire to moan about her sore feet. Instead, she massaged them on the plush oriental rug as she walked across it to deposit her carry-on bags at the foot of the stairs.

Grace finished booking an appointment, then scooted over to greet Marla. "Welcome back!" She gave her a quick hug. "Mm. Love that perfume. Light and flowery. A gift from Warren?"

"Uh-huh. It's a little dainty for me, but I thought I'd wear it for the wedding."

Grace smiled and looked toward the steps. "How about I take your bags upstairs?"

"Thanks. I don't think I could climb two flights right now." During her occasional visits, Marla stayed in the turreted room on the far end of the third floor. Her daughter resided in the remainder of that floor, and client rooms filled the second floor plus part of the first.

Grace marched upstairs with the luggage as Marla folded her long body onto the velvet loveseat. At ease for the first time today, she took in the details of her spa's overhauled reception room—the ornate mahogany woodwork, the curved stained-glass windows, the fireplace with its original mantel. She'd financed the spa's many renovations, expertly completed by local contractor Mitch Mitchell, and now, Grace managed daily operations. The arrangement worked well for both women, as Marla had money but little time, and Grace had time but little money.

Besides, Marla could tolerate living in Port Mariette only in spurts.

Grace danced down the steps and stretched her long, toned arms out to the sides. "So, how does everything look?"

"Terrific. The place smells great too. So clean."

"Thank you." Grace dipped her chin and smiled. "It's been busy, but I do my best to keep the place super clean."

"Remember how musty it used to smell? Poor Aunt Adele just couldn't keep up."

Grace nodded, hands on her hips. "Yeah. Trying to maintain a mansion at her age must have been hard. She's so much happier now living at Sunset Hills." Grace moved closer and perched on the arm of an upholstered chair. "Well, tell me, how was the wedding?"

"Sweet and simple. You should've heard the vows Suzanne and Rob wrote for themselves. So touching." She paused. "And I sang a solo."

"A solo?" Grace's eyes widened, then she chuckled. "I hope it wasn't the same song you did at the reunion."

"Oh! That one?" Marla laughed at the memory. Last year, she'd made up a bawdy tune about her high school memories and belted it out while wearing a Dolly Parton outfit, complete with two perfectly placed balloons. The nuns would not have been amused, but the reunion crowd went wild.

"Seriously, how'd your solo go?" Grace asked.

Marla shrugged. "Judging by the applause, I'd say pretty well."

"Wish I could have been there."

"It was a very small wedding. Only ten guests."

"Oh, I understand. I just wish I could have watched you. It takes such guts to get up in front of people—and then to sing a song! I could never perform in public. I don't think I got a single one of your singing genes."

Marla waved a hand, pushing her daughter's comment aside. "In the City, just about everyone can sing—New York's like Hollywood, everybody's a performer." Her eyes drooped, saddened. "I wish you could have been there today too."

"Well, to be honest, weddings kind of depress me." Grace shifted on the armrest. "Y'know what I mean?"

"I get it." Marla agreed about weddings, but she still longed to have a family. Did Grace feel the same?

They fell silent for a moment. It had been more than a year since Marla had located Grace. Why couldn't they have serious conversations by now? Most of the time, their discussions skimmed the surface, and anytime one of them dipped a little more deeply, the words dried up fast, as if they'd entered treacherous territory.

Marla tried again. "Rob's daughter came to the wedding. I think you'd like her." Marla liked Emily because she was a striver just like herself, but Grace might have appreciated Emily's engaging personality. By the end of the reception, she'd made friends with every person in the room.

"Rob's son didn't make it, though," Marla added.

"How come?"

"No idea. Maybe I'll find out when Suzanne's back from her honeymoon in Boston."

"Boston?"

"Yeah." Marla glanced at the burled wood grandfather clock. "Right about now, in fact, they should be boarding a flight to Logan. Rob's a history buff, and Suzanne used to deliver a lot of her training programs in Boston. It's a hub for the airline she worked for. Anyway, it's one of her favorite cities. Me, I'd choose Paris, but Suzanne claims Boston's romantic too. Walking the Freedom Trail is romantic? Not in *my* book."

Grace shook her head. "Not my cup of *tea*—Boston *Tea* Party, get it?" She laughed at her own weak joke.

Her daughter's sense of humor was nothing at all like Marla's—she must have gotten it from her birth father. Marla leaned forward and hugged her knees, broaching a new topic. "If you went on a honeymoon, where would you go?"

But Grace waved a hand. "New subject, please."

Marla let it go. She should have known better. Anything to do with marriage always put Grace off.

"Can I get you something to eat or maybe a drink?" Grace slid off the armrest and stood with her head tipped to the side, like a waitress taking an order.

"No, thanks. I'm still bloated from that reception." Marla patted her flat tummy with one hand and then the loveseat cushion with the other. "Come sit down. Relax with me for a while." Marla cocked her head as she realized she had no idea what Grace's schedule looked like today. "Do you have time?"

"A little. Kim Kryzwicki's scheduled for a massage in about fifteen minutes." Grace plopped down next to Marla.

"You know her, don't you? She said she graduated with you."

Marla nodded. "She was at our reunion last year. Spent the night on the dance floor. Isn't she married?"

"She's divorced now. Lately, she's become a regular here."

"How about that." Marla forced herself to withhold further comment, although it wasn't easy.

The two went quiet again, then Marla asked, "Latoya's giving Kim the massage today?"

"Uh-huh."

"How's she working out?"

A voice bellowed from above. "She's doing mighty fine." Latoya floated down the steps—quite a feat, considering her size.

"Glad to hear it," Marla said. "And everyone's treating you well?"

"Looky here. I may be the only black person in Port Mariette, but I'm fine with that. I like sticking out in a crowd." Latoya guffawed. "And besides, what's anyone got to complain about? I give marvelous massages."

"So I've heard." Marla laughed at the woman's straightforward style. Hiring Latoya right out of massage school had been a good move on Grace's part. She had a gut feeling Latoya would make a great massage therapist, and she was right. Latoya had a way of making clients feel good on the inside as well as the outside.

Grace glanced out the window. "Here comes Kim now."

The front door burst open, and Kim sashayed into the foyer, dressed in a golf skirt and a tight short-sleeved top with open buttons revealing more than a hint of cleavage.

"Hi ladies. Nice to see you all." Kim fanned herself with her fingers, even though the air conditioning worked perfectly fine. "Just had a round with Mitch. Even with some rain, we managed to squeeze in nine holes. Kinda steamy out there now." Her eyes bore into Marla's. "He's such a sweetheart. So much fun dating him."

Kim's dating Mitch? Marla scrunched her nose. She'd worked closely with him last year during the spa's restoration. As far as she could tell, the guy was married to his work. And if he had a *type*, she'd always assumed it'd be someone modest. Low-key. Religious. Certainly not a sexy divorcee like Kim. Men. Go figure.

"Good to see you too, Kim." Marla forced a smile, then gave Latoya a raised eyebrow.

Latoya picked up the hint and waved Kim toward the stairs. "Everything's ready for you," she singsonged.

"By the way," Kim said over her shoulder as she traipsed upstairs, hips swinging with every step, "Mitch said he'd be here soon to check out your roof."

As soon as she was out of sight, Marla mouthed to Grace. "She's dating *Mitch*?"

Grace shrugged. "News to me too," she replied, her whisper barely audible.

The door upstairs closed with a click. "But you can confirm it with Mitch—he's giving us a quote on repairing the roof after that last storm." Grace looked outside. "There's his green truck coming up the driveway right now."

Marla slid into her heels and strutted out to greet him. "Golfing again, I see," she joked while eyeing his boldly colored outfit.

"Yep. You know me. My passions are God, golf, and construction."

"And Kim Kryzwicki is now your fourth passion?" Marla's eyes teased.

He jutted his chin up dismissively. "Hardly. I'm just giving her some golf lessons."

"And you *hardly* have the time, so what's up?" She raised an eyebrow while waiting for his explanation.

To some, Marla's direct style may have seemed bold, but she felt she had the right. Last year, when they spent so much time working together, she'd cracked through Mitch's exterior. Maybe because she'd shared her own secrets first, he'd opened up to her as if they'd been lifetime friends. Although flawed like everyone else, he'd earned her respect as a trustworthy man and talented contractor, and their deep conversations had encouraged her to question her spiritual beliefs—or the lack thereof.

Mitch kneaded his foot on the asphalt. "Well, when I bought the country club, I knew it'd be an uphill battle to get new members. I sank a lot of money into renovating that place, you know, and Kim had, shall we say, quite the financial windfall from her divorce. She mentioned to Herbie she'd schedule a few parties at the country club if I gave her golf lessons." He took off his ballcap and ran a tan hand through his short hair.

"And since Herbie owns the golf course, he wheedled you into the deal?"

"Right."

"Makes sense. You two have a weird kind of synergy." She poked him in the arm.

"And sometimes Kim and I do a foursome with Herbie and Mary Frances, or maybe with Penny." He kneaded his foot some more.

"Penny? You're kidding—Herbie's still got a thing for her after all she did?" Penny Frampton, Port Mariette's former mayor, used to own the country club and its golf course—until it came out that she'd been conniving to get state funds to cover her gambling debts. Mitch and Herbie saved her from bankruptcy by buying her country club and golf course, and when she confessed her transgressions in front of the whole town, she got off the hook but had to resign as mayor.

"So, how's Herbie doing?" Marla had a rare soft spot for her high school classmate Herbie, who owned several businesses on Main Street along with the golf course. Back in high school, Herbie was the only guy who'd ever said anything nice to her. He'd also been the one to drum up enthusiasm for last year's reunion. Without that, she never would've come back to Port Mariette—and never would have found Grace.

"He still cheats at golf." Mitch chuckled at his inside joke, as he always did, then turned serious. "Herbie's doing okay, but lately he's been a bit down. I'm waiting for him to come out of his cave and talk."

"Why don't you just ask him what's on his mind?"

"It doesn't work that way for us guys. God made men and women different, contrary to what some say." Mitch stuck a thumb in his jeans pocket. "How's Warren, by the way? Is he here with you?"

"He had to get back to New York." She flipped some hair behind her ear. "He's good, just busy."

"Like you?" Mitch lifted a sandy eyebrow.

"Yes." She let out a long sigh. "I'm still way too busy." She looked to the sky. "I know what you're going to say."

"Can't hear God when you're running hard." He twisted his head back and forth slowly as he said it.

"I know, I know. I'm working on it." She put both hands on her hips. "Can we talk about the roof now?"

"Sure. Time's a precious thing, and we sure don't want to waste it talking about God."

"About the roof ... how about stopping in after you've looked it over?"

He gave her a quick salute, and she drifted back inside while contemplating his words, which pierced her once again. Last year, she'd felt like she was filling that hole in her heart with God, but once she returned to Manhattan, she got busy with her foundation, and God slid way down on the priority list. She rubbed her face, stretching her cheeks back and forth, something she rarely did. Ages the skin.

Soon Mitch came inside, clipboard in hand. "Well, ladies, looks like my guys fixed up that roof real good last year. It weathered the storm better than most around here. A few slate shingles blew off, and the flashing looks a little damaged. We can use the leftover supplies stored in your garage. Two hundred oughta cover it."

"A three-digit repair bill, hallelujah!" Marla clapped a few times. Most of her financial outlays on the old mansion had been well into the thousands.

"I can have one of my guys here in the morning."

"How early?" Grace spoke up, a look of concern on her face. "Our first appointment is at ten."

"Not to worry. I'll have Jesse here by eight, gone by ten. We could've done it today, except another storm's coming in. I don't want any of my guys on a roof in bad weather."

"Tomorrow will be perfect." Marla stood. "Thanks, Mitch." Normally she would have expected him to invite her for a round of golf while she was in town. But not now.

Mitch tipped the bill of his ballcap and bounded down the steps to his truck.

Marla shut the door behind him. "Two hundred dollars—what a relief!"

"You're kidding, right?" Grace scrunched her face. "You've got more money than you know what to do with."

Marla let out an uncharacteristic giggle. "True. But it's a joy to write out a small check for a change." The lean days of her early career were long gone, yet she'd never forget them. "How about we celebrate?"

"Celebrate?"

"Sure. Why not?"

"You mean like a bottle of champagne?"

"No, can't do that. I have to be careful about drinking—doctor's orders after the mini-stroke."

Marla wanted to come up with something fun for them to do—not just celebrate a silly roofing bill. That was merely an excuse to spend time with Grace. Her daughter had endured so much over the last year, with both of her adoptive parents dying just months apart. But in a place like Port Mariette, what could they do for enjoyment?

"Not all that much to do around here." Marla looked to Grace, hoping she'd come up with a suggestion.

"How about we take Aunt Adele to dinner at Herbie's pizza place?" Grace said.

"Love that idea!" Feigning enthusiasm, Marla slapped her hands together. She adored her aunt, but Herbie's pizza shop? Hardly the venue she would have chosen.

Then again, she had to keep reminding herself—she was in Port Mariette.

Chapter 6

SUZANNE

SATURDAY

"There's our flight." Suzanne pointed at a departure board at Pittsburgh International Airport. She let out a loud sigh, then rested her head on Rob's shoulder. "Delayed."

"Only for half an hour. Not so bad." He patted her hair. He probably would have run his fingers through it, but the extra-hold hairspray that froze her updo in place curbed any such attempt.

"You don't actually believe what they post about departures, do you, honey?" She gave him a quizzical look. Having spent her career as a flight attendant and then a contract trainer for an airline, Suzanne knew what she was talking about. A major thunderstorm like this could strand them for hours.

"Just trying to be optimistic." Rob hugged her sideways. "Want to grab some fast food, or should we take a chance on ordering a real meal in a restaurant?"

"Let's check the forecast." She flicked open her weather app. "Ugh. That storm still covers the entire eastern seaboard." She showed Rob. "Looks like we won't be flying out of Pittsburgh anytime soon."

"I can't think of anyone I'd rather be grounded with." His eyes twinkled in that darling sexy way she loved.

She stretched up on her tiptoes and planted a kiss on his cheek. "I couldn't agree more."

"Let's find a place to grab a bite." With his hand on the small of her back, he guided her through the undulating crowds until they came to a chain restaurant. "How's this?"

"Suits me fine." She was on such a high from their wedding, even a hot dog stand would be okay with her.

A teenage hostess seated them in a booth and handed them plastic-coated menus. "Your server will be right with you," she said, as animated as one would expect from a sulky teen.

They read the menus, and soon a thin young man with piercings all over head his head and a chain tattoo around his neck showed up to take their order.

Suzanne cringed, imagining the pain he must have gone through to acquire that look. She averted her eyes. "I'll have the salmon salad, please. Medium."

"Turkey wrap for me," Rob said, handing the menus over.

Once the server was out of earshot, Suzanne scrunched her face. "Why do people *do* that to themselves?" Surely Rob could give her an educated answer. He had a marvelous way of explaining human behavior.

He shrugged. "Sometimes they think it makes them look cool. Other times, they're trying to make a statement or shock people." He leaned forward and spread his hands wide. "It can even be a sign of mental illness or a personality disorder."

"Really?" She'd never analyzed the subject before. Rob was so enlightening.

He nodded. "I always pay close attention to what my patients say about their piercings and tattoos."

Suzanne faked a shiver. "I had a hard enough time getting my ears pierced. I could never do anything like that to myself."

"My son's got a lot of tattoos." Rob said it softly, as if he were trying to make it sound casual. "He says the pain's worth it. He likes how it looks."

"Is that so?" She hoped she hadn't offended Rob. "I can't remember seeing any tattoos on him." After all, she'd met Kevin only once. A handsome young man, he was polite and quiet, but that's all she could recall.

"When he's wearing pants and a long-sleeved shirt, you'd never know it."

"What's his reason for the tattoos?" She mimicked Rob's soft, casual tone.

"He says it's a way for him to express his true self." Rob shrugged again. "I don't push the issue. Kevin's a complicated guy. Genius IQ, but he lacks social skills and suffers from rejection."

"Rejection? From whom?"

"Back in school, it was his classmates. At work, it's people on his team. In his social life—well, if you could call it that—he doesn't socialize much, and he's always had trouble holding onto a girlfriend."

"I thought you said he and Suki were doing well together."

"They are. Suki does seem like a good match for him. A little quiet, but very smart. She's a chemist. Kevin needs someone who can engage his brain." Rob massaged his forehead then continued. "I have to admit, Kevin's phone calls this morning unsettled me. He said he was just calling to congratulate us, but he should have realized he was trying to reach me during the ceremony. When I saw his name pop up, I thought he might be having an … an emergency."

"An emergency?" She raised a hand to her heart. "What kind?"

Rob looked down. "Like a suicide attempt."

Her mouth dropped open. "That's happened before?"

Rob nodded. "Twice. So, I'm always watching for triggers. Once, it happened when he was fired from a job and the other time because of a relationship issue."

"I'm so sorry. I had no idea." Suzanne wished she'd known all these details before they'd gotten married. She hadn't held anything back from Rob—details about her father, her daughter, her ex, and even Tony, the guy who dumped her right before the senior prom. Why hadn't Rob given her the same consideration? Would she always have to tread carefully in her marriage, like she'd done all those years married to Mike? Concern engulfed her like the heavy rain smearing across the wall of windows behind them. She bit her lower lip to distract her mind from the shock and disappointment of what Rob had shared.

The server returned and slid their plates onto the table. "Need anything else?" He took a look at Suzanne's face then turned away.

"No, thanks. We're good." Rob said it to the server's receding back.

Suzanne examined Rob's presence, looking for similarities with his son and finding none. But who knows what lurks inside?

"Look, Suzanne, just because I'm a psychologist doesn't mean my family can't be dysfunctional."

"I'm not making a judgment call here, Rob. I'm just trying to understand." She smoothed the napkin on her lap, buying time to think of how to proceed. "Can you tell me why you didn't let me know about this before? After all, I pulled all my skeletons out of the closet for you. I thought you'd done the same for me."

"I should have." He waited a moment before continuing. "But Kevin has been doing well for so long, I didn't think it was a good idea to dredge up his past. Besides, once I told you about his—his *issues*, it would always linger in your mind and affect your relationship with him." He paused. "And maybe with me."

"You didn't have a lot of faith in me, honey, did you?" Suzanne teased him in an attempt to lighten the heavy conversation.

Rob seemed not to notice. "At the beginning," he continued, "I just didn't know you well enough to entrust you with all the details, and then later on, there didn't seem to be a good time to tell you. And frankly, since Kevin was doing fine, I didn't think it was necessary."

"But still, don't you think you should have told me?" She said it sweetly although she was heating up inside. No point in escalating their conversation, especially at the start of their honeymoon.

"I should have. I was wrong. I'm really sorry." He said it slowly and never broke eye contact.

It moved her. She recalled the vows she'd made to him only hours ago, and her heart softened. "Apology accepted." She smiled for a moment, then grew serious again. "Anything else I should know about your family?"

"No, nothing." Rob shook his head with a convincing firmness. "Emily is fine, just overworked and a bit anxious."

"She takes it out on you sometimes, doesn't she?" Suzanne easily recognized that kind of behavior. Jill had put her through the same wringer.

"Yeah. Lately, it seems she needs to let out her frustrations on someone she doesn't work with. It's okay. I can take it for a while, and if it continues, I'll talk with her about it." He flicked a piece of shredded lettuce from his lower lip.

Even with food on his face, Rob still looked appealing to Suzanne, and her heart overflowed with love. One way or another, they'd get past these issues with his kids, she just knew it.

She swallowed her first taste of the salmon. "Mm. This is good."

"On another subject—" Rob raised a finger. "—At the reception, Frank mentioned Marla seemed a little upset because Grace wasn't invited to the wedding."

Suzanne dotted her lips with a napkin. "Marla's trying so hard to tighten her relationship with her daughter. Probably figured singing a solo would impress her." Suzanne put the napkin back on her lap. "What Marla fails to realize is that Grace is already intimidated by her—I mean, who wouldn't be, at least until they got to know her? Anyway, if we'd invited Marla's daughter, then we would've had to invite Rachel's sons, maybe Frank's too, and Warren's girls. I had to draw the line somewhere."

"I see."

"She'll get over it when I tell her the whole ceremony was recorded." Suzanne dismissed it with a wave of her hand.

"It was? I didn't see anyone walking around taking videos."

"The church has a recorder on during all the services, including weddings. I meant to tell her, but I forgot." Suzanne looked down at her plate. She'd been so caught up in her own life that she'd failed to consider Marla's feelings. That woman was a lot more sensitive than she let on, and Suzanne knew it. "I'll have to call her."

"Or maybe you could send her a text right now and put her out of her misery." Rob chuckled, pointing to her phone lying on the table.

Just then his own phone rang. He stared at it as it continued to ring. "It's Kevin again."

Chapter 7

RACHEL

SATURDAY

Lightning flashed as Pete stepped inside the house, shaking water from his arms. "Whoa, get out the ark."

On the living room sofa, Rachel stirred from a nap, the emotion of the day having done her in. "Hi, Petie." She discretely straightened her wig which had gone askew. Had he noticed? If he had, he could easily slip and tell his brothers.

Those blasted sewing scissors. Last week, she'd left them on the coffee table while babysitting her youngest grandson. She'd accidentally nodded off, and who could blame her with the long hours she worked? While she was deep in dreamland, Caleb chopped off fistfuls of her hair. If her sons found out, she'd never be left alone with any grandkids again. All the way to the wig shop, she'd prayed for a way to hide her guilt, and when she spotted something that matched her own cut and color, she gave thanks with a hasty sign of the cross. God apparently did know every hair on her head.

Relieved that Pete hadn't noticed anything, Rachel sat up. "Oh, boy," she said. "What a day."

"All partied out?" Pete grinned.

Rachel's sandals lay under the coffee table, and her dress had twisted itself around her thighs. She yawned as she rolled her shoulders. Suzanne's wedding had thrown her whole day off kilter in more ways than one. "I guess—I guess I fell asleep." At least this time, no one chopped off any of her hair.

Pete plopped onto the armchair.

"What time is it?" Rachel asked, her voice sleepy.

Pete glanced at the grandfather clock. "Four-thirty."

"I must have slept close to an hour. Good thing you woke me up. Otherwise, I wouldn't be able to fall asleep tonight."

He nodded. "How'd everything go?"

What could she tell him? Nothing about Frank, that's for sure. "Well ... the wedding was very moving, and they had quite the spread at the lunch afterwards. Oysters, sushi, caviar." She said it with a straight face.

"Did you eat that stuff?" Pete's upper lip curled.

"Heck, no." Rachel squished her face, just like she'd done at the reception when no one was looking. "I'd never eat that stuff." She giggled. "I had a little filet mignon and some scalloped potatoes."

"Atta girl. I thought maybe you'd want to make some changes to our menu at Food 'n Fuel."

"Never. We'll always be known for our pasta and pierogies." Last year, when she and Pete converted the old service station into a convenience store with fuel pumps, Rachel decided to sell the same kind of meals she used to make for her husband and sons. Simple food for simple people. It never went out of style, at least in Port Mariette.

Pete crossed a leg over his knee, a move he made when he had something on his mind.

"How are things going with Lindsey?" She sensed that might be the right topic. They'd been dating a couple of months, and his mood seemed to improve every time he spent time with her. Having met Lindsey only once, though, Rachel didn't know much about her except she worked in real estate, lived in Lyondale, and had the longest legs Rachel had ever seen. Longer than Marla's or Grace's, and that was saying a lot.

"Fine," Pete replied.

"Fine? C'mon, even a man of few words like you can do better than that."

"Lindsey's a beautiful woman. I enjoy being with her." He bounced his leg a few times. "Sometimes, though, I wonder if she's dating me because she likes me or because she wants to make inroads selling real estate in Port Mariette."

"Hmm." She considered his statement. "As your mother, I can't imagine she wouldn't have fallen madly in love with you on your first date." She winked. "As for real estate sales, you'd think there'd be enough business for her in Lyondale."

"Used to be. But now that the new highway's bringing most of the traffic into Port Mariette, Lyondale's been shrinking."

"Sad but true." Port Mariette was lucky to have gotten the new highway exit—luckier still to have Marla back in town for their fortieth reunion. She'd given local businesses a huge grant to renovate their facades to attract highway travelers, and when the newspaper in Pittsburgh featured a front-page story about Port Mariette's renaissance, the tiny town became a sudden draw.

"Lindsey told me she hopes Mary Frances will retire early, then she'd be the only real estate agent in the area. I think she was only half-joking."

"Oh, boy. If Mary Frances heard that, she'd get a warrant out for Lindsey's arrest." Although Rachel was wildly exaggerating, she'd known Mary Frances since grade school where she'd beaten up a boy a year ahead of them for stealing her peanut butter cup. Even now, everyone knew not to cross her.

Pete leaned back, smiling, with his hands behind his head. "Well, Mary Frances may be Port Mariette's only real estate agent, and even with her being a former councilwoman, I don't think she has quite enough clout to get a warrant issued on those grounds."

"I don't know about that." Rachel played along. "After seeing what Penny Frampton did, I'll never again underestimate anyone in this little town, especially a woman." She slapped her thighs and stood. "But I guess Lindsey would have to do more than hope Mary Frances retires early to get arrested."

"Yep." Pete stood and stretched. "I'm gonna check my emails."

"And I'm going to get out of this fancy outfit." Rachel scooped up her shoes and clutch and went upstairs to her bedroom.

She slipped her dress onto a puffy satin hanger and hung it at the far end of the closet. On tiptoes, she slid her thin clutch onto the high shelf above. Stan used to store his stuff up there, but after she donated his belongings to the church rummage sale, she started using the shelf for items she rarely used. Way at the end, her eye caught what looked like one of his large shoeboxes. *How'd I miss that?*

She hooked the corner of the lid with her fingernail and slid it toward her, but the box tumbled onto the floor. *Shoot!* She dropped to her knees to retrieve the contents. No shoes had fallen out, just mementos—Stan's old Eagle

Scout scarf, drawings from the boys, a wad of greeting cards, and a pile of yellowed articles from the *Port Mariette Gazette* about his and the boys' sports achievements.

Back in high school, Stan had been all-star in three sports. When the boys were old enough to play, he wanted to coach all their teams, but his schedule wouldn't allow it. Instead, he worked the concession stand on game nights, which afforded him the benefit of free food and admission to watch whichever son was on the field. Sure, Stan was away a lot of evenings, but Rachel used the time to catch up on housework, and on Fridays, she'd blow a few bucks at the St. Cyp's bingo. Stan never minded. In fact, he'd do the dinner dishes so she could get there on time.

She looked at the shoebox again. Only one piece of paper remaining—pink in color, wrinkled, with large curlicue handwriting she didn't recognize. A sickening feeling roiled in her stomach as she fingered the paper.

> Dear Stan,
> I'm sorry. I can't do this anymore.
> I will think of you every Friday night the rest of my life.
> Love,
> T ♥

All the air seemed to rush from her lungs. Her heart pounding, she balled up the note and threw it across the room, but the paper seemed to resist, fluttering back toward her. Mocking her attempt like the contents mocked her marriage.

"No!" Stan wasn't with another woman on Fridays—he always volunteered at the concession stand on Fridays. Didn't he?

She shoved herself up from the floor and stomped on the note. *Is that why Stan rushed me out the door for bingo?*

Who was this woman?

What was she doing with Stan?

Who else knew? Shame crept up her body like the slinky dress she just took off. What a fool she'd been. Adultery, the sixth commandment! How could he have done this? She dug her heel on the note and squished it back and forth, as if she could erase it from her life.

She heaved a few times. Her stomach curdled. Cupping both hands over her mouth, she bolted to the bathroom and leaned over the sink. She gagged again, then bent over the toilet, just in time to lose her filet.

Chapter 8

MARLA

SATURDAY

Marla strode into the foyer of Sunset Hills and shook her wet golf umbrella over the brightly patterned carpeting. She spotted the facility's receptionist squinting at a computer screen and did a double take. "Penny? You're working here now?"

An unsmiling Penny shrugged her narrow shoulders. "Disgraced mayors don't qualify for unemployment."

Marla picked up the pen tethered to a string and jotted her arrival time—4:50 p.m. "I see." She spoke in a neutral tone, aware of the rumor Penny had become unstable after all that contentious highway drama. Far be it from Marla to test the theory. She made a mental note to get Aunt Adele's personal belongings locked up. "Can I leave my umbrella here in the foyer?" She could risk *that* being stolen.

"Sure." Penny stood and leaned forward, her slightly mottled hands curled over the inside edge of the counter. "Your aunt's in the dining room. Supper's served at five. Everyone's already in there. They live for the meals, you know." She smirked, looking rather witchy with her pointy nose and thin lips. "So, what brings you to town this time? Suzanne's wedding, I presume?"

Marla nodded, then leaned her umbrella against the wall. "How was it?"

"Perfect. Just perfect." Last thing Marla wanted to do was give Penny material for gossip.

"Sounds like she landed a keeper. Handsome, well off, educated. Lucky girl."

"Rob's a great guy. They're a terrific match." Marla turned to leave.

"By the way, did you hear Mitch is dating Kim Kryzwicki? I wonder if that started before or after her divorce." Penny said it slowly, as if she were trying to decide.

Marla turned back and narrowed her eyes. "He's giving her golf lessons. You know that. You and Herbie have golfed with them, right?"

"It's more like a double date than a foursome, though." Penny tapped her chin with her bony index finger. "I think something's brewing between those two."

Marla pursed her lips.

"What's the matter?" Penny widened her eyes. "Did your spa get a bad review too?" She laughed—it was an unexpectedly throaty one. All she needed to add was *my little pretty* and Marla would have been certain about Penny's true persona.

Marla put a hand on her hip. "What are you talking about?"

A hint of a smile formed on Penny's lips. "Five businesses on Main Street got a one-star review online last week. All anonymous. Herbie's pizza place was the first to get one."

"Oh! That's too bad." Maybe that's why Mitch thought Herbie seemed down. "Any idea who might have written them?" She couldn't help but glare at Penny.

"Don't look at me that way. It wasn't me. You know I wouldn't do anything to harm Herbie or any of his businesses."

Herbie owned about a third of the places along Main Street. Some had been passed down to him by family members, and others were empty storefronts he'd bought last year to expand his grocery store or to convert into new shops.

"Well, I'm sure someone will figure it out." Marla lifted her chin and set out for the dining room. She'd have to discuss this with Grace. The spa was getting off the ground nicely, but bad reviews could set them back. Even worse, a spate of them could damage the entire town's precarious economic rebound.

Marla easily spotted her aunt, who was wearing a hot pink tank top and a matching headband. Although looking thinner than she did a few months ago, Aunt Adele's posture was still straight, and the white hair suited her olive complexion well. Compared to her tablemates, Aunt Adele looked both fit and regal.

Marla gave her a gentle hug and whispered in her ear. "Let's blow this joint, Aunt Adele."

Her aunt laughed. "You're too much, Marla." She excused herself and pushed away from the round table.

"How about a three-course meal at Herbie's pizza shop—salad, soft drink, and veggie pizza?" Marla asked as they linked arms.

"Let's hit it." Aunt Adele patted Marla's hand. "Is Grace coming too?"

"She'll meet us there. Busy at the spa right now."

They signed out while Penny was on a phone call. Marla grabbed the umbrella, and they zipped away in her BMW. She took her eyes off the road to glance at her aunt. "So, how have you been?"

"Terrific." She grinned. "Even better than terrific, now that you're home again."

Home again. Marla smiled. Aunt Adele never could get over how Marla preferred living in Manhattan. When Marla was very young, Aunt Adele had come to New York a few times, but Marla didn't see her again until she was sixteen, when she was banished to Port Mariette to deliver her baby. Grace's adoption was arranged in August, and since Marla's parents were divorcing, they enrolled her at St. Cyprian's Academy for her senior year. For a long time, she winced anytime she recalled that painful period of her life, but after reconnecting with Grace, the memory took on new meaning.

On their way to the pizza shop, Marla and Aunt Adele passed street after street of old frame houses. Marla jutted her chin toward a row of dirty beige homes. "Kind of dreary-looking, aren't they?"

Aunt Adele shrugged. "A lot of them are owned by seniors with fixed incomes. They're more concerned about having money for prescriptions and taxes than making home improvements."

"Understandable." Marla turned onto Main Street, where her grant money had enabled renovation of the facades and installation of Victorian lamp posts. "The town really comes alive here, doesn't it?"

"It certainly does," said Aunt Adele as Marla pulled into a parking space in front of the pizza shop. "You could have spent all that money on yourself, Marla. What you did here was so generous. I'm proud to be your aunt."

Was Grace proud to be her daughter?

Aunt Adele unfastened her seatbelt and put a hand on the door. "You haven't mentioned Warren yet. Everything okay with him?"

"He's fine, just super busy." Marla dug deep into her purse and, with a twinkly-eyed grin, pulled out a piece of paper.

Aunt Adele glanced at it. "That handwriting is totally illegible. Who wrote it? A doctor?"

"A lawyer—Warren. It's a little love note from him." Her eyes still sparkled. "He must have stuck it in my purse this morning when I wasn't paying attention." She looked at the note again silently, then laughed. "I don't think I should read this to you, Aunt Adele. You'd blush."

"Well, as long as you're happy with him." She pushed her door open. "I just want you to have a good man in your life—or maybe I should say, a man in your life who is good for you."

Chapter 9

SUZANNE

SUNDAY

On the outskirts of Port Mariette, Suzanne tapped her heels on the well-worn plank floor at Dom's Restaurant, where she sat alone the day after her wedding. Over and over, she attempted—and failed—to keep her mind off yesterday's bizarre turn of events. She'd never dreamed Rob's son would change her world so suddenly.

She checked her phone. Where were Rachel and Marla? Oh, how she needed their comfort and commiseration tonight.

The last time she was here at Dom's was right before Christmas. Under the fiberglass arch—at that time decked out with fake mistletoe—Rob caught her by surprise with a romantic marriage proposal. Yesterday at the airport, he surprised her again.

"I can't go to Boston," he'd said, holding both her hands in his. "I think Kevin is on the verge of, well, you know, and I need to get to Seattle right away." Suki had left in a huff, carting off her belongings in Kevin's collection of Amazon boxes—evidence, Rob explained, of his son's obsession with online shopping.

"Are you positive you don't want to go with me?" Rob had asked Suzanne three times. But she'd refused. She couldn't imagine a worse way to spend her first nights as Rob's wife than being holed up in her new stepson's apartment while Rob addressed whatever was going on. Besides, Rob had hinted her presence could agitate Kevin. Poor Rob, the man was trying so hard to balance the needs of his son and new wife. Probably an impossible feat.

If the crisis had occurred any other time but their honeymoon, she could have been a lot more sympathetic, even though Rob had promised he'd make it up to her. They'd go on another honeymoon, one even better than what they'd planned. *You do understand, don't you?* he'd said while squeezing her hand, as if expecting a response to ooze out of her fingertips.

"Of course." She'd cooed and made goo-goo eyes at him when she said it. Maybe he'd think she really meant it. She kept her frozen smile in place as he backed away in the direction of the Seattle departure gate.

Not the adventure she'd been expecting the night of her wedding.

She could have gone back to Carmel and continued churning out pieces of art to sell at Creations on Main, the consignment shop she and Andrea owned. But being all alone in California for who knows how long held little appeal.

Instead, she'd caught a ride back to her place overlooking downtown Pittsburgh, a condo she'd held onto after moving to California last fall. She could visit her daughter Jill in the suburbs and run down to Port Mariette to help her sister. Lately, caring for their mom on top of managing the art stop seemed more than Andrea could handle.

With Marla staying in Port Mariette for a while, Suzanne could rely on support from both her and Rachel, thus the reason for tonight's dinner at Dom's. Now, seated at a linen-covered table and waiting for their arrival, Suzanne tapped her heels a little faster. *Where are they?*

A familiar laugh emanated from the bar. Suzanne turned toward the sound and saw Marla dangling her legs from a stool while Dom poured something clear into her glass.

Suzanne pushed up from her chair.

Just then, a high-pitched voice came from behind her. "Aren't you gonna give me a hug?"

It was Rachel, reaching out with both arms, looking all hangdog, probably for Suzanne's benefit—or maybe Rachel was under the weather. Her color wasn't so good. *And is that a wig she's wearing?* Suzanne didn't know whether to ask about it or not.

Marla appeared on the other side of them, a Prada bag slung over her shoulder and a drink in her hand. "Hey, can we turn this into a group hug?"

They hugged hard, then took their seats. A server came along for their drink order. Suzanne asked for a glass of house Merlot, and Rachel a beer.

"I'm good for now," Marla said, her glass still nearly full.

"Are you keeping up with your 'no more than one drink a day' regimen?" Suzanne looked pointedly at the glass of vodka.

"Pretty much." Marla drew it to her lips and took a sip.

"Good girl." Suzanne nodded her approval.

Rachel put a hand on Suzanne's arm. "How are you holdin' up?"

With elbows on the table, Suzanne pressed fists into her cheeks and forced a smile. She'd do anything to prevent herself from crying at Dom's. Already, a couple customers who knew she'd just gotten married had raised their eyebrows when they saw her sitting here alone. She would not give them anything more to gossip about. She choked out a few short sentences. "I know this shouldn't bother me as much as it does. I feel like I'm being so selfish. Kevin's his son, after all, and Rob's a psychologist. Kevin needs him right now. Rob and I can take a honeymoon anytime."

She waved a hand, as if to say she was over it. But she wasn't. She'd been hurt by men too many times, and now those wounds had surfaced again. *Would Rob be the next man in line to hurt her too?*

"I'm so sorry." Rachel's eyes radiated sympathy. "Sorry about Kevin, sorry about your honeymoon, sorry you're here in Port Mariette instead of with Rob."

Marla put an arm around Suzanne and gave her a squeeze. "Believe me, brighter days are ahead."

"Thanks." She gave both of them a red-eyed smile. "I'll survive."

But will my marriage?

Chapter 10

RACHEL

SUNDAY

Rachel took the last gulp of her beer, and with a sigh, thunked the mug on the table. Tonight, one drink would be her limit. Any more than that, she might slip and mention Frank's proposal, or heaven forbid, that awful pink note from Stan's shoebox. This was not the time to raise her own issues. She was here to support Suzanne.

Among the three of them, it had always been Suzanne—certainly not Rachel—who suffered from problems with men. Suzanne having issues, she could understand. But herself? It didn't add up. Why was she having them now, at this stage of life? She pursed her lips as she leaned back in her chair.

"So, anything else on your mind tonight?" Rachel asked Suzanne, who after their lengthy discussion, had paused to take a sip of her wine.

Suzanne held up a hand. "Enough about me and my troubles. How about we move on to another topic, at least for a while. I need some distraction."

Rachel patted her on the arm. "You've survived worse, and I'll bet your marriage will be even stronger because of what you're going through now." Heck, Suzanne could plan another honeymoon, but Rachel would always be tormented by that pink note. With a heart. Signed by T. Who could that be? She wiped her lips with a black cloth napkin, as dark thoughts danced through her mind. Was T the only one—or were there others?

"Here's a new topic," Marla said, swirling the ice around in her empty glass. "Have either of you heard about the negative reviews posted this week about local businesses here in Port Mariette?" She ticked off the names of several stores on Main Street, along with details of the reviews, all too fast for Rachel to absorb. "These reviews had better be a fluke," Marla said. "Otherwise, Port Mariette may have some dark days ahead."

"News to me," Suzanne said, with no emotion, probably still immersed in thoughts of Rob.

Rachel found it difficult to keep up with Marla, especially when more important matters like T occupied her mind. "What are you talking about?"

Marla pointed to one of the reviews on her cell phone. "Look at this one about Hair & Care—*My hair looked better going in than coming out. A filthy place—I swear there were bugs mixed in with the hair on the floor.*" Marla tossed her phone onto the table. "Who would write something like that?"

"And why?" Rachel drummed her fingers on the table. She wouldn't be going to Hair & Care anytime soon. In fact, by her calculation, it would take at least six months for the chopped hair to catch up with the rest, and until she could even it out on her own, she couldn't set foot in there. No secrets in a town like this, especially at Hair & Care—gossip central.

Suzanne lifted a shoulder with indifference. "There are a lot more people coming through town now. Maybe their standards are higher."

"But these reviews are malicious." Marla jabbed her phone with a long, shimmering nail. "There's more to it than someone having higher standards."

"Do you think you might be overreacting a little?" Suzanne asked.

"I don't think so." Marla shook her head. "I've known a lot of businesses in Manhattan who failed because of bad reviews. You have to take them seriously—especially in a town like Port Mariette, where most businesses only get a handful of reviews. That makes a bad one stand out. We're trying to draw people here, not repel them. They rely on reviews to decide where to get off the highway or whether it's worth the drive from Pittsburgh. I'm concerned not just for my spa but for every business on Main Street. After all, my foundation gave this town a lot of grant money. I don't want that investment wasted."

Suzanne shifted in her chair. "You've made a lot of good points, Marla. I guess my mind has been on other things. I wouldn't want the art shop or anyone else's business to suffer because of bad reviews."

"Well, what can we do about it?" Rachel raised her palms. Truth was, she was finding it hard to care. Food 'n Fuel got nothing but great reviews. Well, only three of them, but they were all five-stars, and the one Lindsey posted with Pete's input was a real beaut. Still, maybe those other places needed to improve. Sounded like Hair & Care certainly could. She put a hand over her mouth, realizing that if she didn't go there for six months, they might assume *she* was the one who'd written the bad review.

Marla raised her phone. "Every single Port Mariette business owner should know about these reviews and do something about them. We all need to unite."

"You mean like a union?" Rachel scowled. The unions hadn't saved those steel and coal jobs. Why would she join one now?

"No, not at all like a union," Marla said. "I was thinking we should form some kind of group—"

"Like a chamber of commerce?" Suzanne interrupted, coming alive.

"I get what you're after," Rachel said, "but a chamber of commerce sounds too official for Port Mariette. How about we call it *Main Street Association*?"

Suzanne shook her head. "That won't work. Marla's spa isn't on Main Street. For that matter, nor is the country club, the funeral home, and a bunch of other small businesses like dentists and lawyers." Silence ensued while they mulled their ideas.

Marla's eyes darted back and forth between the other two. "How about *Port Mariette Business Association*?"

Suzanne reacted first. "That's quite a mouthful. But it does fit. We could abbreviate it as P-M-B-A."

"And we could pronounce it 'poom-ba.'" Rachel giggled and looked at the others' straight faces. She cleared her throat. "Just kidding."

Marla leaned forward, all business. "Okay, now we have a name. Next, we need to create a mission statement and decide how we'll operate. I'll ask Warren to draft something for us. Whatever we don't like, we can change. Then we'll invite the other business owners to join."

Rachel sighed. She had only so much energy, and Marla threatened to suck it all up.

But what if she could put Marla's energy to use? Could she enlist Marla to help her figure out who T was? Before she could think of a way to ask, though, their server appeared, balancing a tray of steaming-hot Italian meals—all of them originally made by Rachel in her commercial kitchen at Food 'n Fuel.

Rachel examined the meals. Nice presentation, and Dom hadn't skimped on the red sauce. Stan had always called it her "secret sauce" because she'd never share the recipe with anyone—but it was the same as anyone else's, except her Italian spices were always plucked from plants on a windowsill. Maybe he shared her secret with T. Rachel gritted her teeth.

"I may know how to get stuff done," Marla whispered to Rachel, "but you sure know how to cook."

"Thanks," Rachel replied softly. Dom didn't want anyone to know most of his food was made in a *gas station*, as he called Food 'n Fuel. All he did was reheat it and take the credit.

"You doing okay, Rachel?" Marla was looking at her strangely. "You work such long hours. It must take a toll on you."

"I'm fine," Rachel said. "Maybe just a little tired."

"Why don't you stop by the spa for a massage while I'm in town? It's on me. Get some color back in those cheeks." Marla looked at Suzanne. "You too. Come together or separately, whatever you both prefer."

"Sounds good to me," Rachel said.

Suzanne nodded in agreement as she folded her hands and began saying grace.

Nice how Suzanne always remembered to pray before a meal, even in a public place. The most Rachel would do outside her home was a quick sign of the cross.

"Amen," the women said in unison.

Rachel stabbed a ravioli and shoved half of it in her mouth. The conversation about the new association continued, and her resolve to mention the note dwindled.

Suzanne raised her fork, a chunk of meatball hooked on it. "I'd love to be active in that PMBA group, but obviously I'll be living mainly in California—at least once Rob gets back from Seattle."

"How about your sister?" Marla asked. "Could she get involved?"

"Andrea's okay at running our art shop, but God love her, she's so scattered. She'd never have time for a business owners' association. She's hardly able to keep up with the bookkeeping."

Marla shrugged. "Don't worry, some members will be more active than others. That's just the way it works. Since I'm usually in New York, I hope Grace will get involved, but I can't force her."

"Maybe I could persuade Pete," Rachel said, as she scooped up another bite of ravioli. "But I doubt it. He's not much of an extrovert." She giggled. "I'm not either, so don't look at me."

Both Marla and Suzanne kept silent as they stared at her.

"Well, I guess I could do something." The ravioli slipped off her fork and fell onto the napkin on her lap. Had the others noticed? "Maybe I could take notes at meetings."

"Oh, no." Marla wagged her finger like a doggie's tail. "Secretary? That'll never do. One of us three needs to be calling the shots. It's in our best interests, don't you see? Can you imagine someone like Esther the antique lady being in charge? I'll bet she doesn't even own a computer. Or how about Sharon the hair stylist? She's permanently angry at the world. Who wants an irrational leader? No, we've got to make sure the right person is in charge. Otherwise, someone like Mary Frances will get herself elected just because no one else is willing to do it. You know what she's like—she'd want to focus on real estate issues and nothing else. Herbie would be perfect, but he's already overextended with town council and all his businesses."

Marla gave Suzanne a glance and continued with urgency. "We need someone who has a broad perspective of this region, someone who is beyond reproach in ethics, a person who has a vested interest in Port Mariette's future." Marla's body remained still but her eyes bored into Rachel.

Suzanne kept looking at her too.

"Stop staring at me, you two!" Rachel put down her fork and crossed her arms. "I'm not going to be in charge of Poom-ba. I'm not!"

In spite of Rachel's protests, Marla and Suzanne kept their eyes glued on her. Those two could be relentless. Just look at what they did at the reunion last year, rolling out their plan to overhaul Main Street and ensure the town got its highway exit.

Rachel sighed in resignation. "Okay, okay, I give up." *Maybe, just maybe, Poom-ba will distract me from my troubles.*

Chapter 11

MARLA

MONDAY

A single ray of sun squeezed through the center gap of Marla's velvet bedroom drapes. She opened her eyes to slits and fumbled for her phone on the nightstand.

She googled *Victorian Spa Port Mariette*, then a moment later let out a moan. Grace will be so upset when she sees this.

Marla read the spa's review several times, searching for clues on who might have written it and why, while chewing on the inside of her cheek, a bad habit she'd picked up when she gave up smoking in her thirties. At least she hadn't fallen prey to overeating.

A text popped up from Warren, also an early riser. *You up?*

She tapped his number on her phone.

He answered the call. "Good morning, beautiful."

A smile washed across her face. Warren's voice had a way of soothing her. He'd probably cultivated it to keep his overwrought clients in check, but it worked on her too.

"Hello, handsome." She moved to the edge of her bed, hoping to hear more tender words.

"I got your email about starting a business association in Port Mariette."

So much for sweet talk. She stood and paced the room. "Well, what do you think?"

He chortled. "You just can't help yourself, can you? Manhattan's not big enough for your ambitions?"

In a way, he was right. She'd sold Gemstones Gyms last year, and now, the businesswoman in her needed a fresh challenge. Her strengths had always been marketing and promotion, which came in handy last summer when she, Suzanne, and Rachel had dreamed up a plan to put Port Mariette back on the map. Business had been booming since the plan was implemented, but now, this sudden spate of bad reviews threatened to erase all that progress. "So, can you help us with setting up PMBA?"

"Sure. I've got some boilerplate I can send you."

"Thanks." She bit the inside her cheek again. "Hey. I got some bad news this morning."

"Aunt Adele?" His voice registered sudden concern.

"Oh, no, she's fine."

"Grace?"

"No." She shook her head. "Someone wrote a horrible review about the spa. Really skewered the place."

He swore under his breath. "What did it say?"

She read the first part then stopped. "The last line is the worst—*If you like being black and blue the day after your massage, the Victorian Spa in Port Mariette is the place for you.*"

He groaned. "That's pretty bad. Any idea who wrote it?"

"I hate to say it, but that reference to black and blue could be a hint. Maybe it's someone who doesn't want to get a massage from a black woman."

"Hmm. Sounds like a reach to me. But then again, you did say Latoya can be a little overpowering. Maybe she's a little too vigorous with her massages?" His voice went up at the end.

"She does tend to overwhelm people when they first meet her, but her heart's so big, I can't imagine anyone not liking her, and she does give a great massage. I can personally attest to that." Marla stretched her back and shoulders as she recalled Latoya's massage last night.

"Has anyone ever complained about her?"

"Not that I know of. I'd have to ask Grace." She paused. "Anyway, what do you think we can do about these reviews?"

"You have options," he said immediately, with authority.

"Let me get a pen and paper." She loved how Warren could quickly evaluate all angles of any situation—although at times his ideas could immobilize her, as she preferred action to rumination. Writing things down might enable her to choose the best option.

He took a deep breath and launched his assessment. "A lot depends on the site where the reviews are posted. Sometimes you can flag a review as inappropriate, or you can simply ask the site to remove it. Some sites allow the business owner to reply. In that case, you could ask the reviewer to call you to discuss their situation. If their complaint is legitimate, you could give them a gift card or a refund or somehow make it right for them. You could ask them if they'd be willing to delete or modify their review."

"I'm surprised you didn't say I could sue them. Can I?"

"If the review is inaccurate, you can. But you have a lot of great reviews already, so this is merely one in a sea of good opinions. You might want to just ignore it. After all, a lot of those online reviews are fake. People expect every business to have some bad ones. Maybe somebody is jealous of someone else's success, or they want to ruin their competitor."

"Hmm." Marla squinted in thought. "Lots of options to consider."

"Can you tell if the same person has written all the reviews?" Warren asked.

"I don't know. Every one of them used some kind of nickname. For this review on the spa, for example, the person's name is Amelia Bedelia. I can't imagine a real person has a name like that."

"Amelia Bedelia is a character in a series of children's books."

"Oh," Marla said. Warren had raised two girls, but Marla had missed that part of her own daughter's life.

"By the way, does Grace know about the review yet?"

"I doubt it. It popped up overnight, and she's still in bed." Marla paused as a noise from down the hall caught her attention. "Wait. I think I hear her getting up."

"You might want to keep it low-key when you talk with her."

"What do you mean?" Sometimes Warren could be so obtuse.

"You know how Grace is. She'll feel like she's to blame. Might take it personally. She's not a hard-charger like you."

"What's your point?" Marla demanded.

He sighed. "I'm sure you realize you can be intimidating."

"You think so?" Marla furrowed her brow. "She's never said anything to me about that."

"No? Well, even with knowing Grace as little as I do, how could she? That wouldn't be her style. Keep in mind, you're a businesswoman from Manhattan, not someone born and bred in a small town."

Maybe Warren had a point. Grace was so sensitive. She once told Marla she couldn't watch the nightly news before going to bed—it gave her nightmares.

She finished their conversation and stared out the window. *She intimidated her own daughter?*

After a moment of reflection, Marla trooped downstairs to brew a pot of coffee. Almost eight. The roofer would soon be here making noise. While the coffee percolated, she sat at the table with her elbows on the kitchen table and hands over her eyes. Having a good relationship with her daughter was paramount. But business was her forte, not family relationships. How could she change from intimidating her daughter to being approachable? Should she go to a therapist? Take a class? Read a book?

The answer came in a flash. Warren had raised two girls. She'd get ideas from him when they talked on the phone tomorrow. If there was one thing she could always count on Warren for, it was good counsel. And occasionally, a love note.

Chapter 12

SUZANNE

MONDAY

Suzanne hoisted her heavy carry-on bag out of her sister's trunk and dropped it onto their mother's gravel driveway. "Thanks again for rescuing me, Andrea." Last night, after dinner at Dom's, Marla drove Suzanne back to her condo, where she spent several hours weeping. Two glasses of wine probably hadn't helped.

Regardless, by morning's light, Suzanne had concluded she needed to be around other people until Rob made it back to Carmel—even if it required staying with her mother in Port Mariette. Mom said she'd welcome the company, and Andrea was thrilled to get some help.

"Let me give you a hand, Suzie." Andrea heaved the second suitcase out. Tall, big-boned, and dark-haired, Andrea had clearly taken after their dad's side. "I'm sorry for the reason you're staying here, but I have to admit, I'm glad to get some support. Between Mom and the shop, I've been struggling."

A wave of guilt washed over Suzanne. Their entire drive from Pittsburgh, she'd done nothing but blab about her own troubles. Not once had she asked how her own sister was doing. Although Suzanne had been striving to be less self-centered, backsliding came easy anytime she felt overwhelmed.

Like right now.

They rolled the suitcases along the cracked cement walkway and bounced them up the porch steps. Along the way, Suzanne assessed the house's weathered exterior and its small fenced-in yard. The grass needed to be cut, the shrubs should have been trimmed. And what's all that stuff on the front porch?

Andrea put her hand on the screen door handle then took it back. She dropped her voice to a whisper. "Whatever you do, don't bring up the subject of Mom moving to Sunset Hills, or any other facility, for that matter. Boy, does that set her off."

"She's got to move somewhere, though. It's been one fall after another. What choice is there?"

"Well, she can't lay on the sofa watching TV forever, that's for sure. She needs to be somewhere with hot meals and no steps to fall down." Andrea touched the crook of Suzanne's arm. "Don't worry about it, though. I've got everything under control."

It must run in our family. Suzanne laughed to herself as she fussed with her hair, a wavy tendril now slipping out of a tortoise-shell hair clip.

Andrea continued whispering. "A social worker from the hospital is stopping by tomorrow. She's got a good track record of persuading seniors to move to Sunset Hills. She's gonna take Mom there in one of those access vans. After she's visited the place, maybe she'll give in."

"You do have everything under control." Suzanne gave her sister a sideways hug. "I'm sorry you've had to take care of Mom all by yourself."

"Thanks. I'm doing my best."

"And sorry I rambled on about my own troubles all the way here. You have plenty to whine about too."

"It's okay. I know you needed an ear." Andrea pulled the screen door open.

Suzanne stepped inside first. Same faux leather sofa, same scratched-up end table, same beige telephone with a zero lit up on the answering machine. She sniffed a few times, trying to identify the odor. Why had she never noticed it before?

Andrea called up the stairs. "Mom, we're here."

No response.

"Maybe she's sleeping." Suzanne rolled her carry-on to the bottom of the steps. "How about we take these suitcases up to my old room?"

They climbed the creaky steps as noiselessly as they could.

"I haven't been up here for years, except to use the bathroom." Suzanne smiled in excitement as she turned the wrought-iron knob to her old room. She pushed the door open. "Oh, my goodness." Newspapers, magazines, books, and boxes filled the room, right up to the windowsill.

Musty, that's the smell.

"Holy smokes!" Andrea covered her mouth with her hand, seeming to be more shocked than Suzanne. "Honestly, I had no idea. Mom always told me she kept the spare bedrooms clean herself. Her own room always looked okay, so I figured the other bedrooms were too."

"She was always so meticulous." Suzanne was still whispering, although it clearly wasn't necessary. She could hear her mother snoring down the hall.

"Yeah. Mrs. Clean to the core." Andrea crossed the hallway and opened the other bedroom doors. "Ugh." She covered her nose. "The same."

"No way can she take all this stuff to Sunset Hills." Suzanne put her hands on her hips. "But I'll bet she'll want to keep every single thing."

"Before we can list the house for sale, we'll have to—" Andrea stopped talking and made a beeline to a stack of books near the front window. "Look! It's my collection of Trixie Belden books!" She flipped one open and immediately sneezed. "I'll keep these."

Was hoarding a genetic behavior?

Suzanne stretched for a few seconds, then let out an exhale. "Just *thinking* about everything we have to do here is exhausting."

"Yeah." Andrea dropped the book on top of the pile.

"I know it's been hard on you," Suzanne said. "How are you holding up?"

"Me? Oh, I'm fine." Andrea's overly casual response sounded unconvincing. She gazed out the frilly-curtained window for a few seconds. "Did you notice Mrs. Shevchenko across the street got her house painted yellow? It looks so cheery, doesn't it?"

"Are you trying to change the subject?" Suzanne squinted at her sister. "C'mon. Tell me what's going on. Something with your kids? ... Your ex? ... The business?"

Andrea looked out in the direction of Main Street. "It's—it's the business. I'm having a hard time keeping up. Taxes and utilities need to be paid, the checking account hasn't been balanced in months, and I've got a lot of new inventory to enter into the system."

This was the first time Suzanne had heard of major trouble at the shop—the place that provided her sole source of income. "I had no idea it was this hard on you." She tried not to sound panicky. "Tell me more."

Andrea looked down again at the pile of Trixie Belden books, almost like she was wishing to return to the simpler life of her youth. "There's just too much to do—customers, displays, advertising, bookkeeping, taxes. So much paperwork. Did you know we now have twelve people selling their items on consignment?"

"Really? I didn't know that." Suzanne zigzagged few steps around the junk to get closer to her sister. "I thought it was mainly you, me and Mom."

"It started out that way, but now we have a dollmaker"—she ticked everyone off on her fingers—"a wood carver, a sign maker, a dried flower arranger, a jewelry designer, and a pottery maker—plus other artists like you who use different media like watercolors and oils."

"That's a lot to keep track of." Suzanne sounded sympathetic, but warning bells were going off in her head. Clearly, she'd have to get more involved.

Andrea seemed near tears as she stared at the Belden books.

"So, what can I help you with?"

For a moment, Andrea didn't respond. Then she looked up. "How about the marketing end of things? We sure could use more sales. Foot traffic has been down because of all the rain, and Mom's no longer crocheting. Her stuff has always been our most profitable merchandise. Once her stock runs out, that'll be the end of those commissions."

Suzanne blinked a couple times. She'd been so busy with her new life in California that she'd been oblivious. "Sure, I'll do it." She readily agreed out of guilt—besides, marketing guru Marla would be in town a while longer. Suzanne would pick her brain clean.

"I've got to go open the shop." Andrea gingerly stepped around the books and headed toward the door. "But first, let's find some sheets and a pillow for you. Looks like you'll be spending your nights on the sofa till we get one of these rooms cleared out." She opened a narrow hallway closet. "Ta-da." She pulled out some unmatched linens and a bed pillow and handed them to Suzanne.

"Thanks." Suzanne said it half-heartedly, knowing the condition of the sofa.

Andrea picked up her purse. "Gotta run—I try to open by ten on Mondays. Good luck talking with Mom about those bedrooms." She scooted out the door before Suzanne could protest.

Chapter 13

RACHEL

MONDAY

Ready for work in pressed khakis and a Food 'n Fuel T-shirt, Rachel glanced out her living room picture window. The shimmering puddles in the street showed no sign of drops, only reflected sunshine, yet Monday's forecast predicted more rain, so she grabbed an umbrella from the coat closet.

She squeezed out the front door, thwarting Cinders's attempt to escape. "You were out already, buddy. Go take a nap." She held onto the railing as she made her way down the damp porch steps. Pete had done a masterful job replacing those old boards, but the new steps were more slippery than the old ones. She made it to the sidewalk safely and set out on her walk to work.

Frank appeared on his porch next door, looking like a huggable sleepy bear in his sloppy robe and worn slippers, his graying brown hair desperately in need of a cut and a combing. Poor Frank. He clearly struggled from the lack of a wife's attention.

"Morning, Rachel." He wrapped both his big hands on the porch railing as she ambled along the sidewalk in front of him.

She waved. "Hi, Frank." Her smile was tentative. As of last night, he'd agreed to come over for cards and cookies, but nothing more.

"I'll take Cinders for a walk after I have my coffee."

"You're a doll," Rachel said, feeling a wave of relief. She flashed him a warm smile then continued walking.

"Canasta tomorrow at seven, right?" Frank called as she passed the next house.

"Right. Raisin cookies." Thank goodness it seemed they'd get back into their routine of playing cards one night a week. Maybe they'd go out to dinner on the weekend too. She wouldn't even have to run back and forth from work to let Cinders out. What a bullet she'd dodged.

Strolling to Food 'n Fuel now took about twenty minutes, eight minutes less than when she'd started walking there last year. Breaking the habit of driving to work had initially shaved a few inches off her aging body, with the bonus of sparing wear and tear on her Chevy, but lately, she'd fallen back into bad eating habits. Most of the lost pounds had returned.

She picked up her pace and surprised herself at how quickly she arrived at Food 'n Fuel, already busy with two vehicles at the pumps and another in a parking space. She entered through the front door, gave a thumbs-up to Pete busy behind the counter, and made her way to the other side of the building where they had converted the service bays into a commercial kitchen. A corner in the back contained a metal desk, a cardboard file cabinet, and two ratty chairs—all together called Rachel's office.

She took one look at her desktop and let out a groan. Yesterday, she'd skipped out early to meet Suzanne and

Marla for dinner, leaving herself a fine mess to face this morning. She tossed her purse into a drawer, then sank her hands onto her hips as she surveyed the paperwork scattered across the desk. One of the business lines rang, interrupting her efforts to prioritize.

She recognized the number—her favorite customer and high school crush, Tony Mastriano. It didn't matter to her if Tony now looked like that Humpty Dumpty monk who used to come speak at St. Cyp's. That was Suzanne's opinion, not hers.

Tony owned Signore's, a popular Italian restaurant a few miles south of Pittsburgh. At last year's reunion, he encouraged her to open a commercial kitchen, and once she launched the business, he'd sometimes feature her sausage lasagna on his specials. "Not even an Italian makes it as good as you," he always said. What a boost his encouragement had given her.

A lock of hair fell across Rachel's cheek, and she tucked it behind her ear. *This wig is amazing.* Just like real hair, and even in rainy weather, it always looks great. If only it didn't make her head so hot. She scratched her scalp with a pen as she took his call. "Hi, Tony," she said with a lilt in her voice. The guy did have a way of brightening her mood.

"Ah, it's my sweet angel."

"Ha ha. What d'ya need?"

"Busy, huh? Same here. Hey, some lady just scheduled a huge group in our back room tomorrow. The funeral's at ten. You know how funerals are, everything's last minute. Drives me nuts. She insists on having sausage lasagna, says her husband used to eat it every time we had it on special. "Look, I know you're busy, but any chance you can make up three pans for me?"

"For you, Tony, sure." She smirked, knowing she could never say no to him. Besides, she'd already made a ton of it yesterday afternoon.

"Great. Come to think of it, could you make up two extra pans? Then, between that and the leftovers from the funeral, I'll have enough to put it on my daily specials." He paused. "I'm really short-handed. Another cook just quit on me."

"Good help's hard to find."

"I really hate to ask, but do you have someone who could drive it up here?"

Rachel chuckled. "Sure. I can deliver it this morning. But you know I'm only doing it because it's for you."

"And that's why you're my sweet angel."

Sweet angel. Stan never called her anything but Rachel. *Wonder what he called T?*

"See ya soon." She got her purse back out of the drawer.

The rain still held off, so she took a quick lap around the building to eyeball the premises. The press of daily business made it easy to overlook maintenance; she always had to force herself to do it.

Glass doors are smudged. Plants next to the gas pumps should be replaced. Why hasn't Pete fixed that security camera yet? She pursed her lips. He's too busy, just like me. Heck, she hadn't said a rosary in weeks.

Rachel popped in the front door and saw Pete ringing up a sale. She grabbed a bottle of window cleaner and wiped off the fingerprints. "Those petunias are looking pretty leggy, Pete. We should get something new in there."

"I'll take care of it." He jotted a note.

"How about that outside camera? I thought you were going to fix it."

"I tried, but I had to order a new one. Hasn't come in yet—supply chain issues."

"I hope it wasn't made in China." To Rachel and almost everyone else in the valley, *Buy American* was their way of life. The steel and coal industries may have deserted them, yet their loyalties never wavered.

"Don't worry, Mom, I checked. It's made in America."

"Good. It should arrive soon then since it won't have to cross an ocean." She tossed the rag under the counter. "I've got to run a big order up to Signore's." She went to the other side of the building and loaded the pans into the van.

The drive to Tony's was easy, almost all highway. With the radio playing music from the eighties, her thoughts floated to her high school days. What might life have been like if she had dated Tony instead of Stan? Such a loaded question. Her mind toyed with it all the way to Pittsburgh.

She arrived at Signore's and hopped out to unload.

One of the cooks came out the back door and propped it open with a rock. He wiped his hands on a stained white apron. "Need some help?"

"Sure." She opened the van's rear door and stepped aside to give him access.

"I'll get that." It was Tony's familiar voice. He waved the cook back inside and reached for the first pan. "You just relax. I'll get the rest." He marched back and forth until all five pans had been transported.

She slammed the door shut and pulled her keys from her pocket. "Thanks, Tony." Poor guy, his face had turned red from the exertion. He should have let his cook carry them.

Tony leaned against the side of the van and wiped his forehead with the back of his hand. "I don't know how much longer I'll be able to keep up this pace, y'know what I mean?"

Rachel put the keys back in her pocket. For Tony, she had time to chat. "Yeah. We're in a tough business."

"A big restaurant like Signore's is more than I care to handle at this point in my life. I'm thinking about retiring, at least from here."

"Really?" They were only in their late fifties. Way too soon for retirement, at least in her mind.

Tony's eyes darted all over his building, just like Rachel had done an hour ago with hers. "There's just too much work here for me. A younger person should be running it. Someone who doesn't get overwhelmed with seating two hundred customers and managing forty employees." He shrugged. "My son's ready to take over, but he needs a strong manager as his number two. He can't do it all himself."

"I know what you mean." Pete was terrific, but some days she wished her other sons also lived in Port Mariette and helped with Food 'n Fuel. But they'd established their families and careers elsewhere. The best she could hope for was an occasional babysitting gig, and even that was at risk if word got around about her chopped-off hair.

"I think I might have a solution, though." Tony's eyes lit up. "My former manager called me. She's getting a divorce, just moved back to Pittsburgh from North Carolina. She needs a job." Tony raised an eyebrow, as if in cahoots with Rachel. "Tough break for her but could be a lucky one for me."

"Well, I hope it works out for you." Rachel folded her arms. "Honestly, I haven't given much thought to retirement. I've got too many other things on my mind."

"Like what?"

She couldn't talk with him about Frank, and certainly not about T, so she told him about the online reviews spreading like a virus along Main Street. She'd been hearing some businesses were losing customers over them. What if Food 'n Fuel was next? "Something has to be done."

He nodded. "We get a bad review here and there. I always offer to send them a gift card. Heck, that's probably why people write them—they hope they'll get a freebie."

"Well, we need to do something about those reviews, and we also need to draw more customers into Port Mariette. Last night, I talked with Marla and Suzanne about starting a business owners' association. A united front, y'know."

"Good idea."

"It was Marla's."

"We have a group like that here—South Hills Merchants."

"Is it useful?" Rachel liked their name, shorter and snappier than Port Mariette Business Association.

"Sometimes. A lot depends on the people in charge. Some of them are better equipped to lead than others."

Her mouth turned down at the ends. "Marla and Suzanne want me to run for president."

"President?" Tony jerked his chin.

"You find that shocking?" Rachel hugged her arms a little more tightly around her chest. Why would he underestimate her? Would everyone else too?

"A little surprising, I guess." He looked down and kicked away a pebble on the cracked asphalt. "Being front and center isn't exactly your style—except back when you were head majorette." He winked.

Obviously Tony didn't think she was up to the task. Didn't he know she'd changed since their high school days? Or could it be she hadn't?

She put her hands on her hips and lifted her chin. "I think ... I think I'm going to do it."

Now, she had only herself to convince.

Chapter 14

MARLA

MONDAY

Still pondering Warren's ideas about the online reviews, Marla poured herself a fresh cup of coffee and took in a comforting whiff. She moved to the kitchen window and watched Mitch's roofer leap out of an oversized white pickup truck.

He pulled an extension ladder from the rack, his brisk movements making the task look effortless. A go-getter like Mitch. Not a bad-looking fellow, either, although a little rough around the edges. Looked to be around forty, with plenty of tattoos on muscular arms and long golden curls tamed by a bandana. Yuck. How she hated do-rags.

She tsked, even though no one else could hear her. That Mitch. Him and his habit of hiring guys trying to redeem their pasts. He'd connect with them at some prison in West Virginia, then hire them when they got out. Probably where this fellow came from. Surely Mitch had preached to him just as he'd done with her. Might've gotten the fellow inside his Assembly of God church too, as he had done with Marla last summer.

Grace appeared in the kitchen entry, wearing a long, figure-flattering slitted skirt. "You made coffee." A surprised smile washed across her face, as if Marla should have been incapable of any such kitchen-related accomplishment.

"Good morning, Grace. How pretty you look."

"Thank you," she replied while stepping to the window. "I see Jesse arrived right on time." She waved to him then poured herself some coffee.

"Maybe you and I can have a few minutes to chat before that noise begins on the roof." Marla took a seat at the round table in the turret.

Grace slid onto a chair across from her. "You want to talk about something?" Her voice sounded a note higher than usual.

Marla nodded. She started off with some bland comments about how well she'd slept, then meandered about the rainy weather they'd been having.

Grace furrowed her brow. "You never do small talk. What's wrong?"

Marla swallowed a sip of coffee. "Well ..." She crossed her legs and grabbed hold of a knee. "Looks like those bad reviews are contagious. We just got one too."

"The spa? Oh, no!" Grace covered her mouth with her fingers. "What did it say?"

Marla tapped her phone and showed her the review.

Grace kept her mouth covered as she read, but her wide-open eyes revealed her feelings.

"Don't worry, I've already talked with Warren about what we can do about it." Marla raised her hand straight up, as if that could quell Grace's concerns. "I'm sure there's no truth whatsoever to what this *Amelia Bedelia* wrote."

"Why would someone write that?" Grace squinted. "I wonder if that name's a clue."

"How so?"

"Amelia Bedelia bumbled into all sorts of trouble through no fault of her own." Grace tapped her lips. "I can't imagine a man could identify with her. It's got to be a woman. Probably one who likes to read."

"You should be a detective." Marla forced a chuckle in an attempt to keep the mood light.

Grace smiled wanly. "Who do *you* think might have written it?"

Marla explained her theory about the "black and blue" comment.

"Hmm. Sad to say, I guess that's a possibility, but I hope not."

"Well, whoever it is, we'll get to the bottom of it." Marla raised a finger. "One thing I know for sure—this review has nothing to do with the quality of our employees or our services."

Grace smiled unconvincingly then ran her finger a few times around the rim of her coffee cup. She pushed back from the table. "I'm going outside to see how Jesse's doing with the roof."

Marla let out a sigh of relief. At least Grace didn't overreact. She could be so touchy. Sure didn't get that from me.

She got up from the table in search of something to eat. With little to choose from, cinnamon bagels would have to do. She plunked them into the toaster.

Grace came back inside as Marla was carrying hot bagels and a package of cream cheese to the table. "Something to eat?" Marla took her seat and Grace shrugged, then slid onto hers.

Marla fluttered a napkin open and smoothed it across her lap. What else could they talk about besides that lousy review? She remained still while Grace blessed herself then said a silent prayer.

The roofer banged a few times above them.

Marla glanced up. "Is he another one of Mitch's saved souls?" She hadn't meant to sound sarcastic, but it came so naturally.

Grace arched her back. "I graduated from high school with Jesse." She jabbed her knife into the cream cheese. "He used to be into drugs, but he's clean now."

"How do you know for sure?" Until her mini-stroke, Marla herself had fooled around with recreational drugs. "They say it can be hard to tell if someone's really clean."

"If Mitch hired him, he's clean. You know that. Besides, Jesse's a nice guy. I'm glad he got his life back in order."

"Well, good for him." Marla swallowed a mouthful. "After breakfast, how about we make a list of every female who recently had her first massage appointment. Hopefully it'll be a short list."

Grace nodded. "Then, I could call them and say I'm following up after their visit. See how they react."

"Good. That wouldn't arouse suspicion, and you'll get all sorts of helpful information, even if it's unrelated to the review."

Marla wiped her lips with her napkin and let out a soft chuckle. "When I owned my gyms, a group of women in one of the locations didn't renew their memberships. I had a good relationship with one of them, so I called to ask her what was going on. Turned out one of the other members had been having an affair with an older wealthy man—who happened to be married to one of the women who hadn't renewed her membership."

"What did you do? Grace asked. "You can't change a situation like that."

"Maybe not directly, but you can wield some influence." Grace laughed. "Tell me, what did you do?"

"I didn't do anything, just delegated it to my manager Deanna. She's a deaconess in a Baptist church. Very holy." Marla flattened her hands together in front of her chest and pointed them upward. "She flooded our lobby with Gospel tracts and started a Bible study in a spare room. The atmosphere in the gym changed so much the woman having the affair stopped coming."

"Did the other women return, the ones who hadn't renewed?"

"They did, and they even brought some of their friends. In the end, it boosted the bottom line, so I gave Deanna a raise." Marla hoped the story might inspire Grace to improve the spa's financial picture. Her daughter focused way too much on clients' feelings and not enough on profits.

"But the woman having the affair—what happened with her?"

"I heard she ended it, and then one day, she showed up at the Bible study. With her very own Bible, according to Deanna." Marla chuckled. "Go figure."

"God at work. I love it." Grace stood up straight and strode to the computer. "I'll print out a list of names for us to dig into."

"I'm going to pop over to Main Street. I'll be back in a bit." Anything to get away from that noise on the roof.

Chapter 15

SUZANNE

TUESDAY

Wearing old jeans and a faded Steelers T-shirt, Suzanne wrung out a wet rag and draped it over the side of a bucket. Lucky she'd thrown some old clothes into her suitcase when she hightailed it out of her condo yesterday. Otherwise, she'd be cleaning the art shop in honeymoon attire—silk blouse and dry-clean-only slacks.

Or perhaps a diaphanous nightgown. Why not? She seemed to have no practical use for such an item.

The small cowbell over the front door tinkled, signaling a visitor. Creations on Main wasn't due to open until noon, and since she'd left the *closed* sign on the door, she hadn't bothered to lock herself in. "Andrea, is that you?" Suzanne called from the storage room.

"It's Marla," came the familiar voice, growing louder as she got closer. "I saw the lights on. Figured you or your sister would be here."

"We aren't open yet." Suzanne wiped her hands on her jeans. "I'm just catching up on some cleaning."

Marla stepped into the storage room, her eyes darting around. "Tornado touched down?"

"I know, I know. This room's a disaster. Way too much inventory back here. I don't know why Andrea allows people to drop stuff off when there's no space to display it on the sales floor."

Suzanne picked up a damp cloth and swiped it across a dusty shelf. She may as well keep cleaning. Andrea obviously didn't have time for it, and sure as heck Marla wouldn't be helping. "So, what brings you to Main Street?"

Marla sneezed. "Sorry. Dust gets to me." She pressed her nose with the back of her hand. "I thought I'd make the rounds at some local businesses today."

"Why?"

"To sell them on the concept of Port Mariette Business Association." She lowered her voice, even though they were the only ones there. "Plus, I want to plant the idea that Rachel would be a great choice as the group's president." She looked around. "You're sure Andrea's coming in soon? I wanted to ask her if she could get involved in PMBA."

"She deserted me, just like Rob." Suzanne intended to say it with a laugh, but instead, she felt a stab in her heart, and her words sounded angry. She did feel deserted by her sister—and more so, by her brand new husband. Andrea would show up today to open the shop, but it seemed she'd washed her hands of all other responsibilities.

"What do you mean?" Marla put a hand on her hip.

Suzanne flicked the rag on the frame of one of her own oil paintings. "Oh, don't mind me. I'm just a little disgusted with my life right now. First, Rob skips out on our honeymoon, and now Andrea's dumping her problems on me." Suzanne drew in some air then exhaled loudly. "I shouldn't have said that. This art consignment shop is my responsibility too. I'm co-owner."

"You're just feeling sorry for yourself. It's understandable." Marla leaned against the sink. "You've got a lot on your mind."

"You don't know the half of it," Suzanne said. "My mother's health has been deteriorating fast. Until this week, I had no idea how bad things were. She can't live alone anymore, but she refuses to move into Sunset Hills."

"Aunt Adele loves it there."

"I know, but your aunt is not my mother." Marla's tendency to oversimplify problems drove Suzanne batty. She massaged the skin between her eyebrows, a futile attempt to thwart an oncoming headache. "On top of that, my mom's apparently become a borderline hoarder." There, she'd said it all.

"*Borderline hoarder*? Is that an official diagnosis?" Marla raised a perfectly drawn eyebrow.

"My term. You should see what her spare bedrooms look like—they're ten times worse than this place." She waved her hand around the storeroom. "Anyway, I have to persuade Mom to move without taking all her stuff."

"Hoarding—it must be more common than most people think. Isn't there a TV show about it?"

"I don't know. I hardly ever watch TV. When I was on the road all those years, I didn't want to slip into the habit of watching sitcoms every night, so I forced myself to go to the hotel gyms instead." As pathetic as her life was right now, at least she'd get plenty of exercise cleaning here at the shop and at her mom's.

She yanked out her hairclip and tossed it on a shelf. With fingertips, she combed her wavy hair into place. "I need a break. Let me put this cleaning stuff away, then I'll go with you to visit a few other businesses."

"Great." Marla stood waiting, hand on a hip. "I never knew this storage room was back here." Her eyes danced back and forth across the room. "Maybe you could enclose the sink and the toilet, then turn the rest of the room into selling space."

"Funny you'd say that." Suzanne's face brightened, happy that marketing guru Marla been thinking along the same line as her. As annoying as Marla could sometimes be, she was still the sharpest businesswoman Suzanne had ever met. "Actually, I was thinking of displaying paintings on the walls to increase sales and using the rest of the room for classes."

Marla squinted. "Painting classes?"

"Yes, but even more. Our consignment artists could conduct a whole variety of classes. Andrea could give painting classes, and when I'm in town, I could teach a few myself. Inez, our dollmaker, loves to show others how to make dolls and their clothing. We also have a man in his nineties who does woodcarving. Wouldn't it be wonderful if he could pass along his skills to younger people? And of course, we have plenty of others here who could teach."

"Love your idea." Marla strode around the room, nodding. "You could probably fit twenty people in here."

"At least," Suzanne said. "The classes would draw people to town. After a class, they might want to get a facial, have a meal, or fill up their gas tank. It could be a boon for local businesses."

Marla slapped her hands together. "It's exactly why we need to form a business association. Ideas like this will help every single business in town. What a great idea, Suzanne. Wish I'd thought of it myself."

Suzanne beamed. For the first time today, she forgot her troubles.

Chapter 16

RACHEL

TUESDAY

"Looks like you're a little rusty." Rachel seized the pile of discards and added the top one to the many rows of cards on her side of the table.

Frank's side remained empty. He bit off a chunk of his raisin cookie and leaned back in his chair, chuckling. "You know I'm just letting you win."

The final rays of sun slanted through the front window. He looked into her eyes and held her gaze a second.

Rachel squirmed. He had that same look in his eyes like he did at Suzanne's wedding. She discarded an ace and gave him a wink. "Maybe for a change, I'll let you win."

He ignored the ace and picked a card from the pile. "I thought with your old high school buddies in town, you might be too busy to play Canasta."

"Did you just say *old*?" Leaning forward, Rachel dropped her jaw open, faking offense.

"Well, you know what I mean." His brown eyes twinkled. "They're hardly your *new* high school buddies."

"I know what you mean." She tittered as she pulled back from the table and scrutinized her handful of cards. "I was just teasing. I can always squeeze in a game of Canasta. Once Suzanne and Marla leave, I'll have even more time on my hands. By the way, Marla stopped by Food 'n Fuel this morning. She's talking with all the Main Street merchants about starting up that business association."

"Good for her. She's got more energy than this whole town put together."

Rachel discarded another ace and held her breath. Two aces in that pile might be too much for him to resist.

He seemed not to notice. Instead, he toyed with his mug. "Can I get you another beer?"

"Not for me." She motioned toward the kitchen. "Go right ahead." She was determined to find out if he cheated. Maybe to others, it wouldn't matter so much, but ever since fourth grade when Sister Godfrey drilled the Ten Commandments into her, she'd been a stickler about sin. The way she saw it, if Frank was cheating, he was breaking the eighth commandment by lying and the seventh by stealing her victory.

Frank ambled into the kitchen, opened the refrigerator for a beer, and made his way back to the table. He snapped the can open and poured it into a Steelers mug.

"Your turn," she reminded him as he finished pouring.

He took a card from the pile, pondered his hand for a moment, then discarded a four.

Just the card she needed! If he had glanced at her hand, he would have seen her mittful of fours and never thrown one on the pile. He hadn't been cheating after all. She scarfed up the four and made a canasta.

Relieved he'd passed the test, she ventured to ask something requiring a higher level of honesty. "Let me ask you a question, Frank. You and Stan were such good friends. Did he ever say anything about a woman whose name starts with a T?"

"The letter T? What's her whole name?"

"I can't tell you. Trust me on this. I just need to know if you remember Stan ever talking about a woman whose name begins with the letter T."

Frank rubbed his chin awhile. Finally, he perked up. "How about your sister Theresa?"

My sister? It couldn't be Terrie—could it? No. It couldn't be. But even if it were true, she could never know for sure. Last fall, emphysema cut Terrie's life short.

Rachel's cellphone rang, interrupting her thoughts. She glanced at the screen. "Oh, boy. It's my brother. He never calls unless it's important." She took the call. "Hi, Chip."

"Hey, I'm here with Mom." Chip lived in Florida, a few miles from their mother.

"Everything okay?" Rachel tightened her jaw.

"Yeah, pretty much." He cleared his throat. "Mom—Mom was in an accident."

"Oh, no!" Rachel spread a hand over her heart. "What happened?"

"She was driving her golf cart to yoga class. Some kid was texting while driving. He slammed right into her, toppled the cart over, and Mom fell out."

"Oh, my gosh! Are you at a hospital?"

"We're driving home from it right now. She got banged up and sprained her arm, but the ER doc said they had no reason to keep her."

"Can you put her on speaker?"

"Hi, Rachel." Her mom's voice sounded frail and groggy.

"Mom, do you need me to come help?"

Chip replied instead. "She smiled when you said that, then she nodded off. Pain meds, you know."

"What can I do?" Rachel stood and paced around the dining room table.

First, he said, "Nothing." Then he relented. "Maybe you should come. After all, I can't dress her or bathe her. Heck, I don't even know how to cook."

"I'll—I'll look into flights and let you know when I can be there." She plopped back onto her chair and said goodbye. Her eyes welled with tears of both worry and fear. She'd never flown anywhere alone, much less rented a car and driven in unfamiliar territory. For her mother, though, she'd have to figure out a way.

Frank had already put the cards back into their box. He sat still, with his hands folded on the table.

She repeated the conversation.

"So, your mom's not in any serious danger, but she needs help with recuperation?"

"Right."

"Okay, then. I have an idea. She's only about an hour away from my son Joey in Tampa. You and I can fly into Tampa—it's a direct flight from Pittsburgh. Joey can loan me his car, and I can drive you to your mom's. We can stay as long as you need to, and anytime you need a break, I can pick you up and take you to the beach or out to dinner."

"Wow. Let me think about that." How she feared flying. The plane could get caught in one of those wild storms they'd been having, or her flight could be canceled for some reason. Driving around in a rental car, she might get lost or have an accident. All the worrying made her perspire. She lifted her elbows on the table to allow some air to circulate under her arms. About the heat under the wig, she could do nothing until Frank left.

As much as she dreaded going to Florida by herself, if she traveled with Frank, he could easily read into it, maybe expect more from her. Above all, she didn't want him to misinterpret their relationship.

"That's very thoughtful of you, Frank, but I just don't know." She needed to come up with an excuse. "I—I think I'd feel guilty having fun while my mother's suffering."

"Oh, c'mon. Does she feel guilty because she's been living in Florida having fun ever since your dad died? Of course not. That's life—a mixture of good and bad, suffering and pleasure. You mom will understand if you take a few hours off."

Rachel inhaled deeply as she pushed back from the table. "Okay. Let's book it."

WEDNESDAY

"That's it on the left, the one with light blue shutters and the big palm tree." Rachel pointed to her mom's house as Frank continued driving well under the speed limit. "Let's see how she's doing first, and if she's up for company, I'll make you something to eat." Other than preparing him food, she didn't know how else to show him her appreciation.

He parked along the street, right in front of the house. Before he had time to open his car door, Rachel was already rushing across the lawn, leaving him to deal with her suitcase.

Chip greeted her at the door. "Great timing. Mom just woke up from a nap." He gave Rachel a hug. "You look terrific."

"Thanks." She knew Chip couldn't mean it. Between packing and worrying, she'd barely slept, plus she had to get out of bed at four a.m. to get to the airport on time. The only part of her that looked good—her wig—wasn't really part of her, so if Chip was noticing her hairdo, the compliment didn't count.

"You look terrific too," she said. Her brother did look great—fit, tan, and well dressed. He wore Florida well. Maybe someday she could too.

She motioned toward Frank as he rolled her suitcase up the sidewalk to the front door. "Chip, I'm sure you remember Frank Sowak, my next-door neighbor." Her brother had moved to Florida in his thirties, paving the way for their mother to relocate near him after their father died.

"Sure," Chip said. "Nice to see you again."

The men shook hands and made conversation while Rachel scurried down the hall to her mother's bedroom. Seeing her mother's bruised face, Rachel covered her mouth and burst into tears. "Oh, Mom, what happened?" She dropped onto the edge of the bed.

"I look pretty bad, don't I? Chip told me not to look in a mirror for a while." Her mother gently laughed. "Really, I'm fine. It just hurts when I move." She arched an eyebrow. "Maybe I should just stay in bed a few days till I'm all better."

"I wish it could be that simple." Rachel leaned over and kissed her mother's forehead. "But don't you worry. You'll be back at yoga before you know it."

Chip poked his head into the room. "Frank said he's leaving."

Rachel returned to the foyer.

Frank was standing near the door, jangling the car keys with his big index finger. "We can do that meal another time."

"Okay." Right now, she needed to devote all her energy to her mother. She appreciated he sensed it and gave him a hug, hoping to draw some strength from him. "Let's talk tomorrow."

After he departed, Chip showed Rachel the refrigerator contents. "She's pretty well stocked." He pointed at the kitchen table. "All her meds and the ER's discharge instructions are right there."

She looked over the paperwork and nodded. "I can take over now, Chip. I know you're busy." Chip ran an insurance agency, one of the largest in Orlando, affording him little time for the rest of life. She waved him out the door.

"Call me if you need anything." He hollered as he hopped into his red Corvette.

Rachel returned to the bedroom. "Just you and me now, Mom." She forced a smile.

Chapter 17

MARLA

WEDNESDAY

Standing tall in her platform shoes, Marla smacked the gavel on the carved wood lectern. With everyone already quiet, her action wasn't really necessary, but Marla wanted to heighten the formality of the election process.

"Thank you all for coming, and thank you, Mitch, for hosting this inaugural meeting of the Port Mariette Business Association at your country club." Marla cast a smile his way. "You certainly did a beautiful renovation here."

The attendees clapped from their cushioned seats.

Mitch acknowledged the applause with a nod. Without his ballcap and dressed in pressed slacks instead of jeans, she could see why Kim Kryzwicki was taken with him. But what did he see in Kim? Marla still hadn't figured it out.

She looked out over the group. "We all agree we need to form a business association, with the initial purpose of banding together to take action on the one-star reviews. Most of you have already gotten at least one bad review, and some of you have said it's already costing you business. Clearly, we need to move fast before things get out of hand."

Marla passed papers around at each table as she continued to talk. "My attorney, Warren Hartley, drew up these bylaws and a mission statement for us at no charge. Professional courtesy." She allowed a quick smile. "Please review them at your convenience. Any questions so far?"

The room was quiet except for the rustling of papers.

"To get our organization started, we need to elect officers," Marla said. "I'm sure you've all given considerable thought to who should lead our group. Let's begin with nominations for president."

Except for a few coughs and a single sneeze, everyone was silent. Some pretended they were reading the bylaws. Others crossed their arms, looking expectantly around the room.

"Anyone?" Marla looked directly at Suzanne and Andrea, sitting side by side at the table in front of the lectern, and hoped her interaction with them wouldn't look scripted. But, of course, every word of it was.

Andrea spoke first. "We're making some changes to our business right now and taking care of some health issues with our mom, so neither of us is able to run for office." She turned to her sister.

"However," Suzanne said, "we would like to nominate Rachel Baran. By now, you all probably know her mother was injured yesterday in an accident and that Rachel flew down to Florida this morning to be with her."

No doubt Port Mariette's phone lines were jammed all morning once word got out about the accident, especially since Rachel and Frank had flown to Tampa together. A scandal in the making! Even now, several hours after they'd landed, Suzanne's mention of Rachel's name had set the room abuzz.

Marla rolled her eyes then glanced around the room. Mitch, one of the few not talking, had caught her attention.

He shrugged—shorthand for *that's the way it is around here.* Marla lifted her shoulder in return, and they both let out a chuckle. Herbie wasn't the only one to have inside jokes with Mitch.

Once the chatter died down, Suzanne continued. "Rachel said she'll be back soon, and if nominated, she'd be happy to accept any role in PMBA."

"Thank you, Suzanne." Marla jotted Rachel's name on a lined tablet then glanced around the room. "All right, then. Rachel Baran is our first nominee. Any others?" With Marla spending all that time drumming up support for Rachel, no other names had better surface.

A gravelly male voice came from somewhere in the back of the room. "How about you, Herbie?"

Marla couldn't tell who'd spoken, but it didn't matter, since she and Herbie had already talked. She knew he'd pass.

"Thanks," Herbie said, "but between being on town council and running my businesses, I just don't have the time. I'm sure Rachel will do a fine job." He winked at Marla.

A feathery voice sounded from the side of the room. "I have another nominee." Dollmaker Inez, short and squat, pushed herself from her chair. "Mary Frances. She has lots of business experience. Not as much as Herbie, of course." She flashed a timid smile Herbie's way. "Mary Frances is familiar with every business *and* every house in this town. When she was on town council the past few years, she did fine job, and now that her term is over, she's the logical choice to be PMBA's president."

Inez the dollmaker? Marla mentally smacked herself for overlooking the consignment artists. She could have tamped down the Mary Frances nomination if she'd talked with Inez beforehand.

Mary Frances, sitting next to Herbie, cast him a toothy smile, then stood. "Thank you, Inez. I'm honored to be nominated." She sat back down and smoothed her polyester pants.

Marla pursed her lips and scribbled Mary Frances's name after Rachel's.

Walt Celinski, owner of the *Port Mariette Gazette*, stood with his fingertips touching the mahogany tabletop. "How about you, Marla? You've got more business experience than anyone in this room. We could use a dose of Manhattan right here in Port Mariette."

Some nodded in agreement, but others pursed their lips or looked away.

Will I ever be accepted in this town? "Thanks, Walt, but I've got to pass. I don't spend enough time in Port Mariette to hold that role."

"Maybe your daughter?" He turned and tipped his head toward Grace. "You've got retail management experience, and now, you're running the spa. You'd make a great president, Grace."

Marla had never considered her own daughter as a realistic possibility. Stepping from the lectern, she grinned at Grace near the back of the room. "So, Grace, what do you think?"

Grace raised both hands, palms forward. "No. Not me."

Marla smiled at her, trying to indicate it was okay to say no, then moved back to the lectern. "Any other nominations? If not, we will cast a vote by writing either *Rachel Baran* or *Mary Frances King* on the green index card." She emphasized Rachel's name and bored her eyes into the people who said they'd vote for her.

Mitch offered to tally the votes. He separated the cards into two piles, counted them, then strode to the lectern where he leaned into the mic. "Our new president is—" He glanced sideways at Marla. "—Mary Frances King."

Marla gasped in surprise. How could they ignore her excellent advice? She looked at Suzanne, but all she got from her was a subtle raise of an eyebrow.

Later in the meeting, Walt Celinski was voted in as vice president, and Bob Burns from the bank as treasurer.

Rachel was unanimously elected secretary.

She got her way after all.

Chapter 18

SUZANNE

THURSDAY

After staying up late last night for PMBA and then getting up early today to clean her mother's house, Suzanne needed a break. She reached for her phone and looked at the time. Already a few minutes after nine. Perfect. Six in the morning Pacific Standard Time. Rob was an early riser. She touched his name on her screen and waited.

Five rings, and the call went into voicemail.

She dropped onto the sofa and shoved her face into her bed pillow. *Some adventure, this marriage.*

"Suzanne, are you down there?" Her mother's weak voice called from the master bedroom.

"I'm coming." Suzanne pushed herself off the sofa and raced up the steps. "You okay?"

"I think I had an accident."

"You're in bed. How could you have had an accident?" Suzanne stopped short at the foot of the bed.

Her mother pointed below her waist.

"Oh. *That* kind of accident." Suzanne rolled her mother to the side of the bed, exposing a wet nightgown and sheet.

She had begged her mom to wear a disposable diaper, but she'd refused.

"I'm so sorry."

"It's okay." Suzanne tried to sound like she meant it. "Let's get you into the shower." She slipped her hand around her mother's shoulders, and they shuffled into the bathroom. "Let me get the temperature right before you step in." She turned on the water and adjusted the dial, pulled the nightgown over her mother's head, and helped her get inside the tub and onto the shower seat.

"Let me just sit here alone a while." Her mother spoke with labored breaths. "This water feels delightful."

"You sure you're all right?"

Her mother nodded while waving her away.

Suzanne slipped out of the bathroom, stripped the sheets from the bed, and balled them up with her mother's nightgown. "I'm going to run these down to the washing machine, okay?"

"Sure. Take your time." Her mother looked so peaceful sitting there smiling as the water bounced off her pale veiny skin.

Suzanne lifted the laundry high in her arms and made her way to the basement. As she zigzagged through the clutter leading to the washer, she heard a thud from upstairs. She sprinted up the two flights and found her mother crumpled in the tub. "Oh my gosh—Mom!"

Her mother lifted a hand. "I'm okay. I just lost my balance when I tried to stand."

Suzanne turned off the water and helped her mother back onto the seat.

Quivering, her mother's eyes filled with tears. "I don't want to leave my home, Suzie. Don't make me move." Tears streamed down her cheeks.

Suzanne cried too, while wrapping her mother in a soft faded towel and patting her dry. How could any daughter force her own mother out of the house where she'd raised her family? Guilt washed over her. "Don't worry, Mom. We'll figure something out." What that would be, Suzanne had no idea.

She got her mom into a robe and helped her downstairs to the sofa. "How about watching some TV while I make you a cup of tea?" Suzanne reached for the remote and noticed her cellphone next to it showed a missed call from Rob. She handed the remote to her mom and carried the phone into the kitchen.

As soon Rob said hello, she spoke. "Sorry I missed your call, honey. My mom had an accident—"

"Did she fall again?"

"Well, actually, she had two accidents. First, she wet the bed, then she slipped off the bench in the shower."

"Aw, no! How is she?"

"She seems fine. But I feel so guilty. I shouldn't have run downstairs to put the bedding in the washer. I should have had grab bars installed in her shower too."

"You're doing the best you can. You and Andrea both."

"I wish you were here with me." Suzanne also wished they could go back in time, before they were married, when every day was just the two of them, lapping up life together in beautiful Carmel. In her heart, she knew Rob had been too good to be true, but she'd persuaded herself things would be different this time. What a fool she'd been.

"Any progress on getting your mom into Sunset Hills?"

"Not yet. I think she'd be willing to move if she could take all her stuff with her, but that can't happen. Somehow, I need to get her to part with all this junk."

"Well, honey, to her it's not junk. It's valuable items. Memories. Things she's convinced she'll need someday."

"Okay, Dr. Jackson." Suzanne smiled, happy to be feeling that same emotion she'd felt all those months before they married, even if only momentarily. "If she were your patient, what would you do? How would you convince her to get rid of everything and move into Sunset Hills?"

"It's hard to know without talking with her. I'm not saying I can fix the problem, but maybe I can crack the door open. Can you put her on the phone?"

"Sure." Suzanne hurried into the living room with her arm extended, holding the phone. "Rob wants to say hello." She clicked off the TV and left her mom alone with him.

Suzanne busied herself cleaning refrigerator shelves. She was scraping something brown from the bottom shelf when her mom called her. "Rob wants to talk with you again."

Suzanne brushed her wet fingers over her thighs and hurried into the living room. She took the phone from her mother's hand. "Hi, again."

"We had a nice conversation," Rob said. "I think I understand her better now. I can't give an official opinion as to why she hoards stuff, but I think I can suggest a way to move forward."

"I'm all ears," Suzanne said, while stepping into the kitchen for privacy.

"She admitted she knows she needs to move to Sunset Hills, but as you suspected, her hang-up is leaving her home and all those belongings."

"Well, at least she recognizes she needs to move. That's progress."

"Maybe you can talk with her about the positive aspects of moving—the friends she'll have, the meals that'll be cooked for her, the activities she can be involved in. Get her excited about it."

"But what can I do about all her stuff?"

"Take it slow. That house is paid off, and the taxes are low. There's no rush to sell it. Tell your mom everything will stay in the house for now. Later on, we can figure out the best way to deal with those belongings."

"Okay. Thanks. Sounds like a plan." She hesitated. *Should I ask about his son?* Although she and Rob talked every day, he hadn't said anything to make her optimistic about Kevin's progress. But if she didn't ask, Rob might think she didn't care. She decided it was better to inquire. "How are things going with Kevin?"

"Thanks for asking, hon. He's on some new meds. They seem to be helping, but he's still pretty fragile. He's been working remotely. I think being away from the pressures of working in the office is helping too."

"That's good. He's lucky to have you for his father."

"I may be a good father, but I feel like I'm being a lousy husband." Rob said it softly, his voice cracking.

"Look, honey, maybe we're having a rough start to our marriage, but let's remember what the pastor said about all those adventures ahead." She put on a fake smile. Even though Rob couldn't see her face, she'd once read that people can sense if you're smiling over the phone. "You'll be back in Carmel in a couple days, right?"

"Right."

"And as soon I get Mom moved into Sunset Hills, I'll be home too."

"We can plan a new honeymoon." Rob said it in that deep, sexy voice she loved.

"It'll be just the two of us together again. I can't wait!" Suzanne felt the excitement rising in her.

"Sweetie." Rob cleared his throat. "I don't know how to tell you this, but at least for a while, it can't be just the two of us."

"What do you mean?" Her voice rose more than she'd intended. "You aren't getting that dog you've been talking about, are you?" She'd never been a pet person and didn't plan to start now.

"No. Not a dog." He paused and Suzanne could hear a long, deep breath.

"I hope you'll understand, Suzanne." He paused again. "Kevin—I need to keep an eye on him. He, uh, needs to live with us. Just for a while."

I'd rather have the dog.

Chapter 19

RACHEL

THURSDAY

Stretched out on a cushioned chaise lounge, Rachel fingered her way along a rosary she'd borrowed from her mother, keeping her eyes closed while mouthing the prayers. Concluding, she made the sign of the cross with the crucifix dangling on the end then kissed it. She set the rosary on a plastic coffee table.

Slowly, deeply, and intentionally, she breathed in and out as she pondered her life while absorbing the scent and warmth of Florida. Surely this air has medicinal properties. How else could she explain how good she felt?

The sliding glass door opened part way and her mother gingerly stepped outside. "All done?" she asked while easing herself onto a nearby patio chair.

Rachel nodded. "Thanks for lending me your rosary." She'd packed in such a hurry, she'd forgotten her own—the one time she might actually have time to use it.

"I still say a rosary every day. I think it's the best habit I ever established."

"Wish I could say the same." Rachel looked up at a palm tree, its fronds rustling in the gentle breeze. "I'm just too busy." *Been too busy most of my life.*

"I'm sure you do the best you can." Her mother paused. "So, what's new in Port Mariette?" She pushed her thick-lensed glasses up her nose. Except for lousy vision—which enabled Rachel to maintain the secrecy of her wig—her mother's health was still exceptional.

Rachel filled her mom in on Suzanne's wedding, PMBA, and the recent raft of bad online reviews. "Oh, and Suzanne's mom is going to be moving into Sunset Hills. She's been falling a lot."

"No fun getting older. Especially back home." Her mom shook her head. "All those houses in Port Mariette have flights of stairs up to the bedrooms and down to the basements. Not a single ranch home in the whole town. It's so dangerous. And those northern winters! Snow, ice, and drafty houses. No thanks. Sunset Hills may be a nice place, but I'll take living in Florida anytime."

She shifted her position and winced in pain. "Maybe someday you'll move down here like your brother did."

Rachel shrugged. "Who knows? I sure could get used to this lifestyle. Sunshine, year-round warm weather, one-level living. And no state income tax."

"There are lots of fifty-five-plus communities around here," her mother said, sounding hopeful.

"Living here would be fabulous, Mom, but you know me."

"I sure do. You like to keep things just the way they are." A slight sigh. "But maybe someday you'll retire. I keep hoping you'll move down here while I'm still around. We could have a lot of fun together."

"Maybe someday." Rachel did some more deep breathing and adjusted her position on the chaise lounge. She closed her eyes. *This is even better than a day at Marla's spa.* Not that she could ever spend an entire day there. Who could afford that?

More breaths. She envisioned herself living in Florida, taking up golf, going to yoga with her mother, walking the beach at sunset.

Her mother interrupted the daydream. "I always liked your neighbor, Frank. He's a solid man. Stable."

"Yep. That's Frank, all right, solid and stable."

"He's got feelings for you, doesn't he?" Her mother asked in a tentative voice.

Rachel's eyes popped open. "How can you tell?"

"Well, you're quite the catch, young lady." Her mom giggled, sounding much like Rachel. "You can cook, you have your own money, and you're a lovely woman."

Unaccustomed to compliments from her mother, Rachel could feel the heat rising from her neck up. "You must have ESP, Mom. He asked me to marry him." She said it softly, unsure of how her mother would react.

"Really?" Her mom's mouth dropped open. "You're going to marry him?"

Rachel shook her head. "No. It's not that I don't care for him—I do—but at this stage of my life, I care more for myself. I'm trying to live my life the way I want, not the way someone else wants it to be."

Her mom remained silent for a long moment before speaking. "I get it. You took care of Stan and your boys for a very long time. I can see why you'd want some freedom. It's got its advantages, doesn't it?" She swatted a bug away with her good arm. "Here in Florida, we have a saying about older single men on the hunt for a wife—*they're looking for a nurse or a purse.* I don't think that's true of Frank, though. He's a good man, and it's obvious he cares for you. You'll find out—the older you get, the harder it is to find someone like that."

"But I don't love him." She blurted it out, surprising herself at the rush of emotion that accompanied her words.

"Well then, if you don't want to marry him, don't." Her mother shrugged. "After all, Stan's a hard one to replace—a good provider, nice-looking, not a big drinker, fun to be around."

Rachel nodded. Her mom always had a way of cutting through the clutter to make her point. "Mom, I need to ask you something."

"Go right ahead, I'm not going anywhere." She let out a chuckle.

"Did you ever hear Stan talk about a woman whose name starts with a T?"

"The letter T?" Her mom cocked her head. "How about your sister, Theresa?"

Rachel felt that pang in her heart once again. "Can you think of anyone else?"

Her mom pondered a moment then shook her head. "Not really. Why are you asking? What's the big mystery?"

In a halting voice, Rachel explained the pink note.

Her mother touched the cross on her necklace chain. "Oh, dear. I hope Stan never wandered. But we all know there's evil lurking in everyone's heart." She looked Rachel in the eye. "That includes your heart and mine. As for Stan, I guess you'll never know. But if he did wander, it's water over the dam. Forgive him."

"Easier said than done."

"Just tell God you forgive Stan of anything he might have done. Even if you don't mean it, God will help your heart to heal."

Rachel pursed her lips and vowed to find out who that woman was. She couldn't forgive what she didn't know.

Chapter 20

MARLA

THURSDAY

Positioned in the turret of her spacious bedroom, Marla leaned on a marble windowsill and took in the panoramic view. Deep in the valley below, the river raged from yet another overnight storm that flooded its banks.

Her eyes followed the river into town, where homes had been built on elevated land to keep them and the people within safe. Her eyes traveled upward to survey the horizon, a blue sky smeared by streaks of stratus clouds.

Stratus. One of the three kinds of clouds—cirrus, cumulus, and stratus. She remembered that from St. Cyprian's Academy, where the nuns held such fascination for all things ethereal. For Marla, though, earthly matters were the only ones on her mind. That negative review about the spa—who wrote it and why? She still hadn't figured it out.

She slipped her feet into sandals and padded down to the kitchen, where she plucked a few eggs from the refrigerator. Gently scrambling them over low heat, her mind continued to churn.

If the spa had been the only business to get a negative review, that would be one thing—but now, many other business owners had gotten them too. She'd obsess over the situation until she resolved it, even though no one else seemed as concerned as she was. Here in Port Mariette, they just didn't understand business like she did.

At last night's PMBA meeting, instead of voting for Rachel—as so many had promised but failed to do—the business owners spent more time yakking about Rachel's mom and her golf cart accident than the election. What's wrong with them? The woman wasn't even admitted to a hospital.

Now, PMBA was stuck with Mary Frances as its president. She'd take action on the reviews only if they affected local housing prices. Her narrow mind didn't understand the urgency. Bad reviews could eventually affect the whole town's economy.

After last night's meeting, Marla discussed the situation with Warren for the umpteenth time. With only so much tolerance for *nitpicking nonsense*, he cut her off, telling her they had talked enough—it was high time she got back home.

In a way, she had to agree. The people of Port Mariette were getting on her nerves.

She spooned some eggs out of the pan and considered when to book a flight back home.

A loud vehicle pulling up outside interrupted her thoughts. The spa's first appointment wasn't due for a couple of hours—who could that be? She peered outside and spotted a white pickup truck hauling a trailer. It came to a halt just beneath the kitchen window, and someone jumped out of the cab.

The do-rag guy. What's he doing here? The roof's fine.

He slammed his door shut and clanged open the trailer. With all this noise, she may as well be in Manhattan.

Seconds later, Grace appeared downstairs, dressed in a flowery summer dress. "Good morning," she said with a smile. "I see Jesse's here to cut the grass."

Marla cocked her head. "The roofing guy also cuts our grass?"

"Jesse mainly does house painting and landscaping work. He only works for Mitch when he can squeeze something in." She flipped her long hair over a shoulder. "Jesse said Mitch has jobs for him all the time. It's hard to find guys willing to climb ladders and work on roofs."

"I admire Jesse's industriousness, but couldn't you have hired someone without a criminal record?" Marla pointed her fork toward the stove. "There are more eggs in the pan, if you're interested."

"No, thanks." Grace turned on her heel and walked outside.

Marla tried to read their lips as they chatted and laughed, then she watched as Grace moved an arm toward him, probably to pay him.

Marla toyed with her scrambled eggs until Grace came back inside. "How much does he charge to cut the grass?" Most of the property she'd inherited from Aunt Adele was wooded, but the landscaped part was still substantial.

"We have a barter deal." Grace responded while looking in the refrigerator, her back to Marla. "I pay Latoya to give him a massage, and I manicure his hands. With the work he does, they get pretty rough and dirty."

"When did you become a manicurist? I thought only Hannah did our mani-pedis."

"Oh, I only do it for Jesse. I'd do the massages, too, if I were as strong as Latoya."

"Well, it sounds like a good financial arrangement, but I can't imagine it's much fun cleaning those dirty hands." Marla scrunched her nose.

Grace closed the refrigerator door and faced Marla, her feet spread apart and her jaw set.

"What's wrong?" Marla set her fork down.

"I don't believe you." Grace shook her head. "Why are you so critical of Jesse? For that matter, why are you so critical of everyone here in Port Mariette?"

"*Everyone*?" Marla's face registered shock.

"Just about."

"I'm not critical." Marla recovered her poise. "Merely honest."

"You think so? Let's take Mitch—even *Mitch*, a guy you really get along with. You criticize him because he hires guys with a record. But look at all the good Mitch does."

Marla gasped. Grace was lashing out at her for no good reason.

"And Mary Frances—what did she ever do to you?" Grace thrust a hand on her hip. "Sure, she can be a little self-serving, but isn't that like you looking in a mirror?"

Marla's jaw dropped open, but no words came out.

"Even my Aunt Sissy—Rachel—you think you're better than her because she's never lived anywhere but Port Mariette."

"Not true!" Marla protested.

"Yes, it is. I heard you talking with Warren about her the other day."

Marla cringed. She had been venting with Warren about a lot of people lately. Had she gone too far?

"I'm tired of biting my tongue when you're here." Grace turned and walked away. She stopped, as if she were going to say more but changed her mind, then stomped up the stairs and slammed a door.

Marla closed her mouth. For once she didn't know what to say, and even if she did, Grace couldn't hear it.

Chapter 21

SUZANNE

THURSDAY

Not long after Rob's pronouncement about Kevin, Suzanne walled herself in the art shop's back room, hanging artwork with a vengeance, attempting to burn off her frustrations. An hour or so into it, she needed a breather. She dumped her petite frame onto a folding chair and stretched her legs straight in front of her.

All those years she worked as a traveling contract trainer for the airline, she'd never needed so many breaks. Maybe they were right for letting her go before her entire body failed. Or maybe it really was age discrimination. Whatever. She'd never uncover the truth, and besides, being an artist was much more fulfilling.

Too bad the rest of her life was in such a shambles. Like a teapot ready to squeal, she blew some air out of her taut lips. Not only did she need a break, she also needed someone to talk to.

The doorbell jingled and Suzanne scurried to the front. "Marla! What a nice surprise."

"I was on my way to the Dairy Mart. Thought I'd see if you were here."

Suzanne grabbed Marla's arm and gave it a squeeze. "Your timing's perfect. I've got a mess on my hands."

"A mess?" Marla's eyes darted around the room. "Here at the shop?"

Suzanne shook her head and waved Marla into the back room. "Let's find some privacy."

They each took a seat, then Suzanne's words came tumbling out. "I'm talking about my life! It's turned into a complete mess."

"Oh, it can't be that bad."

"But it is! A year ago, I had a great job doing training for an airline, flying all over the place, making good money, swimming at hotel pools every night. Then I met Rob, and right after that—boom! Everything changed."

"For the better, right?" Marla said.

"At first, yes, but then I lost my job." Suzanne threw her hands up in the air.

"And you moved to California to be near Rob and became an artist. I'd say that's pretty exciting, wouldn't you?"

Suzanne ran a hand through her hair. Didn't Marla understand? Suzanne needed someone to sympathize with her, not minimize her troubles. "I guess so."

Marla got up and stepped over to a large oil painting, her back to Suzanne. "I dunno, sounds like a wonderful life to me."

"But now, everything's changed. Don't you see?" Suzanne spread her hands wide, wanting to grab Marla's full attention. "When Rob canceled our honeymoon to take care of his son, it was it was like I was being fired from being Rob's wife."

"Oh, that's ridiculous." Marla turned her head back to Suzanne. "It's just a temporary situation. You two will go off on a fabulous honeymoon sometime soon and live happily ever after."

Suzanne pursed her lips. "That's what I thought at first too."

"So, what are you talking about?" Marla sat back down. "Is it Rob? Or because you're here in Port Mariette taking care of your mother? Or maybe it's because you're stuck cleaning up this art shop?"

Emotions clouding her perspective, Suzanne had to stop and think before replying. She let out a loud sigh. "I—I guess it's *everything* you mentioned. I'm losing sleep over Rob, I need to move Mom into Sunset Hills, and I have to stick around here until I'm sure the art shop is on solid footing."

"Solid footing?" Marla leaned forward, fully alert. "What do you mean?"

Finally, she'd captured Marla's attention. That always happened anytime a conversation shifted to business matters. "Turns out our mom's crocheted items are what's been keeping this store afloat. Now that she's not producing, it's up to me to make this place more profitable."

"She can't crochet at Sunset Hills?"

"She can't crochet anywhere. Her arthritis has become too painful."

"That's too bad." Marla tapped her lips with her index finger a few times before continuing. "Well, I love your idea about offering classes in the back room. They'll generate income and increase foot traffic for the whole town too."

"I hope so. But that's solving only part of the problem."

"Ease up on yourself, Suzanne. You'll take care of a few things here in Port Mariette then go back to Carmel. Everything will be fine."

"I'm not so sure about that. At least not with Rob."

Marla cocked her head. "Why not?"

Suzanne heaved another big sigh. "Rob has invited his son to live with us." She held back her tears, reserving them for another restless night on the lumpy sofa.

"You're kidding."

"I wouldn't kid about something like that."

"Why did you agree to that?"

"I didn't. I learned about it after he already invited him."

"Rob didn't ask you beforehand?"

Suzanne shook her head.

"Why on earth did he do that?"

"Rob said he felt he had no choice." Suzanne wanted to respect Kevin's privacy, but she also needed Marla to understand the situation. "Kevin apparently has some ... some mental health issues."

"I see." Marla crossed her arms. "What are you going to do?"

"What *can* I do? Rob's made it clear his son is more important than I am. If he wants Kevin to live with us for a while, I'll have to adjust." She was not about to have a second failed marriage on the books. She looked up at Marla. "Remember what you sang at our wedding—*A cord of three strands is not easily broken*? I know that's true, but what's happening now is more trying than I ever expected. And it's only the first week of our marriage. God only knows what will happen down the road."

"I feel bad for you, Suzanne. I really do. You and Rob seemed like the perfect couple with such a bright future."

Seemed? What was she inferring? Suzanne inhaled, proud she continued to hold back her tears, especially in front of Marla, who always seemed to be in control of everything, including her emotions. "I'm—I'm just taking it a day at a time."

"One day at a time. That sounds like an outstanding plan." Marla let out an artificial laugh, an obvious attempt to change the tone of their weighty conversation. "I have to tell you, Suzanne, your wedding was so touching it got me thinking maybe Warren and I should get married too."

"Really?" Suzanne's eyes registered surprise. Marla never mentioned Warren and marriage in the same sentence. "What's holding you back?"

"Oh, I've been single all my life. It's better I keep things that way. Besides, Grace and I had a weird conversation early this morning. She's my focus now."

"A weird conversation?" Venting about Rob had been helpful, but Suzanne wasn't a fool. Marla of all people would never come up with any good advice about husbands. Moving on to Marla's problems might be what she needed more than anything. "Want to talk about it?"

Marla's mouth twitched in irritation. "Grace told me I'm too critical of people."

Suzanne paused to think of what she should say instead of agreeing with Grace. "Well ... do you think Grace is right?"

Marla hesitated. "I guess I guess people in Port Mariette might say I'm too critical. But they have to remember, I've lived most of my life in Manhattan. It's just *different* there." She stretched out in her chair, her shoes nearly touching Suzanne's.

"That may be true, but what are you going to do to patch things up with Grace?"

"No clue. I'm not used to having to get along with a daughter."

"I always ask Rob for advice on dealing with my daughter, Jill. He knows how to strike at the heart of an issue. If you were talking with him now, I think he'd say something like, *the only behavior we can change is our own.*

Then, he'd probably ask, *what do you think you could do differently to get a better outcome?*"

Marla rolled her eyes and let out a sigh. "Maybe I could act like I like people even when I don't."

The moment of total honesty caught Suzanne by surprise. She laughed a little louder than she'd intended.

"It wasn't *that* funny, was it?" Marla's face registered surprise.

"No," Suzanne said, eyes averted. "Sorry for laughing."

"That's okay. But I still don't know how I'm going to act so Grace doesn't get upset with me."

Suzanne's eyes lit up. "How about faking it? You know, like, *fake it till you make it?*"

Marla crossed her arms and tapped an index finger on one of them. "Y'know what, that's really not bad advice. Back when I owned my gyms, I had to pretend I liked my clients even when I couldn't stand them. I guess I could do the same around here."

"Good girl." Suzanne managed not to laugh. "Here's another idea. Rob always quotes that platitude *actions speak louder than words*. Maybe if you behaved differently, Grace will notice, and you won't have to talk about things like this anymore."

Marla shrugged, dismissing further discussion. "We'll see."

"So," Suzanne said, changing the subject, "you claim you'll never marry Warren, but when it comes to matters of the heart, who knows? Maybe you will. For that matter, maybe Rachel will marry Frank someday." Too bad she couldn't be here right now. Rachel was a much better listener than Marla, and although her advice was plain and simple, it was usually sound.

"Rachel marry Frank? I can't imagine her making such a huge change," Marla said. "But who knows? Going with him to Florida might jar her into doing something impetuous."

Suzanne chuckled, knowing how unlikely rash behavior would be for Rachel. "I doubt it. Anyway, she'll probably be too busy with her mother to give Frank much attention while they're down there." Suzanne glanced at the clock. "Speaking of mothers—I've got to run some errands for mine." She lifted her purse from a hook on the wall and turned off the lights as they made their way to the front of the shop.

"I can't believe Rachel left town right before our PMBA meeting." Marla tsked. "If she'd been there, I think she would have been elected president."

"Well, she hardly had a choice. Her mother needed her." *Just like mine does.* Suzanne flipped the front door sign from *open* to *closed*. "Let's hope Mary Frances pays attention to other issues besides real estate sales. And at least Rachel will be our secretary. She'll keep on top of everything going on."

"We need to strategize about that," Marla said. "We should have a video call with Rachel so she'll be prepared to drive the agenda."

Suzanne looked across the street and squinted. "What's Mary Frances doing over there on the sidewalk?"

Marla looked. "Cleaning her window?"

"But she's carrying her purse, not a rag."

"Picking up a coin?" People in Port Mariette, Marla had often commented, never hesitated to scoop up even a single penny.

"No. Something's wrong over there." Suzanne hurried across the street, Marla right behind her. They stopped short as they neared Mary Frances's real estate office.

Shards of glass from a smashed front window littered the sidewalk.

"What on earth—?" Suzanne tiptoed with care.

A red-faced Mary Frances balled her hands into fists and gave them a shake. "Who would do this?"

"And *why* would they?" Suzanne looked at Marla, hoping her big brain would have an answer.

But Marla only shrugged.

"Oh! I forgot to lock the art shop." Suzanne hollered over her shoulder as she hustled back across the street. Who knew where that vandal could strike next? She waved her phone in the air. "I'll call Sergeant Dan."

Chapter 22

RACHEL

THURSDAY

"Me out of town, and both of you in Port Mariette? This video call is all backwards." Rachel held her cellphone in front of her face as she plopped onto her mother's old leather sofa. Bright sun streamed through the picture window, warming Rachel's pale shoulders.

Last year, before their fortieth reunion, Marla had always phoned in from New York, and Suzanne had called from whatever city she was working in. Rachel had been the only Port Mariette caller.

Suzanne smirked. "And our lives are a bit upside down too. How's your mom?"

"She's able to get around pretty good now. I'll know more when I take her to the doctor first thing tomorrow. How about your mom, Suzanne?"

"Only one fall since I've been here, so she thinks she doesn't need to move to Sunset Hills. I wish she were as healthy as your mom."

Rachel nodded, sympathetic but pleased her own mother was aging so well.

"Is Frank staying there with you?" Marla asked.

"Good grief, no." Rachel fluffed a throw pillow and leaned back on it. "I don't have time to take care of him too. He's staying with his son, Joey. This is the first time I've sat down to relax. Been cooking up a storm. Mom's freezer will be fully stocked by the time I leave." She smiled, satisfied she was fulfilling the role of a good daughter at this stage of life.

"Any idea when you'll be back?" Marla asked. "PMBA is meeting again on Tuesday. Now that we have officers in place and our mission statement has been agreed to, we need to get going on the agenda items."

"I know, I know. I expect to get home this weekend. It's only Thursday, but Mom's doing well, and Pete told me we're almost out of pierogies at Food 'n Fuel, can you believe it?" Rachel's eyes brimmed with pride. Her son had been handling her absence so well. Funny how you raise your kid to be a responsible adult, and when he proves he's become one, you're surprised. "Don't worry, Marla, those online reviews will be at the top of our agenda."

Suzanne raised a finger. "It *might* have to be the second item of business." She paused for effect.

Suzanne could be so dramatic. All those years working as a trainer, having to hold an audience's attention, was probably the reason for the theatrics. "How come?" Rachel finally asked.

Suzanne bent closer to her screen, as if releasing a secret. "Someone smashed the front window of Mary Frances's real estate office."

"Oh, my gosh!" Rachel's hand flew to her mouth. Suzanne did have reason to be dramatic after all.

"Glass went everywhere, but nothing was stolen from inside," Marla added.

"Anyone know who did it?" Rachel asked.

"No," Suzanne said. "But Sergeant Dan's already working on it."

"Does Mary Frances use security cameras?" Rachel asked.

"No. No cameras anywhere near there." Suzanne shook her head.

"Sounds like security cameras oughta be the first item on the agenda." Rachel scratched herself two reminders—one, to add security cameras to the agenda, and the second, to check with Pete about the one he had ordered for Food 'n Fuel. Thank goodness he'd installed those cameras last year when they were plagued with shoplifting and even a drug dealer. Now this!

"With that new highway, all sorts of strangers are coming through town, just like Penny warned," Suzanne said. "Maybe she was right, at least about that."

Rachel nodded while observing Suzanne on the screen. She must still have a soft spot for the former mayor. It was Suzanne, after all, who got Penny to admit she'd been trying to get a payoff from someone in state government in order to erase her gambling debts.

"Well," Rachel said, "I'll check with Mary Frances before I finalize the agenda." Official business taken care of, she put down her pen and wished she were back in Port Mariette with her friends. "So, what's new with the two of you?"

"Not much here." Marla glanced at her watch. "I'm meeting with Mitch in about fifteen minutes. Not sure what's on his mind. He just said it was business-related."

Rachel stretched her neck to lean into the screen. "Is he still giving golf lessons to Kim Kryzwicki?" Mitch meeting with Marla about business matters made sense, but golfing with Kim? That, Rachel couldn't grasp.

"I have no idea what's going on with the two of them." Marla waved the question away.

"O-kay." Rachel chalked up the dismissal to irritation over the bad reviews, and now a smashed storefront window on top of it. She moved on. "How about you, Suzanne? What's new with you?"

"The best I can say is that Rob and I been having a lot of interesting phone conversations." Suzanne gave a weak smile then took a few minutes to detail Kevin's anticipated move-in with her and Rob.

While Suzanne vented about Rob's son, Rachel's mind drifted. Is that what happens when you marry later in life? You're burdened with issues from a family you hardly know? Or do you end up with the wrong person altogether, like Mitch and Kim, just because you're lonely or the other person makes you feel young again?

Rachel heard her mother's high-pitched voice from down the hall. "Who's there with you?"

"Mom's up," Rachel said, "Gotta run. I'll call Mary Frances later today and let you know if she wants any other changes to the agenda."

Rachel disconnected the call and hurried to her mother's bedroom. "I was on a video call." She slid her phone into a pocket and sat on the edge of the bed. "Did you have a good night's sleep?"

"Mm-hmm." Her mother yawned, exposing teeth that might've once worn braces if they'd been invented in time.

"Looks like your bruises are healing well. They're turning green and yellow now."

"Actually, I think I look better in black and blue." Her mother smirked, rolling to her side and facing Rachel.

"Were you talking with Frank just now?"

"No—Suzanne and Marla."

"But he's still taking you to the beach tomorrow, isn't he?"

"Uh-huh. Right after your doctor's appointment."

"He's such a nice man." Her mom inhaled, as if preparing for a speech.

Rachel didn't want to hear it. She slid off the bed. "How about some ham and home fries for breakfast?"

Chapter 23

MARLA

THURSDAY

At least from the outside, Mitch's was the finest of all the mansions on Hilltop Lane, nicknamed Millionaire's Row by the locals. The lush green lawn with thick hedges trimmed square and a columned wraparound porch worked together to create unequaled sidewalk appeal.

Although she would have preferred making a grand entrance through the front door, the drive-up entrance on the side would enable Marla to avoid getting soaked by the heavy rain. She eased her car under the porte cochere and for a moment pretended she had just entered with a horse and buggy instead of a BMW. She stepped out of her car and gave a quick wave to Mitch, who was waiting a few feet away at the side door, a smile on his deeply tanned face.

"Hi, Marla, come on in." He led her along wood-carved halls heavy with sepia-toned photographs from Port Mariette's early days. He pointed out a few details about each picture—*this fellow riding the horse is Herbie's grandfather ... the bank was the first commercial building on Main Street ... this is the original St. Cyprian's Church before they renovated it back in the nineties.* Why Mitch had never left Port Mariette was apparent—he had a deep and lasting love for this town, its people, and its past.

They reached Mitch's office, and he motioned her inside.

"This was originally the living room?" Marla asked, looking around. Stacks of papers inundated the carved kidney-shaped desk, as well as the leather armchairs opposite it.

"Yes, it was." He pointed to two damask loveseats facing one another, a coffee table between them. "Let's sit over there. It'll be more conducive for our conversation."

"Conducive?" Marla always got a kick out of pointing out Mitch's tendency to use big words. She wondered what people in this town thought of that. She also wondered how many of them appreciated how much Mitch had done for them. With his capabilities, he could have made far more money working on stately old homes in Pittsburgh or any big city, for that matter. Instead, he'd chosen to remain in Port Mariette, marshaling whatever forces he could in order to keep at least some parts of the town looking as beautiful as they'd once been.

She took a seat across from him, set her handbag on the plush carpeting, and crossed her legs.

He stared.

She adjusted her skirt to make sure she was properly covered. Mitch was a straight arrow, and she knew how to behave around him.

"I'll get right to the point," Mitch said in his strong, deep voice. "I've got to make a change at the country club, and while you're in town, I wanted to get your opinion."

Seriously, if it weren't for Warren, she could enjoy getting to know Mitch better. The guy loved talking business, and he knew how to get right to the point. Those things alone appealed to Marla, weird as that might sound to others. And even in his mid-sixties, Mitch was easy on the eyes. He reminded her of Clint Eastwood. Parsed his words like him too.

"So," she asked, "what kind of change do you have in mind?"

"You know I bought the country club when Penny was in dire straits last year. Got it at a decent price, poured some money into renovations."

"You did a phenomenal job. The place is gorgeous. So why the change now?"

"We just don't have enough people in this area who can afford membership in a country club. I figured I'd eliminate the country club memberships and turn it into a venue for special events."

"And you want some marketing ideas from me?" Already, she was imagining ways to promote it.

"Not quite." He leaned forward, clasped hands between his knees. "I've already met with our members, and they've agreed to dissolve the country club. The steel and coal executives who were members are long gone, and those who remain are business owners like Herbie and professionals like doctors and lawyers. They're happy to be released from having to pay monthly dues."

"Then what's your question for me?"

"I'm not convinced turning it into a venue is the best way to go. Lately I've been thinking bigger—like converting it into a boutique resort with lots of space for special events. There's only one hotel in this whole area, a run-down little place in Lyondale." He grabbed a rolled-up drawing on the table and spread it open. "I have a few extra acres of land over here." He pointed. "I'm thinking of adding about thirty hotel rooms and some high-end amenities like a gym, maybe a pool and a sauna." He looked up, his eyes seeking Marla's reaction.

"That's a huge undertaking." Her eyes bounced back and forth between Mitch and his drawing.

"This town needs an anchor to attract more travelers from the highway. And now that the drive from Pittsburgh is so short, I think this could draw weddings, family reunions, holiday parties—you name it. I've been praying about this, and I believe it's the way to go."

"I see." Praying about it. Not exactly her method for making a sound business decision, but that's the way Mitch operated. His money, his choice. At least he'd asked for her opinion too. "You could also create some package deals with other places in town," she said. "People would stay at your hotel and eat meals there, shop on Main Street, then they could golf at Herbie's golf course or come to my place for spa treatments."

"You could even set up a space over here for massages." He brushed his hand across the drawings. "But those are the kinds of details we can work out later."

Marla's eyes lit up like they always did when she sensed a good business opportunity. "It's a solid idea, so what's the delay? God put you on hold, or what?" Her curiosity was genuine. She'd like to know how Mitch got his answers.

"We need to solve our town's mysteries first. Who's writing those bad reviews? And who smashed that window on Main Street? I'm not putting money into this hotel idea until someone figures out who's doing what and why. Port Mariette may have recovered from losing the steel and coal industries, but we're still in a precarious position. Bad reviews or a reputation for vandalism could prevent visitors from coming here. You've invested a lot of grant money in this town, and as the contractor who did the renovations, both of us have a vested interest in making sure bad reviews don't impact the town."

"I hear what you're saying, and I agree." Marla nodded. "Well, do you have any suspects in mind?"

Mitch leaned back and laced his hands behind his head. "Nope. I was hoping you did."

"Me?"

"Yeah, you. Remember last year when Rachel was having issues at Food 'n Fuel with shoplifting and drug deals? You got that resolved in a matter of days."

Marla downplayed his comment with a wave of her hand. "All I did was tell her to set up security cameras." She leaned forward. "Are you presuming whoever smashed the window is the same person who wrote all the bad reviews? I'm thinking it's probably different people. And I'm thinking that at least one of them might be racist." She told him her concern about the black-and-blue comment.

He stiffened. "Port Mariette is no bastion of diversity, that's for sure. But don't assume that just because the population around here is almost all Caucasian that anyone's racist."

"Sorry if you thought I assumed that." She hadn't meant to ruffle him. "I'm just digging for clues."

"I get it." He crossed his leg over his knee and grabbed hold of the ankle. "I've been talking with Herbie about this too."

"Oh, so he finally came out of his cave?"

Mitch nodded. "Yeah. That bad review made him take stock of his businesses. He takes a lot of pride in every single one of them, and he thought he might be slipping. Took him a while to put things into perspective. Since all his businesses except for the golf course are along Main Street, he's going to arrange for security cameras there."

"That'll help if there's more vandalism, but we still need to figure out who's writing the reviews." Marla raised a finger. "I'm thinking it's a business owner, maybe more than one, from either Lyondale or Dunham City. They didn't get a highway exit like we did, and their businesses have suffered."

"Interesting. I've been thinking that too." Mitch said. "They're closing businesses faster than windows in a thunderstorm. But I don't have the time to investigate all the possibilities in two towns."

"I know what you mean. Warren gave me a bunch of ideas on how we could handle the reviews, but it's overwhelming."

"Look," Mitch said, "Maybe you could identify a couple competitors for everyone who's had a bad review. Take a drive over to some other towns. Strike up a conversation with business owners or their employees. See if you can dig something up."

Marla laughed. "Do I look like Columbo?"

"Hardly." Mitch looked away. "But you're the only person around here who has the brains and the time to figure it out."

"Can't be me." She shook her head. "I won't be in town much longer."

"How come?"

"Oh ... Grace is pretty fed up with me. I seem to make things worse every time I talk with her. I thought I'd stay clear of her for a while."

"And you think running back to Manhattan will solve the problem?"

She squirmed. "Maybe not, but I'm not so good at healing broken relationships." They went silent for a long minute, then Marla continued. "She thinks I'm too critical of people."

"Anyone in particular?"

"Well, Grace rattled off a long list of names, but what triggered the outburst was some comments I made about that roofer of yours, Jesse."

Mitch threw back his head, laughing. "You were critical of Jesse? In front of Grace?"

"Why do you find that so funny?"

"Didn't you know? She's nuts about the guy."

"Really?" Marla groaned. "I had no idea." She looked plaintively at Mitch. "How can I be so clueless about people—especially the ones I love?"

"Don't be so hard on yourself, Marla. We all have our blind spots." Mitch stretched an arm across the back of the loveseat. "Well, maybe you can stay in town a while longer so you can patch up your relationship with Grace." He chuckled. "Sounds to me like you'll have plenty of time to be Port Mariette's investigative reporter."

Unfortunately, she had to agree.

Chapter 24

SUZANNE

THURSDAY

Suzanne ended a phone conversation with Rob just as Marla returned from Mitch's and careened into a parking space in front of the art shop. Lucky no pet was tethered to the dog post—Marla might've taken him out.

In an instant, an old memory surfaced, causing Suzanne to shiver. Many years ago, a drunk driver had nearly killed her grade school friend, the youngest Sanders child, right where Marla had just parked. The sweet little girl was only eight, and neither she nor the town ever fully recovered.

That tragedy was one of the legitimate reasons Penny fought the new highway exits for Port Mariette last year when she was mayor. She claimed strangers would come to town and cause accidents and assorted crimes. Despite her efforts, though, the exits were approved, and Penny retaliated by having iron dog posts drilled into the sidewalks.

Last summer, the post in front of the antique shop prevented a careless driver from smashing into Suzanne's mother as she carried an old lampshade to her car. No matter how much trouble Penny had caused the town, Suzanne would always be grateful for Penny's foresight.

Suzanne picked up a feather duster and stood watching Marla popping out of her BMW as if she'd hit an ejector button.

What's the rush?

Rob seemed to be in a hurry this morning too. Was he in a rush to get her off the phone—or was it just her imagination?

Maybe she'd bored him with details about her mother—her physical state, the condition of her house, what to do with all that clutter. Or maybe he didn't want to hear about her plans for the art shop's back room or the latest online reviews. Regardless, Rob sure wasn't behaving like a man yearning for his bride to get home.

She leaned over and dusted some pieces of pottery. If she looked busy, maybe Marla would leave her alone in her thoughts.

Who was she kidding? Marla was always a woman on a mission—her own mission. Everyone else's priorities took a back seat when she was around. "Love people as they are, not as you want them to be," Rob always said. Sometimes Marla made that difficult for Suzanne.

Marla whooshed into the art shop and launched into a quick summary of her conversation with Mitch.

"Sounds like it was a productive meeting," Suzanne said, trailing the duster over some mugs.

Marla nodded. "So, are you free?"

"Free?" Suzanne stopped dusting.

"You and I need to do some digging in Lyondale and Dunham City."

"You and I?" Suzanne jerked her chin back. She certainly didn't have time to be roped into doing detective work. "I promised Andrea I'd work in the shop today."

"How about tomorrow then?"

Suzanne didn't have anything specific planned. She took a second to consider her options. It might be good for her own mental health to get out of Port Mariette for a day, especially with Marla. As annoying as she could sometimes be, Suzanne did enjoy Marla's company. "Tomorrow's fine. But why *me*?"

Marla chuckled. "I don't know a thing about Lyondale or Dunham City, and Rachel's in Florida. So that leaves you."

"Gee, what an honor. But I haven't been to either of those towns in about forty years."

Marla continued as if she hadn't heard Suzanne's retort. "Mitch said there's a pizza shop in Lyondale. The owner might be the one who gave Herbie's pizza shop a bad review. We can start there. I'll search online for other businesses we can check out."

At least she wouldn't have to do anything tomorrow other than show up.

Marla looked up at the ceiling, her mind apparently in overdrive. "Once that's done, we need to come up with an idea for a special event here in Port Mariette. Something that'll draw plenty of people. We need to overcome this spate of negative publicity."

"Like a two-pronged attack," Suzanne said. "Find out who's behind the reviews and the vandalism *and* boost Port Mariette's reputation with a special event."

"Right."

Suzanne's eyes twinkled as she ran the duster along the rim of a ceramic pitcher. "I already have an idea for something."

"Really?"

The idea had just popped into her head as she was dusting, and although she hadn't fully thought it through, it seemed like a good one. "Yes," she said. "An arts festival."

Marla raised her eyebrows, as if she were the only one who could come up with anything worth doing. "That sounds fabulous!"

Boosted by Marla's enthusiasm, Suzanne added some details. "Just imagine it—music, food, and all our artists lined up on Main Street. And business owners like you selling products and promoting their businesses. Art would be the main focus, of course, but we'd make it broader than that."

"Love your idea. The spa could give out samples of facial creams or a discount coupon. Maybe even have Latoya do chair massages." Marla paused. "We should call Rachel again. She'll need to get your arts festival idea on the PMBA agenda."

Suzanne tapped her finger on her lips and remained silent for a few moments. "Speaking of Rachel, I have been thinking, maybe we should remind her not to be out in the sun a lot while she's in Florida. Not good for someone with her ... uh ... condition."

"Her condition?" Marla's eyes widened. "You—you noticed that wig too?" Her voice dropped. "Do you think she has some kind of cancer?"

Suzanne shrugged. "I don't know and I didn't want to ask her. Figured she'd talk about it when she was ready—but if both of us have noticed something's going on with her, she may be wondering if we care."

"Yeah. Maybe you can bring it up. I'm not so good at delicate topics."

No kidding. "If she's getting chemo, she needs to stay out of the sun. Her doctor might not know she's in Florida for a while." Suzanne swiped her phone. "Let's see if she can talk right now."

Rachel answered the call, giggling. "Two times in one day! What's up now?"

"Nothing major," Suzanne said. "Marla and I came up with a couple new things to run by you. She just met with Mitch and he suggested we do some local detective work."

Marla gave her the highlights and asked Rachel for suggestions on logical businesses to visit. "Suzanne and I will make the rounds while you're in Florida, and hopefully by the time you're back, we'll have some possibilities to mull over at Tuesday's PMBA meeting," Marla said.

Rachel laughed. "Apparently you never sleep, Marla. You've always got something in the works." She gave them suggestions of businesses to visit, then Suzanne piped up about the arts festival.

"I love that idea, Suzanne." Rachel said with enthusiasm. "Sounds like you haven't been sleeping either."

"Sleep ... uh. How have you been ... *sleeping*, Rachel?" Suzanne asked in a halting manner, wishing she had a better way to initiate a conversation about cancer.

"I've been sleeping fine." Rachel screwed up her face. "Why do you ask?"

"Well, uh." Suzanne had expected Rachel to say she'd been sleeping poorly. At a loss for words, she looked pleadingly at Marla.

"What she's talking about," Marla said, "is, you know, the cancer."

"The *cancer*?" Rachel repeated.

"Yeah, the wig, the cancer," Marla said.

"Oh, my goodness. You think I've got cancer? And you noticed my wig?" Rachel put her hand on her head. "Is it that obvious?"

"Who cares about the wig?" Suzanne waved a hand. "Tell us, how are you doing? What are the doctors telling you?"

"I don't have cancer!" Rachel squealed each word.

"You don't?" Marla and Suzanne said it in unison.

"No, and I can't believe you thought I did." Rachel described in detail how her hair happened to get chopped off the weekend before Suzanne's wedding. "I couldn't let my boys find out. They'd never let me be alone with my grandkids again. Not that they come home all that often, but still. Pete, of course, doesn't have any kids, but I have to keep it a secret from him too. He might slip and tell his brothers."

She let out a loud sigh. "It just made sense to keep it secret from everyone. Otherwise, I'd have to worry about when to wear the wig and when not to. It was either buy a wig or get a ridiculously short pixie cut. You know me, I don't like to make a scene, so I decided on the wig."

Suzanne and Marla took turns trying to apologize, but Rachel just giggled. "That's okay, I'm touched that you were both so concerned about me." She paused a moment. "Here, let me show you how bad my hair looks, then you'll know why I was so desperate to cover it." She yanked off the wig, revealing multiple bare spots. "What do you think?"

"Pitch that wig and move to Manhattan," Marla said, laughing. "You can start a new trend."

"What a relief it's just a weird haircut, not cancer!" Suzanne said. "You had me worried." She couldn't help but wonder what Frank thought of it. Hard to imagine a man liking to run his fingers through a wig. Heck, Rob didn't even like when she used a lot of hair spray. Maybe someday soon he'd once again be touching her hair ... her face ... her body.

But when?

Chapter 25

RACHEL

FRIDAY

Seagulls swarmed overhead as Rachel positioned a basket of lunch on the hot sand. "You'll get some bread when we're done," she called to the birds, laughing. She spread beach towels for herself and Frank, and after easing herself down on one, scanned the surroundings—waves and water, children playing in the sand, a distant boombox playing lively music. What a fabulous way to spend the day before flying home.

She handed Frank a ham sandwich, heavy on the mayo, just as he'd asked. Serving others had always been her style. Since Stan died, her life may have changed, but she'd never stop serving others.

"Thanks." Frank lifted the bread to examine the mayo. He smiled, pleased.

She inhaled a deep breath of the salty summer fragrance, then reached for her soda. She wasn't used to this kind of heat. Florida's sun felt good on her body, but underneath her wig, she could already feel the sweat starting to drip from her scalp to her temples. She had to get this thing off.

"Frank, I have something to tell you."

His sandwich halfway to his mouth, he reversed direction and put it on a paper napkin. "What's on your mind?"

She quickly added, "Nothing serious." She sipped again. "But I need to tell you something." Perspiration dripped straight down her forehead onto her nose. She wiped it away with a finger. "I don't know if you've noticed, but I'm wearing a wig."

"You're kidding." He stared at her head, then reached to touch the hair. "It feels so real. I didn't know wigs could feel that way." He paused. "Well, why are you wearing it? Are you ... sick?"

"No, I don't have cancer, if that's what you mean."

"Then why the wig?" He asked, a perplexed look on his pink face.

Rachel told him about Caleb and how mad her sons would be. "Falling asleep while watching my grandson was bad enough. Failing to wake up while he clipped off my hair with sewing scissors? That's practically a mortal sin for a grandma. I had to keep it a secret."

"So, why are you telling me now?"

"Suzanne and Marla noticed my wig. They thought I had cancer. I thought you might be thinking the same thing, and I didn't want you to be concerned."

"That's very thoughtful of you." He pushed his glasses up the bridge of his wide nose and scrutinized her hair. "I guess my eyes aren't as good as theirs. I never noticed anything different—all I remember is you said your hairdresser took a couple inches off."

"Uh-huh. The wig's a little shorter than my hair was. I had to have an explanation."

He stared at her head. "Take it off," he said, a little forcefully.

"Huh?"

"Take the wig off. I'll keep your secret, I promise. No wonder you're sweating so much. I don't want you to be miserable here at the beach."

She looked around. No one was looking her way. Eh, why not? She slipped it off. Her real hair—at least what remained of it—was a sticky, uneven mess. She massaged her scalp with a hand towel. "Whew. That feels so much better." She smiled. "Thanks for not laughing when you saw my hair."

He reached for her hand. "I don't care what your hair looks like. I still love you."

Her eyes went wide. *Love*. He'd never before used that word with her.

"Rachel, I hope you'll say yes this time." He let go of her hand and motioned toward the waves lapping up the sand. "We could have such a great life here in Florida. I know you're a few years younger than I am, and you might want to work a little longer. You could work if you wanted to, but I've got a good pension, so you wouldn't have to. Living here would be so much healthier for both of us. We'd walk the beach, swim in a pool. You could go to yoga class with your mom."

He turned his face to her, a serious look on it. "Or if you really wanted to stay in Port Mariette, I'd even be willing to do that."

She put her hand over her loudly beating heart. He made it all sound so easy and so wonderful. "Oh, Frank. I don't know what to say. You're such a good man. You—you've become such an important part of my life, and I enjoy being with you." She looked down at the sand, uncertain how to explain herself. "But I don't know if I can ever get married again. At my age, that's a huge step. Can't we just leave things the way they are?"

Frank ran his fingers through the sand for a few moments. He grabbed a handful and let it pour out slowly, then fast. "The days go slowly, Rachel, but the years go fast. With my health problems, I don't know how many years I have left. I want to enjoy every one of them, and I want to spend them with someone I love."

Love. There's that word again. "That's so ... touching." She didn't know what else to say.

He dropped the rest of the sand onto the beach, and his face turned sad. "I've given this a lot of thought, Rachel. I meant it when I said you wouldn't have to work if we lived in Florida or that I'd even stay in Port Mariette. But it looks like it doesn't matter. Sounds to me like your mind's made up."

Rachel kept her hand on her heart. With Frank, she had the opportunity to create an entirely different life for herself. She wouldn't have to work anymore. She could live near her mother and brother. All her boys and their families would want to visit her in the winter. Her mother was right, Frank's a good man. Chance of a lifetime! Don't be a fool. Say yes!

But no words escaped her lips. The waves and the laughter of children sounded louder and louder as the silence between them lingered.

Finally, Frank pushed himself up from the wrinkled beach towel and brushed the sand from his hands. "Don't worry, I won't be bringing up marriage again." He plodded to the water's edge and dipped his feet into the waves. He turned to face her again, holding his arms out wide, as if to say *all this could be ours.*

She didn't move.

Chapter 26

MARLA

FRIDAY

Sun slanted into the spa as Marla entered through the front door, hoping to initiate a conversation with her daughter before things got any more awkward than they already were.

Yesterday, Grace had avoided her, and today, Marla had been busy investigating businesses in Lyondale and Dunham City. She hoped by now enough time had passed for Grace to cool down.

Marla followed her nose to the kitchen where she found Grace standing over the stove cooking chicken tenders in a pan. "Hi, Grace." She tossed her handbag on the countertop. "Making dinner?" Marla said it in a tentative voice.

"Uh-huh." Grace answered, her back to Marla.

Looked like enough for the two of them, unless Grace had invited someone over. Jesse? Marla hadn't eaten anything but a slice of cheese pizza all day long. "Anyone else coming over?"

"Nope." Grace turned on a burner for a pot of peas and flipped the chicken.

Marla took a step closer and inhaled. "Smells good."

"Probably the poultry seasoning."

More than a one-word answer, but Grace's reply still sounded that way to Marla. She inhaled again. "I'm starved. Suzanne and I spent the day wandering around Lyondale and Dunham City trying to figure out who might have reason to write those nasty reviews."

"Is that so?" Grace said, in a chilly voice.

Marla forged ahead. "We visited pizza shops, hair salons, and even a real estate agent's office."

"Lindsey's?"

"No, the one in Dunham City. We skipped Lindsey's. Figured she'd know what we were up to, and besides, if she had any information, she would've already shared it with Pete." To lighten the mood, Marla forced a chuckle. "Suzanne and I dreamed up some fine tales about why we were stopping by to chat, but eventually we ran out of places to visit." Even worse, they hadn't come up with a single clue.

Marla leaned against the counter to get in range of her daughter's eyes. "Look, Grace, I want you to know I heard what you said the other day." She reached down to smooth the wrinkles in her linen slacks. Linen slacks! What was she thinking, bringing them to Port Mariette? There's not a single dry cleaner for miles around here.

Grace kept her eyes on the stove as she stirred the peas and poked the chicken around in the pan.

"I need to apologize to you." Apologies were something Marla rarely gave, but when she did, she could do a thorough job. She'd keep talking until Grace cracked. "I never realized how I came across to you—or probably a lot of other people too. You gave me a wake-up call."

Grace allowed a wan smile but said nothing.

"I have to admit I get easily annoyed by people and I don't hesitate to voice my opinions about them. I don't have a lot of patience, and I rush to judgment." Marla paused before her final punch. She looked directly into Grace's eyes. "I can be blunt, I'm competitive, and I have a low tolerance for stupidity."

Grace burst out laughing. "You know yourself pretty well, don't you?"

Happy that Grace was laughing, a smile spread across Marla's face. "Did I miss anything?"

This time, they laughed together.

"I'm sorry for offending you about Jesse," Marla said, her voice soft. "Mitch says he's a really good guy. I made a snap judgment about him, didn't I?"

"Uh-huh." Grace turned off the burners. "Want some dinner?"

"Sure." They arranged their plates and sat to eat.

"So, tell me about Jesse."

Grace didn't blush, but her expression looked like she might. "He's so wonderful!" She blinked a few times. "Hardworking, smart, ethical, generous, thoughtful, strong, fun, handsome." After a pause, she giggled. "You can probably tell, I'm wild about him."

Marla smiled. "Sounds like a great guy to me. Are you—are you two dating? Has it progressed to that point?"

"Sort of." Grace prodded her peas onto her fork. "We're both so busy, though. I work long hours at the spa and he's trying to establish himself in landscaping and house painting. When we have time, we get a pizza, watch some TV. We usually meet Sunday mornings for Mass too."

Do-rag goes to Mass? Marla was stunned. Even Jesse was a better Christian than she was. "Is he divorced? Any kids?"

Grace shook her head. "Never married. He lives alone, in an apartment over a bar in Lyondale." She put down her fork. "He's just as lonely as I am."

Lonely? Grace was surrounded by people all day long. "You mean your nights are lonely?"

"No, I mean I'm lonely. Almost all the time." Grace fussed with her napkin. "Last year, when Mom and Dad were both so sick, I quit my job in Pittsburgh and moved in with them." She let out a puff of a laugh. "Let me tell you, living in Port Mariette with your parents isn't ideal for hanging out with friends, much less dating." She looked away. "But of course, for them, I'd do it all over again; I have no regrets." She blotted her teary eyes with a napkin. "I miss my mom and dad."

She got up for a tissue then returned to the table. "I mean, I know you're my birth mother, and I'm glad we finally reconnected last year, but they're the ones who raised me. I can't help but think of them as my mom and dad."

"I get it. They'll always be your parents. And I hope there will be a place for me in your life too."

Grace smiled at Marla but didn't comment, so Marla continued. "I can sympathize with you about your grief. My dad died last year, and then my mom went a few months later. It's a one-two punch when you lose both parents so fast."

"It is." Grace nodded then sniffled. "Maybe that's why God allowed you and me to finally find one another after all those years. He knew we'd need to comfort each other."

Moved that her daughter was opening up to her, but shocked at how sad Grace was, Marla reached across the round table and placed her hand on Grace's. How could she not have realized how Grace felt? "I'm so sorry. I didn't know you were so lonely. I had no idea. Forgive me." She stumbled with her words, uncertain about what to say and how to say it. Expressing emotions felt so unnatural. Maybe that's why she and Warren were a great match. He couldn't express emotions in any way except a written note. Herself? She could barely do it any way at all.

A tear rolled down Grace's cheek. She brushed it away.

Not knowing what else she could possibly say, Marla stood and held her arms out toward her daughter. She wished she could shed tears like Grace, but her eyes remained dry. At least she knew how to hug.

Grace bubbled into sobs and pushed herself up from the table. She embraced Marla.

Marla patted her daughter's back and smoothed her hair. "It's okay, it's okay." Marla repeated it over and over. She didn't want to stop. Even without tears, she'd never before felt so much like a real mother.

But what could she do that would make everything all right for Grace?

Chapter 27

SUZANNE

SATURDAY

Wide-eyed, Suzanne stared at the bright phone screen as she read a one-star review that popped up for Creations on Main. Mostly, the review attacked Inez's dolls, but it also jabbed the art shop itself. What would drive someone to write such awful things? She could understand if somebody didn't appreciate one of her caricatures or even her landscapes, but who would be cruel enough to criticize Inez's precious hand-painted dolls?

She'd call Rob about it. He'd understand. He'd say something to make her feel better.

It rang four times. How could he could be so busy? He's only helping Kevin pack up a two-bedroom apartment.

On the fifth ring, he answered. At least she didn't have to leave him a voicemail.

"Hi, honey." Rob's deep voice sent a tingle through her, in spite of her mood. "How's it going?"

"Not so good. These bad online reviews keep pouring in, and someone just posted one about the art shop—mainly about Inez's dolls, but about the art shop itself too."

He groaned. "Just what you need. What does it say?"

"It's really long. I don't feel like reading it again right now. It'll just irritate me more. I'll send you the link."

"Any chance you recognize who wrote it?"

"No idea. Marla and I spent all day yesterday talking to business owners in Lyondale and Dunham City trying to piece things together. We didn't get anywhere."

"Could the police help?"

"I doubt it. It's not really their job. Besides, this is not exactly NYPD here in Port Mariette."

"How about Warren?"

"He already helped us start up PMBA, and he told Marla the options we could look into for the reviews. But he doesn't have the time to follow up, and frankly, neither do I."

"How about Marla—does she have the time? Or anyone else?"

Suzanne ticked off the names. "Marla's been distracted by a problem with Grace. Rachel's tied up with her mom in Florida. Mitch and Herbie are too busy, plus they don't know much about technology. The rest of the business owners are just sloughing it off. Even Mary Frances. Now that her insurance agent assured her she'd be reimbursed for the smashed window, she seems unconcerned."

"That's too bad. I wish I could be there with you, if only to put my arms around you and tell you it'll be okay—because it will be. I'm sorry you're going through this without me. I wish I could be helpful in some way."

"You're helping, honey, just by listening to me rant." Thank goodness she'd married a psychologist. Her ex-husband Mike never had the time or patience to listen. Letting off steam with Rob made her feel better already.

"By the way," Suzanne continued, "on a happier note, Marla liked my arts festival idea. I'm going to present it at the PMBA meeting on Tuesday. They'll need to set a date for it as soon as possible."

"It'll take weeks to plan an event like that and help from a lot of people. I hope they can put together a good committee."

"I know. I'm just presenting the idea. It's up to them how they want to implement it."

"Tell them to have plenty of umbrellas on hand." Rob chuckled.

"You're not kidding. This weather has been unbelievable. They say we've had rain every day for almost three weeks. I can't wait to get out of here."

"I feel the same way about Seattle. But not because of the weather." Rob let out a sigh. "I think—I think I made a mistake coming here, like I should have let Kevin handle his problems on his own."

"Really?" Suzanne tried not to sound overly thrilled by his admission, but her voice gave her away.

"Yeah, I have to admit it, I did make a mistake. I let my fear of losing him override my logic. As a psychologist, I should have known better. You know that saying about a shoemaker's kids going without shoes? Well, I've been guilty of not being a good psychologist to my own son."

Taken aback by his admission, Suzanne didn't know what to say. Rather than say the wrong thing, she remained silent.

"I—I ruined the start of our marriage." Rob sounded like he was choking up.

Her heart went out to him, and he probably expected her to say *no, not at all*, but she couldn't lie. He *had* ruined the start of their marriage. She wasn't sure if or when she could forgive him for that. "That's a pretty strong statement, Rob."

There. She'd said something that was truthful but didn't let him off the hook.

"Yes, and it's a true statement." He sounded so sad.

As upset as she'd been this whole week, her heart now ached for him. "We'll get through this, honey. And one day, although it might be a long time from now ..." She chuckled. "... maybe we'll even laugh about it."

Rob chuckled, too, although a little weakly. "I sure hope we can do that soon." He let out a deep sigh. "Well, anything else going on?"

"Oh, I forgot to tell you. Sunset Hills called. They have a room opening up, maybe as soon as tomorrow."

"That's wonderful news. Is your mom willing to move in?"

"She's still balking, but she knows it's inevitable, so I think so. Andrea said she'd help me with the move but I'm not counting on her." Suzanne paused. "Speaking of moving—is Kevin all packed up?"

"He is. We had to buy some boxes for packing since Suki cleaned him out, but that was the only glitch." Rob cleared his throat. "You know, Kevin's going to be working out of our house while he's with us in Carmel, and uh, he'll need a lot of space for that."

"Uh-huh." What's Rob driving at? "It's too bad I turned the casita into my art studio. That would have been perfect." He'd better not ask her to convert the studio into an apartment for his son. She'd just gotten everything arranged the way she wanted.

"Right. So, uh, I was thinking he'll probably find a new place to live in a few weeks, but since he'll need a lot of working space—he uses three computer screens at the same time, can you believe that?—you and I could switch to that small spare bedroom temporarily, and Kevin could turn the master bedroom into his office."

"Really?" The word came out with force. "Have you already discussed this with Kevin?"

"Sort of." Rob mumbled.

"Sounds to me like it's a done deal." Suzanne struggled to maintain a calm voice.

"Well, we really don't have any other option."

"Can't you find him an apartment near us right away?" Suzanne said it more like a statement than a question.

"I need to keep a close watch on him, just for a while."

"What? A few minutes ago you told me you had made a mistake watching over him in Seattle. What's the difference when he's in Carmel?"

"It's only until he gets established with his new doctor and adjusts to his meds. It shouldn't be long. I just need to make sure he's on an even keel."

"But what if he doesn't get on an even keel? Or what if he gets used to living in daddy's home for free?" She didn't intend to snap her response, but it came out that way.

"Look, Suzanne, I have to do this for my son. If Jill was in the same situation, I'm sure you'd want to help her in the same way."

Suzanne pictured Kevin living at their house. Would he have dinner with them every night? Would he leave a lot of clutter around? Did he smoke or drink? Play heavy metal? Would he sleep in our bed? *Omigosh*—"Is Kevin going to be sleeping in our bed?"

Rob let out a huge sigh, as if gearing up to answer a tough question. "I'm sorry, sweetheart. He'll have to. That king-size bed won't fit into the spare bedroom. You and I will have to make do with a queen-size for a while. After all, I want to keep you close to me all night long." He said it with that deep sexy voice she normally loved. "And don't worry about your clothes and shoes. I'll move everything into that closet down the hall. You won't have to do a thing."

Chapter 28

RACHEL

SATURDAY

Rachel boosted herself onto the back seat of Pete's truck as it idled in the passenger pick-up lane of Pittsburgh International Airport. "The front seat is better for lumbar support," she said to Frank, motioning him in that direction. But the truth was, she didn't feel like talking. If she sat in the back of the cab, Pete would drive, Frank would talk, and she could feign an inability to hear over the sound of windshield wipers.

What a lie. *Eighth commandment: thou shall not bear false witness.* If she ever found time to go to confession, would she remember to confess that? Or how about her lies to Frank, telling him how hard a decision his proposal was for her.

All lies.

She closed her eyes and leaned her head against the foggy window. Soon, they were on the highway and Frank was droning on about Florida. The rhythm of the sounds lulled her into a nap, making their trip home seem like only minutes.

They all popped open their doors, and after that, their umbrellas. Pete pulled Rachel's hefty suitcase out first and dropped it onto the driveway. With no idea how long she'd be away, she had packed for the worst-case scenario, and her suitcase showed it. Ending up in Florida only four days, she could've gotten away with a carry-on, but how could she have guessed her mom would recuperate so fast?

She looked up at Frank, clutching the long handle of his suitcase in one hand and an umbrella in the other. "Thanks again for everything, Frank." She tried to give him a hug, but he was so stiff it was like hugging one of those life-size cardboard pictures with the face cut out for a photo opportunity. She let go and stepped back. No point in saying anything more—they'd talked everything out already, and now more than ever, Frank's body language made it clear he was cutting ties with her—with all of Port Mariette, in fact. At least that's what he'd told her on the flight back to Pittsburgh.

So that was that. Soon, Frank would put his house up for sale, he'd move to Florida, and Rachel would have to adapt. Ever since Stan died, she'd been adjusting to one change after another. Suzanne and Marla were good at that. She wasn't.

Suzanne once told her in order to have something new happen in your life, you have to create space for it, which could be an act as simple as getting rid of papers on your desk or clearing out a cluttered room. Inspired by Suzanne's concept, she had emptied Stan's clothes from their bedroom closet. What a change *that* had made space for!—a letter from T and a marriage proposal from Frank.

Even so, the concept still appealed to Rachel, and maybe Frank's departure would create space for something wonderful, like that tour of Poland she took last year with her bingo buddy Sandy Roczinski. After that trip, and now this one to Florida, she could finally imagine herself capable of flying somewhere on her own.

Yes, she could travel alone now. She was sure of it. Stan would be proud of her.

Stan. She bristled thinking of him and whatever he might have done with T. Could she ever be proud of *him* again? Maybe never, and definitely not until she got to the bottom of that pink note.

Pete rolled her suitcase up to the porch and pulled the front door open for her.

Cinders bounded out and leaped onto her stomach, knocking her back a step.

"Good to see you, too, Cinders." She hugged him for a moment, then he pranced down the steps to visit a shrub. She left her wet umbrella on the porch and stepped inside.

After being away only four days, the house felt different to her. It looked different, even smelled different. Someone else besides Pete had been spending time there. She was sure of it. She lifted an eyebrow and looked at Pete, on his way up the stairs. "Any chance you had Lindsey over while I was away?"

He pivoted and gawked at Rachel. "How could you tell?"

"I've lived in this house all my adult life. I can just tell." She shrugged. "Look, Pete, you're a grown man and I'm not going to tell you how to run your life. Just remember what Father Obringer always said, "Give Satan an inch and he'll become ruler of your life."

"I know, I know." Pete tramped up the stairs. "By the way," he said over his shoulder, "Tony Mastriano called while you were away. I told him you and Frank were in Florida for a while."

"What?" Her voice went unnaturally shrill. "You told Tony I was away with Frank?"

"Don't worry, I told him about Grandma being in an accident. He wants you to call him."

"Did he say why? Does he need something catered?"

"I have no idea." He smirked. "I try to mind my own business."

Chapter 29

MARLA

SUNDAY

Marla didn't even let Warren finish saying hello when she blurted, "I finally have some good news!"

"You're coming home!" His voice boomed.

Marla winced. She should have realized he'd misinterpret her excitement. "Mm ... Not quite yet." She said it in an unnaturally soft voice, hoping for his support.

He swore under his breath, then in a testy voice said, "Well, then, what's your good news?"

Their conversation going south, she kept it short. "I apologized to Grace and she forgave me. Then we hugged. It was like a real mother-daughter hug."

"Great. I'm glad for you. Now when are you coming back home?"

"Do you miss me?" Marla teased in an effort to lift his mood, although her own had also turned sour.

"Of course I miss you." He sounded irritated she'd ask such a question. "But that's not the point. Remember, you have obligations here, and as legal counsel for your foundation, I need to remind you there are matters needing your attention."

"Like what? You're handling the legal stuff. The accounting firm handles all the finances. And Deanna is a very capable administrator. I *do* know how to use the internet as well as my phone. There isn't a thing requiring my attention I can't do just as well here in Port Mariette." If Warren had said a few sweet nothings about how much he missed her, she might not have sounded so huffy. But he hadn't.

"I need your signature on a few documents."

"Can't I sign them online?"

"Not these. They're financial matters and some proposed revisions to your initial filing. We need to discuss them."

"Overnight them to me, and then we can talk about them over the phone."

He sighed.

"Well, I've got to run. I'm going to church this morning. Talk to you tomorrow." For the first time she could remember, she disconnected the call without a single term of endearment.

★★★★

Marla slipped into the last pew of New Life Assembly of God. Hoping to blend into the crowd, she wore no jewelry, a beige sleeveless dress, and a matching sweater in case the air conditioning was set too low like it was last summer when Mitch brought her here. Back then, his church wanted to establish a retreat center and Marla hadn't yet decided what to do with her aunt's mansion. She'd considered selling it to the church, but in the end, she chose to convert it to a day spa.

She recognized a few people in nearby pews but didn't try to catch their eye. On the other side of the church, she spotted Mitch, sitting alone. Last year, while working on renovations, they'd become trusted friends and occasional golf partners. Ordinarily, she would have walked over and sat with him, but now that he was dating Kim Kryzwicki, she didn't want to cross that line. Tongues would wag—even in a church.

Besides, she needed to sit by herself so she could figure a few things out, including how to pray about her relationship with Grace—that's why she came to church in the first place.

Here and there, people chatted and waved at one another. To avoid the distraction, Marla closed her eyes. She needed to pray, but what should she say? How exactly does one pray? Suzanne and Rob knew how to pray, and so did Mitch.

Marla didn't.

Soft organ music soothed her mind and she sat still, waiting for inspiration. Words finally came in a simple but earnest prayer. *God, please help me be the mother Grace needs.*

The first notes of a lively song blared from the front of the church, jarring Marla from her brief time of prayer. So loud. How can anyone think? Maybe being here was a mistake. She should have come when no one else was around. Silence would be more *conducive*, as Mitch would say, to prayer.

But she was here now, so she went along with everyone else, sitting, standing, singing, and listening to the preaching—everything, it seemed, but praying.

Soon the service was over. She blended into the crowd filing out of the church and opened her folding umbrella, still wet from more than an hour ago. She was nearly to her car when a familiar deep voice rose from behind her.

"Marla?" The voice came from underneath a striped golf umbrella.

She turned and smiled. "Hi, Mitch."

"You were at the service?" His eyes were open so wide it made Marla laugh.

"Aren't sinners allowed to go to church?" A hand on her hip, Marla feigned offense.

"I didn't mean it that way." Flustered, Mitch continued. "I mean, you never go to church when you're in Port Mariette—do you?"

"Sometimes I do." It was the truth, just barely. The last time she'd set foot in a Port Mariette church was last summer when she zipped into the basement at St. Cyp's to use a bathroom.

She continued walking to her car. Mitch stayed at her side.

"Isn't Kim here with you?" Marla asked.

"Why would she be here?" He lifted a hand toward the church. "Does this look like a golf course?"

"Oh! I thought you two were dating."

"An unsubstantiated rumor."

Marla laughed at his word choice. "Then maybe we can golf sometime." Although Kim had given the impression Mitch was off limits for golf with anyone but her, Marla's relationship with him was strictly business. Even Warren, who leaned toward the jealous side, didn't mind her golfing with her contractor. He recognized such an activity enhanced working relationships.

"I'll give you a call." He pulled Marla's car door open for her, then walked away.

Why was he so abrupt? Had she said something that offended him?

People. She'd never figure them out.

Chapter 30

SUZANNE

SUNDAY

Suzanne hopped onto the new highway and headed north to Pittsburgh. *The new highway.* How long would it take for everyone to stop calling it the new highway? It had been almost a year since the ribbon-cutting ceremony. But then again, change came hard in Port Mariette.

The cloudy skies matched Suzanne's mood, but with little traffic on the road, she quickly arrived at Living Water Church. Hard to believe just one week ago, she and Rob had gotten married in this church. Last week, she loved being here, but today, she *needed* to be here.

The moment she entered the building, she felt the difference in her mood. No one had touched her but she felt embraced. No one had conversed with her but she felt heard. She slipped into a seat in the section where she used to sit and waved to a few people she recognized.

The praise team started with a rousing, uplifting song. She stood, clapping and singing like everyone else. A few more up-tempo songs fueled her, then the music softened for one of her favorites, "I Surrender All." How that song had affected her the first time she heard it. Surrender all? How could a person do that? Lord knows, she'd tried again and again to hand over her whole life. But each time, she took it back bit by bit. How could she do it for once and for all? *Do it every day*, the Lord seemed to say to her.

She stretched her arms as high as they'd go and mouthed a sincere prayer surrendering everything to Jesus and thanking him for speaking to her heart.

At the end of the service, she walked up front for prayer. Pastor Rick greeted her warmly but with a concerned look. "You're still here in Pittsburgh? I thought you and Rob were going to be living in California."

She explained how Rob's son had upended their honeymoon plans, then described the demands her mother, her sister, and the art shop had placed on her shoulders. "I'd—I'd just like to walk away from everyone and everything." She looked up into Pastor Rick's weathered and understanding face and hoped he'd have an answer.

He merely nodded.

"Look, I know I can't walk away. They need me," Suzanne said. "But this sure isn't how I'd like to be spending my honeymoon. I know God has a reason for everything unfolding this way, and I know I need to surrender to his will, but with all these moving parts in my life, what would that look like? I just don't know."

"I don't know, either, but I know someone who does." Pastor Rick looked up to the ceiling and smiled. "How about we pray?" He rested his tattooed hands on Suzanne's shoulders and prayed God would guide her. After the amen, he arched an eyebrow. "Remember that sentence you added to your vows? The one about choosing to be married to Rob the rest of your life?"

Suzanne nodded. "I can't believe you remembered that line."

"When you told me you felt led to add it, I thought—she's going to be tested. I didn't expect it would happen this fast, but you're being tested, don't you see?"

"Tested. Hmm. I never looked at it that way. I've been too busy reacting to everything that's happening."

"That's when Satan loves to hop into our lives, when we're too busy to notice his arrival."

"I get it." She tilted her head. "Well, I still don't know what I should do."

"Pray about it, Suzanne. Listen for answers. Trust and obey."

"Pray, listen, trust, and obey. Okay, I got it. Thanks, Pastor Rick."

She pivoted and exited the church. Another downpour. She opened her umbrella, hurried to her mother's car, and left the parking lot.

Pray. Listen. Trust. Obey. She pressed the accelerator a little harder. Easy for him to say. Pastors had all sorts of time for praying and hearing God's voice. How about people like her, people busy with the problems of everyday life?

She pondered a little more, and before long reached her daughter's house. Jill and her family had just returned from a short vacation at Lake Erie where the weather had been dry and in the eighties. If they'd gotten enough sleep, they ought to be in a good mood. She parked in the driveway and hopped out, carrying her purse, a wet umbrella, and a stuffed zebra for Elizabeth.

Jill greeted her at the front door, holding her index finger to her lips. "Elizabeth's napping." She gave Suzanne a warm hug. "Good to see you, Mom. Drew's downstairs watching something on TV so we'll have a chance to catch up." Was that the real reason for Drew's absence? She chose to believe it was. They'd had their differences, but she was confident they were on a good track now. Rob had been so helpful with that. Why couldn't he solve his own family's problems?

Suzanne walked around the first floor, complimenting Jill on the improvements she'd made since her last visit. "You painted every room! How'd you manage to do that?"

Jill smiled like a shy six-year-old. "Made good use of nap times."

"Love those pastels. So warm and inviting."

They curled up at opposite ends of a corduroy sofa, just like they used to when Jill would come home from school and unload her day onto Suzanne—only now, Suzanne would instead unload her week onto Jill.

It took a while, but Suzanne covered all her topics—Rob, Kevin, her mom, her sister, and the art shop.

"Oh, my," Jill said. "After all this, you're the one who needs a vacation."

"Skip the vacation. I'm just hoping to have a honeymoon."

"It'll all be fine, Mom. Remember what you used to tell me when I was having issues with Drew?"

"No. Tell me."

"Two things—give him space, and pray for him."

"That's it?" Suzanne usually gave far more than two short pieces of advice.

"Well, that's all I remember, and that's all I did. And it worked. You can see how well things are going for us."

A small cry came from upstairs.

"Elizabeth's awake. You want to go get her?" Jill asked.

Suzanne grabbed the stuffed zebra and headed to the steps, a smile wide across her face. "Grandma's coming, Elizabeth!"

Chapter 31

RACHEL

SUNDAY

Rachel yanked a grocery cart from the line-up in the Dairy Mart's entrance, then shook her wet umbrella and hooked it on the side of the buggy.

"Nice sunburn," came a high-pitched voice from behind her.

"Oh. Penny. Hi." A long shopping list in hand, Rachel hoped to avoid a conversation. That woman could talk the stripes off a flag.

"Did you and Frank enjoy your vacation?" Penny singsonged loudly as she followed Rachel into the produce section.

Rachel glanced around, relieved no one was within earshot. "It wasn't a vacation. I was helping my mother with her recovery, and Frank stayed with his son Joey."

"Oh." Penny sounded disappointed.

"Well, did I miss anything while I was away?" Rachel asked as she selected a container of blueberries. She'd never admit it, but she was a teensy bit glad she'd run into Penny. Pete never paid much attention to local happenings, and neither Suzanne nor Marla were part of the grapevine. After a few minutes with Penny, Rachel would be all caught up.

"Let's see." Penny squinted. "More bad reviews showed up yesterday. Suzanne's art shop got a really bad one."

"Aw, no!" Rachel dropped the berries into her cart. "That's terrible. She must be beyond upset." Rachel would have to call her later.

"There were a couple others, but I can't remember them all."

"Not Food 'n Fuel, I hope?"

"Oh, no," Penny said, eyes to the ceiling. "I think I would have remembered that."

"There haven't been any more broken windows along Main Street, have there?"

"None I know of," Penny said with a degree of uncertainty. "What a pity there are only two security cameras on the entire street—one at your place, and the other all the way at the other end, at the bank. Even though the middle of the street doesn't have any security, I guess two cameras are better than nothing."

"Actually, our camera's out of commission," Rachel said. "Pete ordered a new one, but it's still not in. Supply chain issues, you know." She rolled a head of iceberg lettuce into her cart. "Anything else I missed?"

"Let's see." Penny squeezed an avocado, then tossed it back on the display. "Oh, we're going to have a room available at Sunset Hills. I already called Suzanne about it. I think she'll be moving her mother in soon."

"Is that so?" Rachel tilted her head. "Isn't that kind of information confidential?"

Penny shrugged.

"Well, in any event, poor Suzanne's as busy as popcorn on a skillet." Rachel would definitely call to offer help. "Anything else?"

Penny nodded, a gleam in her eyes. "Kim Kryzwicki is dating some guy she met online. Ray, Roy, I can't remember his name." She lowered her voice. "I ran into them the other day. They were holding hands, all lovey-dovey."

"Really? Where'd you see them? On Main Street?"

"No, silly." Penny poked Rachel in the arm. "On the riverwalk. You should see it down there—what a mess! After all that wind and rain we've been having, trees have fallen all over the place."

"Is that so?" Rachel's face registered surprise. She'd have to check out those pines in her backyard. Their root systems were so shallow. Stan never should have planted them.

She pushed her cart to the baked goods section, Penny right behind her. "I thought Kim was dating Mitch."

"She liked to make it sound that way, but Mitch claimed he was just giving her golf lessons. The truth's probably somewhere in between." Penny cackled. "Besides, he's better off without her. She cheated on her husband, you know."

Rachel had been unaware of that too.

Chapter 32

MARLA

SUNDAY

The best thing about Sunday on Main Street was it was easy to snag a parking spot. Marla found one in right in front of the Dairy Mart and pulled in just as Rachel passed by, loaded down with groceries.

Marla tooted her horn.

Rachel jumped at the sound. "Oh, hi, Marla." She stuck her index finger up in the air then set the bags on the hood of her Chevy. She hurried back to Marla, waiting on the sidewalk

"Welcome home." Marla gave her a hug. "How's your mom doing?"

"Great. The doctor said she had the speediest recovery he's ever seen."

An elderly woman walked by and interrupted their conversation to ask about Rachel's mom. And Frank. After she moved on, Rachel said, "Wanna sit down over there and catch up?" She pointed to a bench in front of the antique shop.

"Sure." They took a few steps then sat down.

Rachel gave Marla a once-over. "You're wearing a dress."

"I went to church."

"I didn't see you there."

"I went to the Assembly of God church."

"Oh." Rachel was silent for a moment. "Why didn't you come to St. Cyp's?"

Marla chuckled at Rachel's unexpected directness. "Mitch took me to his church once last year when they were looking for a retreat house. He thought I might want to sell Aunt Adele's house to them."

"But you turned it into a spa, so why did you go back there today?"

"Boy, Rachel, you sound like Warren interrogating someone on a witness stand."

Rachel giggled. "Sorry, I'm just curious. People who are raised Catholic usually stay Catholic. I guess you and Suzanne are exceptions."

Marla did always like to be an exception, but that was not why she'd gone to the Assembly of God church. She shrugged. "I just feel more comfortable there."

"How come?"

"Why do you ask?" Marla laughed. "Are you thinking of switching denominations?"

"No way. But why do you feel more comfortable there?"

"It's hard to explain, because it's so different from St. Cyp's." Marla squinted in thought. "I guess the reason is because last summer Mitch and I had a lot of conversations about God."

"*You* talked about *God*?" Rachel's eyes widened.

Marla laughed again. "Is that so hard to believe?"

"Well, uh. It's just that you don't come across as being some holy person."

"Believe me, I know. My daughter, for one, has let me know I'm far from holy. Maybe that's one reason I like Mitch's church. Everyone's very open about discussing spiritual matters like sin and backsliding. Someone got up today and gave a testimony about where he used to be and where he is today. It was powerful to see how God worked in his life." Marla shrugged. "Made me think I'm not a lost cause."

"Boy, you're really being hard on yourself, Marla. How come?"

Marla told her about what Grace said a few days ago. "She was right. I have been doing a lot of backsliding since last summer. I've been super critical of people in Port Mariette. Been self-centered too."

Rachel opened her mouth to reply, but Marla held up a hand to stop her. "It's true. Grace was right. So now I'm trying to get myself back on track."

"Have you talked with Warren about this?"

"Not yet. He's upset with me too. Wants me to get back home. He claims I need to sign some documents in person, but I know the real reason he's irritated is because he's had to attend a few social events alone. He hates that." Marla paused. "It would be nice if he'd say he missed me instead of telling me to come home to sign documents."

"Men." Rachel sighed. "What else can I say?"

Marla laughed. "Well, enough of that. "How did it go in Florida with Frank?" In such a beautiful setting, maybe their relationship had accelerated.

Rachel's face suddenly turned a little redder than it already was from the sunburn. "It didn't go so well," she finally said.

"Oh! I'm sorry." Marla felt genuinely sorry, and it caught her by surprise. "Do you want to talk about it?"

Rachel rolled her eyes. "It all started at Suzanne's wedding." She explained how Marla and Warren had unwittingly interrupted Frank's marriage proposal.

"I *thought* you two were acting a little strange, but I didn't say anything. I didn't want to ruin anyone's mood at a wedding, but it turns out I did—a proposal!" She touched Rachel's arm. "I'm so sorry."

"That's okay. I was so shocked, I didn't know what to say to him anyway."

Marla looked down at Rachel's left hand. No ring. "So, he hasn't attempted another proposal?"

"In Florida, he asked again. He said he wanted me to move with him to Florida. I could retire, and we'd live off his pension, or if I wanted, I could find a job down there."

"And?"

"Let me just say, things didn't end on a pretty note."

Marla wrapped an arm around her friend. "I'm so sorry—so sorry it didn't work out. I had no idea. I—I guess I've been too wrapped up in my own life." She held onto Rachel for a few seconds, feeling emotionally connected to her and on top of that, pleased that the hug came so naturally. Maybe going to church had been a good idea after all.

"That's okay. I didn't want to talk about it until everything was decided." Rachel shrugged. "So now, Frank's going to be selling his house and moving to Florida. Life sure changes fast."

"Frank's moving?" Marla said, her eyes widening.

Rachel nodded.

"Has Mary Frances listed the house yet?"

"I doubt it. We only got home yesterday afternoon. But Frank's not relaying the details of his life to me anymore." Rachel raised an eyebrow. "Why are you so interested in Frank's house, anyway?"

Marla smiled. "It seems Grace has a man in her life, a guy named Jesse. He lives in a dumpy apartment above a bar in Lyondale. I'm thinking maybe Jesse would be interested in buying Frank's house. If he made an offer before Mary Frances got the listing, he could save a few bucks not having to pay a commission."

"Hmm. Well, I hope Jesse's handy. Frank prefers sitting on his porch to doing home maintenance, if you know what I mean."

"Jesse's as handy as they come." Marla cocked her head. "Is Pete interested in the house?"

"Never dawned on me to ask him," said Rachel. "He was only going to stay with me for a few months. Been almost a year now."

"Can you check with Pete? If he's not interested, let me know right away."

Chapter 33

SUZANNE

MONDAY

Last night when she got home from Jill's, Suzanne had planned to broach the topic of Sunset Hills with her mother, but she changed her mind. Rob had once told her not to talk about serious matters when she was hungry, angry, tired, and something else. He said to remember an acronym—H-A-L-T. But what did that L stand for? Late? Didn't matter. Being so tired had been enough to make her hold off, and instead, she joined her mother in watching some ancient reruns of *Bonanza*.

But this morning, it dawned on her. *Lonely.* That's what the L stood for. Yep, last night Suzanne was tired *and* lonely. Good thing she waited till this morning to have that conversation. She still missed Rob but at least her mother was around.

She could hear her rustling upstairs. "You up, Mom?" Suzanne called from the foot of the stairs.

"Yes. Almost dressed."

Suzanne marched up the steps, wondering how the conversation would go. "Morning, Mom." She gave her a squeeze then perched herself on the edge of the bed, hands on either side to hold her in place. She took a loud and deep breath.

"Uh-oh. What is it?" Her mother let herself down gently beside her daughter. "Did someone die?"

"No, nothing like that." But how should she start? She took her mother's hand. "Let talk."

"Oh," her mother said softly. "I get it. Sunset Hills called, didn't they?"

Suzanne gave a single nod.

Her mother let out a sarcastic chuckle. "So obviously, someone *did* die. Probably a woman. Those places always advertise pictures of old men sitting around laughing with women, but that's a lie. Everyone knows women outlive their husbands. They wait on their husbands all their lives then get carted off to an assisted living facility to die alone."

"Oh, Mom. I'm so sorry." Suzanne put an arm around her. "I wish you could live here in your house the rest of your life, but you know it's just not safe anymore."

"Maybe Andrea could move in with me?" She wrinkled her forehead.

"You're kidding, right?"

"Yeah, I'm kidding." She shrugged. "Andrea's a lousy cook and a worse housekeeper. Well, I wonder who created a vacancy for me."

"No idea," Suzanne said. "Penny did tell me the room is one of their nicer ones. You know how it is, you have to take what's available, so I guess we're lucky you'll get a nice room." Suzanne was trying to put a positive spin on matters, for her mother's sake as well as her own. Forcing her mom to move to a place she didn't want to go broke Suzanne's heart. Why couldn't her mother move in with her and Rob instead? After all, Kevin would be moving out one of these days and then her mom could use the spare bedroom. How could Rob object, after he'd so readily welcomed his son?

"I hope it wasn't Marla's aunt who died," said her mother, jarring Suzanne back to the conversation at hand. "I always liked Adele."

"Marla would have told me if anything happened with her aunt." Suzanne paused a moment. "Why don't you move out to California and live with me and Rob?" The words tumbled out of her mouth before she knew it. She flattened a hand on her chest. *I'm just like Rob!* He had invited Kevin without asking her, and now she'd done the same with her mother.

"California?" Her mother guffawed. "I've never traveled out of the tri-state area, and you're asking me to move to California? You can't be serious, Suzanne." Her mother shook her head, then smiled. "But that's really sweet of you to offer. Next time I talk with Rob, I'll thank him too."

"Actually, uh, I never mentioned it to Rob."

"Ha. I guess you're lucky I said no, then."

Suzanne ignored the comment. "I really think you'll like it at Sunset Hills, Mom. No more steps. No more cooking. Lots of activities. You'll make new friends and see old ones too. Marla's aunt says she loves it there. I'm sure she'll show you the ropes."

"So I can hang myself." Her mother lowered her chin.

"Oh, Mom, please!" Suzanne pleaded with her eyes. This wasn't going as well as she'd hoped. "I wish you could live here in your home forever, but something's got to give. I'll be going back to California, and Andrea can't handle everything on her own."

"I know, I know. I'm just feeling sorry for myself. You have no idea how hard this is. It's like facing the final step. After that, it's heaven." She smirked. "Maybe I shouldn't be complaining, huh? Heaven's a pretty fantastic destination."

"That's right. Nice place to spend eternity."

They remained silent for a while, then her mom jerked to attention, "How about all my stuff? What are you going to do with it?" Her eyes darted around the room. "Can I take my perfume bottle collection with me? My crossword puzzle magazines? My own bed?"

"I honestly don't know." Suzanne knew the perfume bottle collection would never make it, but magazines seemed like a reasonable request. "How about we run over there today find out? We can decide what you should take right away, then later on, Andrea or I can bring things over as you need them. Anything you leave behind can stay here for now. After all, you don't need to sell your house right away."

"Right." She got up from the bed and pushed her shoulders back. "Okay, let's go now and get this over with."

Suzanne leaped from the bed, grabbed her purse, and helped her mother to the car. It wasn't long before they entered Sunset Hills's parking lot.

Penny pulled into the spot next to them then came over to open the passenger side car door. "Well, good morning, Mrs. Schwartz," gushed Penny. "So nice to see you today." As she led both women to the entrance she glanced at Suzanne. "Have you two had any breakfast yet?"

"Actually, we haven't," Suzanne said with a guilty giggle. "We started talking about coming over here as soon as Mom got up, and we ran out of the house without so much as a cup of coffee." No point in giving her mother time to change her mind.

"Well, then, c'mon in." A grinning Penny held the door open for them, then guided them to the dining room. "Let's get something in your stomachs."

They took their seats at an empty table as Penny called to an aproned woman wiping a nearby table. "Carla, could you set these ladies up with some breakfast?" Then to Suzanne and her mother she said, "I've got to get to my desk. Carla will take care of you for now, and I'll stop back in a little bit."

Suzanne tilted her head, squinting at Penny, who only a year ago had confessed her transgressions to Suzanne—everything from massive gambling debt to trying to bilk the State out of money she'd pocketed for her own purposes. Maybe Rob could figure her out. Suzanne sure couldn't.

Marla's aunt came over from another table and gave them both a hug. "Hello, ladies. I'd love to take you on a tour," Adele said. "I can give you the inside scoop."

"That's so kind of you," Suzanne said. "Let me check with Penny to make sure that's okay." She left them at the table and went to the reception desk, where Penny sat staring at her computer with an annoyed expression. Suzanne leaned over the counter and peeked at the screen. Why was Penny on the funeral home's website? "Everything okay?"

Penny leaped up and blocked Suzanne's view of the screen. "It's—it's something confidential."

"Oh, of course. Sorry." No doubt Sunset Hills had frequent reasons to be in touch with Lipton's Funeral Home.

Penny regained her composure. "Would your mother like to see the room that's available?"

Suzanne nodded. "Adele wants to give her a tour."

"She can come along, but a staff member has to lead the tour." Penny turned off her computer and got up from her desk. "I'll get the key to the vacant room. Maintenance always locks them up once they're sanitized."

Penny and Adele, competing for who could provide the most information, considerably lengthened the tour. Finally, the four of them reached the vacancy.

"You're going to love this room," Penny said as she unlocked the door. "You'll be close to everything, but far enough away from the activities that you can nap undisturbed."

The room looked tidy, smelled clean, and a heavenly morning sun streamed through two large windows. Suzanne raised her eyebrows, waiting for her mother's reaction.

Instead of examining the room, though, her mother kept staring at something outside one of the windows. "Oh, my! Look at all those beautiful hydrangeas. They're my favorite plant!" She turned toward Penny, smiling. "This room is perfect. I'll take it."

"A good choice, Mrs. Schwartz," said Penny, with a nod of her head.

"How about we sign the paperwork, Mom?" Suzanne tried not to sound overly eager. "Then we can go home to pack a few things."

Mom chuckled. "Yeah, let's sign those papers before I change my mind."

Suzanne put an arm around her and gave her a squeeze. "It's a hard decision, but it's the right one."

"I know." Mom's eyes suddenly welled. "I know." She repeated the words a few more times, as if trying to convince herself. She dabbed her eyes with a fingertip, then straightened her spine. "Okay, I'm ready to sign."

Chapter 34

RACHEL

MONDAY

Port Mariette's gossip-in-chief Penny probably already knew all about T, but no way would Rachel subject herself to hearing the truth from her. She'd figure it out on her own.

Still in her pajamas, she flicked on the bare light bulb in her unfinished basement. How many times had she asked Stan to turn that dark and dank room into a playroom for the boys? He'd always been too busy. Doing what?

She opened one dusty storage container after another and finally unearthed their old high school yearbooks. Sitting on the steps she flipped through the class photos, searching for every female whose first name began with a T.

A couple of times, her heart skipped a beat when she thought she'd found the answer, but in the end, for one reason or another, none of the women from St. Cyp's could have been involved with Stan. That meant T had to be someone who had attended the public school or possibly someone who moved here as an adult, although in Port Mariette that was a longshot.

Enough of this. She needed to get to work. Mondays were always busy, and today she had to replenish the stock of food at Food 'n Fuel. She changed into work clothes and within a half-hour was stuffing cabbage leaves as quickly as she used to change the boys' diapers. She didn't even bother to look up when the side door opened. Pete could get whatever he needed without her help.

"Hi, Rachel." It was Tony's cheerful voice.

She jerked her head up. "Tony!" She should have called him back after she landed, or at least first thing this morning, but her mind had been on other matters. "Are you here to pick up an order?" She wiped her hands on her apron and stepped toward him, hoping she had enough stock of whatever he wanted.

"Nope. Nothing on order. Just popping in to see you while I'm in town."

She gave him a quizzical look then jutted her chin toward her desk. "Wanna sit down?"

"Sure." Tony let himself down onto a metal folding chair. "Herbie wanted me to check out one of his storefronts. He's going to have a vacant one soon. That little gift shop is closing—the owner's retiring. It'd be perfect for me."

"You're interested in running the gift shop?" Rachel furrowed her brow.

Tony waved a hand. "No, no." His eyes twinkled as he explained. "I have a side business making candy."

"Really? You never mentioned that."

"I've kept it under the radar. It's a small operation, just online sales."

"That's amazing." No wonder Tony was weary. Running a candy business on top of Signore's would exhaust anyone. Maybe even Marla.

"At the reunion last summer, I talked with Herbie about it. I told him once the candy business turned a profit, I wanted to open a shop. Candy ought to sell better in a shop than online."

Rachel nodded, although she knew nothing about selling candy. Eating it, that was a different story.

"Seems to me Main Street in revitalized Port Mariette would be the ideal place to set up my shop. It would fit in well with the small-town, homemade vibe."

"I'm confused. I thought you were going to retire." Rachel tilted her head. "Sounds like you're going to be busier than ever."

"For a while, yeah. My son's ready to take over Signore's. I just have to make sure Gia works out. After that, I'll have time on my hands."

"Gia?"

"She's the manager we rehired, the one who moved back home after her divorce."

"Oh. Now I remember."

"Once that happens, I can devote myself to the candy shop."

"Wow. How about that." Rachel took a moment to process this piece of news. "Are you really going to do it?"

"I am."

"So you *will* have extra time on your hands."

"I will." He chuckled. "In fact, I was thinking of coming back to Port Mariette some night this week for dinner at Dom's." He paused. "I was thinking of ... asking you to join me." He gave her a sheepish look.

"Me?" Rachel put a hand on her chest.

"Yes, you." He knit his brows. "Am I off base for asking you out? Herbie told me you're, uh, available now. He said Frank is moving to Florida—alone."

"Herbie knew all that a day after I got home from Florida?" Penny could learn a few things from him.

Tony nodded. His forehead was dampening. "Well, uh, whatcha think? Wanna go out to dinner with me?"

Chapter 35

MARLA

TUESDAY

Marla stood at the railing of the spa's front porch, pushing cuticles back with her thumbnail. Even with living in her very own spa, she'd been too busy for a manicure. How could that be? She stopped toying with her nails as soon as Grace and Jesse pulled up in his truck. He hopped out first then opened the door for Grace, who balanced a box of leftover pizza as she leaped out.

"Thanks for holding down the fort for me," Grace said to Marla as she and Jesse walked up the porch steps. She glanced back and forth at Marla and Jesse. I guess—I guess you two haven't formally met yet, have you?" To Jesse, Grace said, "This is my birth mother, Marla Galani."

"Nice to meet you—." He stopped short, as if uncertain how to address her.

"Call me Marla." She extended a hard. "Want to sit out here for a while? I dried off the rocking chairs. It's not supposed to rain again until this evening."

"Let me put this pizza in the fridge. I'll be back in a sec." Grace pivoted and went inside.

Marla and Jesse took their seats. "You've been doing a nice job keeping our property in shape," Marla said.

"Thank you, ma'am," Jesse replied, nervously lurching back and forth on his rocking chair.

"Call me Marla," she reminded him with a smile. Without a do-rag, and dressed in a polo shirt and khakis, Jesse looked quite presentable, even ruggedly good-looking. She could see the attraction he held for Grace.

The front door opened and Grace rejoined them. "I told Jesse about Frank getting his house ready for sale."

Jesse nodded. "I've been looking for a fixer-upper here in Port Mariette. Since the new highway opened, though, housing prices have gone up. Sounds like Frank's place might be something I could afford." He paused. "Do you know how much he's asking?"

Right to the point, that Jesse. Marla liked that. "Rachel said she didn't have any idea about the price, just that the place needs work." And her son Pete had no interest in tackling a renovation.

"You got Frank's number?" Jesse asked.

Marla read it aloud as he typed the number on his phone.

Jesse stood and walked to the railing, thumb in his pocket. After a quick conversation, he said, "Let's go."

A man who takes action. Marla liked that too. She gave Grace a smile of approval.

"Can you come with us, Marla?" he asked. "I'd appreciate your input."

"Let's take my SUV." Grace pulled a keychain from her purse.

They piled in, arriving few minutes later. Frank answered the door. "This place is a mess," he said, sounding like a busy housewife. "Ignore all the dust and clutter."

The three of them trooped in, and Marla immediately sneezed. "Sorry. Allergies." She pulled a tissue from her purse. The house looked almost as bad as Aunt Adele's before she and Grace cleaned it up.

"You're welcome to look around for yourselves." Frank waved a hand. "If you have any questions, give a holler."

They made their way through every room. Jesse took notes, then they went outside. He borrowed Frank's extension ladder to climb to the roof while Marla and Grace chatted with Frank.

"It's a nice house, Frank, but it does need some work," Marla said.

"I know. It's been hard to keep up since Wendy died, and Jesse's probably gonna get off that ladder and tell me I need a new roof."

The aluminum steps creaked as Jesse made his way down. "I hate to say it, Frank, but it looks like you need a new roof up there."

Frank looked at Marla. "What did I tell ya?" He shrugged. "Well, Jesse, are you interested?"

Jesse put his hands on his hips. "How about you and I go inside to talk?"

The two of them made their way into the house while Marla and Grace waited on the front lawn.

Marla brushed the tall grass back and forth with her foot. "Well, at the very least, Jesse ought to be able to sign Frank up as a customer for his landscaping business."

"You're not kidding." Grace chuckled. "This place needs some serious TLC—inside and out." She waved her foot through the grass, mimicking Marla. "Thanks for teeing this up for Jesse. I appreciate it, and I'm sure he does too."

"Not a problem. I'm just glad Rachel told me about Frank moving." Marla smiled warmly at Grace. "I know you and Jesse want to live closer to one another." A tender silence followed, then Marla said, "I can see why you like him. He's a good man. I hope it works out for you."

But please don't get so caught up in Jesse that you forget about me.

Chapter 36

SUZANNE

TUESDAY

"Me?" Suzanne's hand flew to her throat. "But Mary Frances, I don't even live here." Her eyes bounced around the meeting room in search of another PMBA member who could run the arts festival. *Marla? Rachel? Herbie? Andrea?* She sized up the capabilities and availability of every attendee—and came up with no one.

"It *is* an arts festival, after all, and you were the one who dreamed up the idea." Mary Frances stood at the podium, hands locked on the edges, as she looked down over reading glasses at Suzanne. "If we're going to do it at all, it has to be a success. A lot of effort and money will be riding on it."

"I have to get back home to California," Suzanne said weakly. *I have a honeymoon on hold and a marriage that's teetering.*

Mary Frances leaned forward. "Look, Suzanne, this arts festival was your idea, and we've all agreed it's a good one. Since most of the activity centers on the artists of Creations on Main, either you or Andrea need to head it up. If Andrea can't do it, maybe you can fly back and forth a few times."

Andrea leaned over and whispered, "You *have* to do it, Suzanne. You know I can't."

"I'll help any way I can," Rachel called from her note-taking table at the front of the room.

"So will I," added Marla from her seat across from Suzanne.

Others nodded or said they'd help.

Clearly she'd have support, but that didn't change the fact she still needed to get home. After all, she'd just told Rob she would fly home in a few days. She stood to address the group. "I appreciate all your offers to help, but I really need to go back to California. Flying back and forth is just not realistic for me." No need to tell them about Kevin, her postponed honeymoon, and her wobbly marriage. Heck, most of them probably already knew anyway.

The room went silent, except for a loud, exasperated sigh from Mary Frances.

After a long and awkward moment, Walt Celinski, owner of the *Port Mariette News*, called out from the back of the room. "I have an idea. How about we plan to have it next Saturday?"

"Next Saturday?" Suzanne did a quick count. "That's only eleven days away! We couldn't possibly promote the event in such a short period of time."

"I'm not saying it'd be easy, but there are ways," Walt said. "I have contacts with all the Pittsburgh newspapers. I can call in a few favors to make sure they give us advance coverage. And of course, it'll be front page news in our local paper. Everyone in Lyondale and Dunham City will read about it there."

Walt's wife Rosemarie spoke up. "I'll get coverage on social media too."

"For that matter, all of us can post on social media," said Mary Frances.

Suzanne let out a loud sigh. She *could* stretch her time in Port Mariette another week and a half. Moving up the date might not be so bad. After all, like Rob always said, work expands to fill the time allotted, and if they had months to plan, they'd end up dragging out the process. By staying here longer, she'd be able to check on her mother a while longer, clean up some of her clutter, get the art shop back in shape, *and* avoid being around Kevin. Not a bad deal, when you think about it.

She looked across the table at her sister. Andrea was holding her hands up, folded. "Please," she mouthed to Suzanne.

How could Suzanne refuse? "I'll do it under one condition." She raised her index finger. "I'd like all major promotional announcements to include information about the classes we'll be offering at the art shop."

"Consider it done." Walt said. "Send me the details and I'll take care of the design."

Mary Frances flashed a smile. "Thank you for your willingness to head up the arts festival, Suzanne. You'll do a wonderful job."

Oh my. What have I agreed to? In only eleven days, she'd have to organize the festival, create a schedule for the art classes, and find a way to tell Rob this time, she'd be the one to postpone their life together.

Mary Frances looked down at her notes. "Next on our agenda is discussion of the negative reviews. Oh, by the way, Sergeant Dan sends his regrets for not attending. He's out with the flu. He did tell me online review issues are outside the purview of the police department, so we are on our own here. According to my last count, sixteen businesses have gotten at least one negative review. Any new ones surface today?"

Everyone remained silent, so Mary Frances continued. "Glad to hear there are no new ones, but we still have to figure out who's been writing them. Anybody have an idea?"

Marla piped up. "Suzanne and I spent a day in Lyondale and Dunham City investigating, but so far, we have nothing."

"We thought we'd go back again later this week," said Suzanne, "but now I don't think we'll have time."

Mary Frances smiled with the most warmth Suzanne had ever seen from her. "What would this town do without the two of you? How can I persuade you ladies to move here permanently?"

"Hear, hear!" Mitch called out from across the room.

"Well said, Mitch," said Mary Frances, still smiling for a moment longer. She looked from one table to another. "Does anyone else want to comment on those reviews?"

The room fell silent.

Mary Frances continued. "So far, I haven't noticed any impact on real estate sales, so let's table that topic until after the festival. If we get a lot of good publicity from the event, it ought to counteract the negative reviews, at least for a while." She shuffled her papers. "That's all we have on our agenda for tonight, unless Suzanne would like to talk about specifics for the arts festival."

"Yes, I'd like to." Suzanne strode to the front of the room, a tablet and pen in hand. "How about we decide who will do what and how?" Suddenly, she felt like she used to when she worked as a trainer for the airlines. In charge.

Authoritative. Knowledgeable. Not only could she handle this assignment, she'd do a masterful job.

But how would she do with her explanation to Rob?

Chapter 37

RACHEL

FRIDAY

"Tonight, I'm going out on a limb. I'm gonna order the chicken parmesan." Rachel said it with a straight face as she slid her menu aside. The selection certainly wasn't outside her comfort zone, but agreeing to this date with Tony? About that she felt less sure.

"You consider chicken parm high risk?" Tony chuckled.

She leaned toward Tony and whispered, "It's one of the few meals Dom makes. But it's our little secret, okay?" She winked at him.

Tony would keep the secret. After all, at Signore's, he often passed off her sausage lasagna as his own. "Mum's the word." He grinned as he placed his hand on top of hers.

Electricity. Yes, that's what she felt! She'd sometimes heard women talking about a special jolt from a man, but personally, she'd never experienced it, even from her own husband. Last year, when she and Tony danced together at the reunion, she hadn't felt it either. Odd. Maybe back then, she was still numb from the newness of being a widow. In any event, she felt the electricity now, and it put all her senses on alert.

A server interrupted the connection. "What'll you have?" asked the ponytailed young woman. She took their selections, then pivoted toward the kitchen.

Tony leaned into Rachel, an earnest look in his eyes. "I'm—I'm glad you decided to come to dinner with me. You probably never knew this, but back in high school, I always had a thing for you."

"You did?" Her eyes widened at his sudden admission. "Why didn't you ever say anything to me?"

"I couldn't. I didn't want to hurt Suzanne. We'd been dating since tenth grade. You probably knew our relationship wasn't perfect, but it was comfortable. You're not the only one who likes predictability, you know." He chuckled. "Even after Suzanne and I broke up right before the senior prom, it wouldn't have been right to ask her best friend to go in her place."

"So that's why you asked Mary Frances? I always wondered about that." Mystery solved, more than forty years later.

"Right. Anyway, remember that long walk you and I took on our senior mission trip in Guatemala?"

Rachel gave a knowing smile.

"Yeah, I remember a lot about you from those high school years—the way you looked twirling those batons on the football field and how you were always laughing and smiling." He shifted in his seat. "Last summer, at our fortieth reunion, I thought about asking you out, but you know how it is, it takes a long time to recover from losing your spouse. I wasn't ready, and I didn't know if you were either."

"I wasn't." Rachel shook her head. She'd helped organize the reunion merely as a way to take her mind off her troubles, not to meet a man.

"Then you got involved with your neighbor Frank. I didn't want to interfere with that. But as soon as Herbie told me your relationship had gone kaput, I figured I'd ask you out right away, before some other guy swept you off your feet." His eyes twinkled and a smile spread over his broad face. "I'm sure I'm not the only guy who's thought about asking you out."

Rachel giggled. "I don't think there's much chance of that happening in Port Mariette. Not a lot of single men in my age group here." She tilted her head coquettishly. In the span of a few minutes, Tony was making her feel like a vibrant, exciting woman. With Frank, she'd always felt she was trudging into old age.

"Well, I didn't want to miss my opportunity." He patted her hand, then turned serious. "Look, Rachel, you and I have a lot of shared history. We have a lot in common. It's taken me a while, but I'm ready to date now. You said you are too." He furrowed his forehead, bringing his dark eyebrows close together. "But at our age, dating is a little awkward, isn't it?"

"You'd better believe it." She tittered.

"What I'm going to suggest is that you and I just jump right into this and see what happens. No holding back, no games. We're too old for that kind of nonsense." He paused. "What do you think?"

Her mouth dropped open. How could he be so bold?

Suzanne had always said she liked bold men. No wonder she liked Tony—they didn't come any bolder. But Rachel wasn't Suzanne, and she was still on edge over that pink note in Stan's shoebox. Tony had broken Suzanne's heart back in high school—how could she trust him not to break her heart now?

Tony continued to stare at her, waiting for her reply.

"Um," she said, then fortuitously the server showed up with their meals. Rachel unfurled her napkin and avoided Tony's eyes as she made the sign of the cross and softly said grace.

They said *amen* in unison, then with his eyebrows lifted expectantly, Tony repeated himself. "Well, what do you think?" He touched her hand and she felt that electricity again.

She looked at their hands for a moment, then lifted her eyes to his. "We'll see."

Chapter 38

MARLA

TUESDAY

Marla opened the spa's front door in the midst of a downpour to welcome Rachel. "Get yourself in here before you get washed away!"

Rachel dropped her umbrella on the porch and hurried inside, holding up a large insulated bag. "Three-cheese ziti—straight from the oven."

"Smells wonderful." Marla hadn't eaten a bite since late yesterday afternoon, so she could afford to binge.

"Remember last year when we met at Suzanne's, how you pulled that bottle of champagne out of your purse?" Rachel giggled.

"Did I hear my name?" Suzanne appeared from the kitchen, wiping her hands with a paper towel. "Group hug, ladies!" She stretched her arms out to them.

"I wish you both lived in Port Mariette," said Rachel. "I love it when you're in town, but we never seem to have enough time together."

"Well, today I don't have a champagne surprise for you ladies," Marla said, "but I do have fresh-squeezed lemonade. The table's all set, and Suzanne just tossed a beautiful salad, so while the ziti's still hot, why don't we sit down and eat?"

As they headed toward the table, the spa's phone rang. "Grace is out. I've got to take that call." Marla waved Rachel and Suzanne forward while picking up the phone. "Good morning, Victorian Spa." She said the greeting in a soft and soothing voice, mimicking what she'd expect from a spa. No wonder Grace sounded perfect on the phone. Soft and soothing was her natural voice.

"Grace?" The caller sounded uncertain.

"This is Marla. How can I help you?"

"Oh, Marla. I should have recognized your voice. It's Mary Frances. I wanted to schedule a facial with Hannah. Does she have anything open Thursday morning?"

Marla checked the schedule. "Would ten o'clock work?"

"That's perfect." Mary Frances dropped her voice. "By the way, someone just posted a one-star review about my business. Thought you'd want to know."

"Sorry to hear that." Now that Mary Frances had gotten one of her own, maybe she'd get a little more worked up about them. "Any idea who wrote it?"

"No. I can't imagine who hates me enough to call me *arrogant and egotistic*."

"I have no idea." Marla had to contain herself. Whoever wrote the review must know Mary Frances pretty well. "It just doesn't add up," Marla said. "Well, thanks for letting me know, and you're confirmed for Thursday at ten with Hannah."

She set the phone down and tapped her nails on the desk. Mary Frances might not be a magnetic personality, but her reputation in real estate was impeccable. Since no one would question her business acumen, maybe a jealous competitor felt the need to attack Mary Frances personally.

Marla pondered that idea as she joined Rachel and Suzanne at the round table. "Sorry for the interruption. Would you like to say the blessing, Suzanne?"

"Sure." Suzanne bowed her head. "Heavenly Father, we acknowledge you as the provider of everything in our lives, including this meal today. We give you thanks for it and pray you would bless it. In Jesus's name we pray. Amen."

"That was short," Marla said. She'd been expecting Suzanne to go on for at least a few more sentences. Even hoped she would. Might give Marla some ideas on how to pray herself.

Suzanne shrugged. "Sometimes I do get carried away, but that's all I felt led to say today."

Strange how people like Suzanne and Mitch say they *felt led*. It'd be nice to have that kind of guidance. She smoothed the napkin on her lap. "Not to start off our meal with something negative," Marla said, "but that was Mary Frances on the phone. Someone wrote a bad review about her."

"You mean about her business, not her, right?" Suzanne asked.

"Actually, it was about Mary Frances herself," Marla said. "Called her arrogant and egotistic. Makes me wonder if a jealous competitor wrote it."

"Oh, my." Rachel's mouth went down at the sides. "I hope it wasn't Lindsey."

"Don't say anything to her," said Marla. "Or to Pete."

"Why not?" Rachel asked.

"We've got to stay focused on the arts festival for now," said Marla. "It's only five days away." Maybe they should have stopped to talk with Lindsay when they were in Lyondale after all. She cast a sideways glance at Suzanne, who was staring back at Marla and probably thinking along the same lines.

Rachel dug a fork into her ziti. "I think we all need to pray about the arts festival. I keep feeling like someone wants to ruin it."

"Like with one-star reviews?" Suzanne asked.

"You didn't get one, did you, Rachel?" Marla chimed in.

"Not a review." Rachel shook her head. "Something else. I didn't want to ruin our fun today by talking about it, but last night, someone painted graffiti on the front windows of Food 'n Fuel. Luckily, Pete replaced our security camera just the other day, so I thought for sure we'd see who did it, but the video isn't clear enough. Sergeant Dan couldn't figure it out either."

"What a shame," Suzanne sighed. "Maybe we should ask the police to take turns patrolling Main Street all night long until the arts festival is over."

"That wouldn't be a bad idea if we had a large police force," said Rachel, "but there are only three officers, and one of them is part-time."

"Let's just focus on what we need to do to get ready for Saturday," said Marla.

"Okay." Suzanne nodded. "I've never organized a public event in my entire life. And certainly never in a week and a half. I'm just a *teensy* bit concerned I'll overlook a key detail."

"*Teensy* bit?" Marla teased.

"All right, I'm worried *a lot*." Suzanne pulled out a legal pad and launched into a detailed description of who was doing what, along with what still needed to be done and by whom. She showed them her sketch of Main Street, with the artists assigned to their booths like a spine down the center of the road and the other participants spaced along the sidewalks. "Have I missed anything?" she asked.

"I'm making plenty of finger foods to make it easy for people to eat while they walk around." Rachel talked as

Suzanne jotted down Rachel's list. "We'll have napkins, too, so don't worry, people won't get anything on your paintings."

"You've sure been busy." Suzanne tapped her pen.

"Uh, yeah, I've been busy. Busy at work, busy getting ready for the festival, busy with other things too." Rachel squirmed.

"Like what?" Suzanne put down her pen.

"I've ... I've been dating Tony." Rachel's neck turned a vivid shade of pink.

"Really?" Suzanne's eyes went wide. "That's wonderful. Tony's a good guy. I'm glad for both of you. To tell you the truth, I'm not surprised. At the reunion, it looked like you two were hitting it off."

Rachel smiled, averting her eyes. "We were. But neither of us was ready to date back then. Now, the stars seem aligned." Rachel got a dreamy look on her face.

"Well, I'm happy for you too," Marla said. But her heart felt heavy. Half of her was happy to see Rachel excited about Tony. The other half wished she felt the same way about Warren. But at least her relationship with Grace was on the upswing.

"Grace has everything in order for the spa," Marla said. "She's going to set up the chair massage. We'll also have a tableful of products to sell, free samples, and discount coupons. I swear Grace must have gotten my marketing genes. I haven't had to do much of anything."

"Speaking of Grace, where is she?" Rachel asked, looking around. "Upstairs?"

"She's at Frank's house," Marla replied.

"Frank's house?" Suzanne tilted her head. "I'm really out of the loop today."

"Rachel told me Frank was going to be putting his house up for sale," Marla said. "Pete wasn't interested in buying it, so I let Grace know, and she told Jesse about it."

"Jesse? Who's that?" Suzanne asked, her confusion still evident.

"He's the guy Grace is crazy about." Marla chuckled. "That was news to me, but I'm learning more every day."

"I saw Jesse next door yesterday," Rachel said. "He's a hard worker."

Marla ran her finger up and down the side of her glass of lemonade. "By the way, Jesse is going to paint the exterior yellow, like he did at Mrs. Shevchenko's." She looked over at Rachel. "I thought you'd like to know beforehand."

Rachel scrunched her nose. "Why such a bright color?"

"Jesse told Grace he wants to brighten people's moods around here." Marla chuckled. "And let's face it, a lot of these frame houses *are* kind of drab."

"How about that." Rachel said. "Maybe someday he could paint my house. Pete could help him so it wouldn't cost so much." She squinted. "I'm kind of partial to baby blue."

"I should talk with him about painting my mother's house—inside and out," Suzanne said. "Cheery paint colors would help sell that place." Her cell phone rang a distinctive tone. "That's Rob."

"If you want some privacy, you can go into one of the open rooms down the hall," Marla said.

Suzanne shook her head. She let the call go into voicemail. "Thanks, but I'll call him back later."

"Is Rob coming in for the arts festival?" Marla asked. "Warren's arriving early Saturday morning, and we'll probably fly back to New York on Sunday."

Suzanne smoothed the napkin on her lap. "Rob has never said a word about coming to the festival. I haven't bothered to ask because I know what he'll say—he's either busy with Kevin or with clients."

Marla had never heard of anyone's marriage getting off to such a shaky start. "So, when do you plan to go back to California?"

"Not sure." Suzanne swirled the straw in her lemonade. "I've got the art shop in good shape, but my mom's house is still filled with clutter, and at the moment, I'm too focused on the arts festival to think of anything else."

Suzanne put her hand to her mouth. "Oh, I almost forgot! We're going to have an opening ceremony for the festival. Some kids in the St. Cyp's Academy band are going to march Main Street alongside the artist booths, then at that little park at the end of the street, they're going to play *The Star-Spangled Banner*." With a pleading look in her eyes, she looked at Marla. "Would you be willing to sing it?"

A hint of a smile started across Marla's face, then it spread into a wide grin. "I'd love to."

Chapter 39

SUZANNE

WEDNESDAY

Those darned new traffic signals. Once again, Suzanne had forgotten about the recently installed lights on Main Street. She stomped on the brake, causing her mother's clothing and toiletries to lurch forward from the back seat and scatter who knows where.

Fine. Everything could just stay where it landed until she arrived at Sunset Hills, where she'd check off another task on her interminable to-do list.

All alone, she allowed herself a noisy yawn. Last night, instead of sleeping, her thoughts had bounced from her mother to the arts festival to the classes she was setting up at the shop.

Those online reviews bothered her too. Now, even the local funeral home had gotten a bad one. When would it end? She had even lost sleep thinking about Rachel and Tony, praying he wouldn't hurt Rachel like he'd hurt her.

Most of all, though, her mind had dwelt on Rob. When they talked yesterday afternoon, he assured her they'd make new honeymoon plans soon. Soon? When would that be? She didn't care where they might go. Only that they could be together, just the two of them. This separation wasn't helping them or their marriage.

She'd go home to him right after the arts festival, even if it meant adjusting to living with Kevin. Poor Rob, torn between his only son and his new bride. In such a situation, how could any man satisfy both of them?

She'd been so hard on Rob—and Kevin, too, for that matter. Where was her compassion? How about showing a little kindness? Hadn't she just made a vow to stick by her husband no matter what? Next time they talked, she'd have to apologize.

Maybe she'd even confess she'd invited her mom to live with them.

Or maybe not.

Yawning again, she pulled into a parking spot in the Sunset Hills parking lot. She scooped up her mother's belongings and dashed to the entrance.

At the registration desk, Suzanne gave her umbrella a shake, grabbed a pen, and signed in. "Hi, Penny. How are you doing on this lovely Wednesday?"

Like a tiny bird, Penny flitted up from her chair. Her eyes darted back and forth between Suzanne's face and her dripping umbrella. "Still raining, I see. They're predicting thunderstorms for the next couple of days." Penny turned her computer screen away from Suzanne and leaned closer to the registration pad. "Maybe you should cancel that arts festival."

"The show will go on!" Suzanne forced a laugh, although she would have much rather screamed. No way would she go through planning the event a second time. "If it rains, we'll just hold it inside the shops instead of in the middle of the street. Or we can borrow Mitch's tents from the country club. We have options."

Ignoring Suzanne's upbeat response, Penny pursed her lips. "My goodness. First, it's those awful reviews, then it's vandalism on Main Street. All this town needs now is thunderstorms the day of the arts festival."

Something about Penny's expression brought back to Suzanne's memory that bizarre evening last summer when she confronted Penny about her gambling. That conversation was the beginning of Penny's undoing. In some weird way, could history be repeating itself?

Lord, give me wisdom and discernment. She stared at Penny's face, waiting for inspiration.

Then it dawned on her. The funeral home. Right after she'd seen the funeral home's website on Penny's computer screen, a negative review about Lipton's had shown up. There had to be a connection.

Suzanne glanced around to make sure no one else was within earshot. She leaned closer to Penny and said in a hushed tone, "Did you know Rachel's son Pete put a new security camera on the outside of Food 'n Fuel a couple days ago?"

Penny's small eyes widened and her mouth dropped open. "No!" She backed away an inch.

"Yes. It's true." Suzanne continued, feeling confident she was on the right track. "The camera had been on order for weeks. It finally arrived, in the nick of time." Just like last summer, Suzanne was bluffing again, hoping to draw out another confession from Penny.

Color drained from the woman's face. She didn't say a word, just clutched the arms of her chair and let herself down.

"They know what you did, Penny," Suzanne whispered. "Sergeant Dan already has the tape." She glanced at the front door, as if expecting someone. "He's probably on his way here right now to talk with you. I thought you'd appreciate a heads-up."

A gasp escaped Penny's gaping mouth. She covered her face with her hands and slowly shook her head. "What am I going to do?" she whimpered.

"I'd suggest you tell the truth."

"The truth?" Tears welled in Penny's eyes. "No one would understand. No one."

"Help me understand, Penny. Then maybe I can help you." Suzanne said it softly.

Penny shrank in her chair. "You wouldn't understand. You've got everything—a husband, a daughter, a granddaughter, even a new career. Me?" She sniffled. "I'm a widow with no kids, no money, and a lousy job."

She stiffened in her chair and her voice turned angry. "Last year, I owned the country club and golf course, I was the mayor, and I was in love with Herbie. Then, I lost everything, including Herbie, who turned around and started dating my *former* best friend, Mary Frances."

"Oh my." Not sure what to say, Suzanne expanded the syllables. "So ... you smashed her windows to get even?" It was a guess.

Penny jutted her chin out. "Right."

"But why all the other things?" That sounded vague enough. Suzanne still wasn't sure if Penny had posted all those one-star reviews.

"Well, I had to give Herbie's businesses some bad reviews so people wouldn't suspect me. Then Inez had the nerve to nominate Mary Frances as president of PMBA."

"But there were *so* many other bad reviews," Suzanne said. "Why?"

"Mary Frances gets her hair done at Hair & Care, and she gets her facials at the spa. I kept adding the other places as a way to punish the whole town for what it did to me."

"What the town did to *you*? Seems to me you have it backwards."

"They could have let me continue as mayor. They stripped me of all my pride. Look at where I am now, a receptionist in an assisted living facility."

"What's wrong with that, Penny? Think of all the residents and visitors you talk with every day. You have the chance to make everyone's day brighter just by your behavior. And it's probably a lot less stressful than being mayor."

"That may be true, but being mayor made me who I am—or rather who I used to be. Now I'm nothing."

Suzanne shook her head, trying to absorb what Penny had said. If only Rob were here. He'd understand Penny's motivations. He'd know the right thing to say. She paused, imagining what to say next.

"I'm so sorry you feel that way, Penny. You are not *nothing*. You were created in God's image. He loves you as much as he loves me." Her words seemed to have no effect. She paused again, then said, "When's the last time you prayed, Penny?"

Penny rolled her eyes. "I have no idea."

"Would you mind if I prayed for you right now?"

Penny shrugged.

Suzanne took it as an assent. "Lord, we are all sinners and have all fallen short in many ways. We ask your forgiveness. Penny has done things she shouldn't have. Show her your compassion and your mercy. Above, all let her know who she is in you. I ask this in Jesus's name."

"Thank you." Penny's eyes searched Suzanne's. "And thank you for praying for me instead of judging me."

Touched, Suzanne's eyes teared up. Poor Penny—what would happen to her now? Suzanne would have to call Sergeant Dan, and Penny would be punished again.

Suzanne tilted her head. "One more thing I have to ask—why the graffiti at Food 'n Fuel? Why not just a bad review?"

"Can't you see? Penny smirked. "Vandalism scares visitors away. The arts festival would be a flop, and that would be an embarrassment for the whole town. Like I said, they've taken everything away from me so I wanted to punish everyone." She dropped her chin. "It was the only way I knew how."

Chapter 40

RACHEL

WEDNESDAY

Rachel felt like a school girl as she and Tony held hands, strolling alongside the river. All her life, she'd driven by and barely noticed the view, but today, with her senses on high alert, she noticed every detail—the glistening rocks, the rushing water, the grasses growing tall on both banks.

How quickly she and Tony had become a couple. It had taken days, not months or even weeks for the shift to occur. Being with Tony felt natural and right, not merely a comfortable convenience like her companionship with Frank. With Stan, it had been different too. He'd been a good provider and an admirable father, but if she was being honest, as a husband, Stan was just *there*.

Already, she knew where this relationship with Tony was headed. She knew he felt it, too, just by the way he looked at her. He awakened in her something that had been dormant all these years. He made her feel fully alive, beautiful, interesting, wanted, valued. All of which seemed too good to be true. That's why she'd responded cautiously on their first date, in spite of Tony's boldness. But she quickly decided she'd be foolish not to trust him. Heck, even Suzanne encouraged their relationship.

As they neared the old wrought iron bridge, Tony pointed to it. "How about we go up there? We'll have a great view of the river."

Hand in hand, they walked to the bridge, then leaned against the rail and stared at the rushing water below.

Tony slid an arm around her shoulder. "Look how high the water is on the banks. When it's that high for a long time, it's hard on the tree roots. In fact, look way down there." He pointed in the distance. "See all those trees that have fallen into the water? Someone's going to have to remove them. They'll cause a boating accident."

She nodded, dreamily. "Remember when we were about fourteen and St. Cyp's had a summer camp? One of the parents took all of us for rides on his pontoon boat."

"I remember that. I remember being with you on the boat too."

"Really?"

"Yeah." He smiled sheepishly. "You were so full of joy on that boat, talking, laughing, acting silly. The sun was shining on your hair. You had a summer tan. You found some kind of fishing net and held it in the water, and when you caught a little minnow, you yelped in excitement." He paused to gaze into her eyes. "I think that's when I first fell in love with you."

Rachel's breath caught. "That's—that's so touching."

He pulled her closer and kissed her gently on the lips. "I'm trying not to rush things between us, but I just had to do that. I hope you don't mind." As he smiled, his eyes looked deeply into hers.

A few huge raindrops plunked on their shoulders. Tony opened his umbrella and held it over them.

She rested her head on his shoulder, feeling a contentedness she'd never experienced, wishing the moment could last forever. Soon, though, the raindrops increased, pummeling the umbrella and dancing on the water beneath them.

"I guess we should get out of here," Tony said. "The forecast said there might be thunderstorms today."

They made their way off the bridge, onto the path, then into his car.

"How about we go sit on my porch?" Rachel asked. Moments later they arrived and took seats side by side on matching rocking chairs.

"I can see why you like living in Port Mariette," said Tony, rocking. "It's not perfect, but it's darned close to it."

"I feel the same way. I never understood why Marla and Suzanne couldn't wait to leave town right after graduation."

A text came in from Suzanne. *Call me when you have a minute.* Rachel ignored it and kept rocking.

"Yeah, leaving was their loss." He rocked a little faster. "I'm so relieved I hired that restaurant manager I was telling you about. Now that my son has the support he needs to run Signore's, I think I might follow through on my candy store idea."

Rachel stopped rocking. "Really? That's fantastic." Rachel could feel her hand getting moist from the excitement. How could the pieces of her future be falling into place so quickly?

"For the moment, though, I still have to make sure the transition at Signore's goes well."

He smacked his forehead with his palm. "I almost forgot to ask, any chance you could make up a batch of pierogies for me? I know you'll be busy getting ready for the arts festival, but someone booked the back room for a party

Friday evening. The birthday boy's turning a hundred, God bless him. He's been a regular customer for ages, and since he's Polish, his family wants us to serve pierogies. We'll need about ten dozen, potato and ricotta cheese filling. I can send someone to pick them up Friday afternoon. Can you do it?"

"Sure, Tony." She'd be losing sleep over him anyway, so why not make pierogies instead of tossing and turning?

Chapter 41

MARLA

THURSDAY

"Maybe Penny's off on Thursdays." Marla said to Grace as her eyes darted around the empty registration area at Sunset Hills.

"Or she might be out sick." Grace signed both of them in.

"I hope nothing's going around." Marla pursed her lips. Two of the spa's appointments had canceled due to a flu bug, which allowed her and Grace to visit Aunt Adele together in the middle of the day. "We don't need any excuse for people to miss the arts festival." Only two days away, Marla couldn't help but wonder if there'd be another bad review or more vandalism on Main Street. Maybe that's what Suzanne had texted her about last night. She'd have to squeeze in a call to her today.

They walked to Aunt Adele's room, and Marla rapped on the door. "Are you decent? It's me and Grace."

"Decent?" Aunt Adele guffawed. "I'm dressed for success, like always. C'mon in." She waved them toward a couple of chairs. "My goodness, both of my favorite people here at the same time! What an unexpected pleasure." Her eyes widened and she lurched her head forward suddenly, looking like a turtle with wavy white hair. "Oh, my. Something bad must have happened, that's why you both came, isn't it? Did someone die?" She clutched the arms of her chair.

Marla shook her head. "Nothing's wrong, no one's died." She answered quickly, wanting to put her aunt at ease.

"Actually—," Grace interrupted. "It's not why we came, but someone did die—Tiffany Sanders."

"Oh, my, I'm sorry to hear that." Aunt Adele placed a hand over her heart. "How she suffered all these years. I remember when she used to come into the library as a little girl. She always checked out wholesome books. Lives of the saints and that sort of thing."

"How can you remember details like that?" Marla looked at her aunt, amazed.

"Who could forget that horrible accident? The doctors didn't know if she'd survive, or what condition she'd be in if she did. It was all so emotional. Everyone in town was talking about her and praying for her. I remember thinking that if she died, at least I knew she'd be going to heaven."

"But you couldn't know that based on the books she read." Marla shook her head. "They didn't prove she was a good person."

"Maybe not, but her heart was in the right place. If a little girl was reading books like that, she must have known God or at least wanted to know him."

"Besides, being a good person is not the reason anyone goes to heaven." Grace said it softly.

"I know, I know." Marla crossed her arms. This was turning into a conversation like she'd had last year with Mitch.

Aunt Adele smiled. "When I was little, one of the nuns at St. Cyp's told our class if we said *Jesus* as our last word before dying, we'd go to heaven."

"That's ridiculous!" Marla scoffed.

"For years, I thought so too," said Aunt Adele. "But one day I realized she was probably right. Imagine you're on your deathbed—what's on your mind? Your family? Your money? Your regrets? ... Or is Jesus on your mind? If he is, that tells you everything about a person's heart."

"Can we change topics?" Marla interrupted. "All this death and dying makes for a pretty morose conversation."

Aunt Adele's eyes softened. "Okay, but maybe one of you could take me to the funeral home so I can pay my respects."

"Sure," said Grace. "We'll find out the hours and let you know."

"Thanks." Aunt Adele patted her lap. "Now, what would you like to talk about instead?"

Marla crossed her legs and gave her knee a hug. "Well. Nothing in particular. It's just that I'll be going home soon. I know Sunset Hills will be bringing you to the arts festival in their van, but since Grace and I expect to be busy, we might not have much time to talk with you there. I wanted to stop by today to say goodbye."

"Goodbye? That's a pretty sad topic too." Aunt Adele frowned. "When will you be back?"

Marla shrugged. "I don't know. I've been running the spa for Grace so she could help Jesse clean up Frank's house. They've made good progress."

"Oh, I see. Jesse. He's quite the guy, isn't he?" Aunt Adele winked at Grace. "Maybe you'll want Marla to come back in a month or two to give you another break from the spa?"

"Well, maybe ..." Grace smiled, her eyes averted. "Jesse and I are having a lot of fun getting that house ready for him to move into. Lots of work, but we're enjoying it."

Marla smiled at her daughter. "I'll come back anytime you need me." She'd been working hard to strengthen her relationship with Grace, but it sounded like Jesse was becoming her priority.

Would Grace want her back for more than filling in at the spa?

Chapter 42

SUZANNE

THURSDAY

Hurrying through the reception area at Sunset Hills, Suzanne shook her head in wonder at yesterday's turn of events. How quickly Penny had caved in, after just a few carefully selected words. God had certainly orchestrated that conversation. Suzanne couldn't have done it on her own.

Glad to have that mess behind her, she now focused on the clutter in her mother's house. She needed permission to clear things out while she was still in town. How could she explain it in a way her mother could accept? Suzanne mouthed a few words she might say to persuade her.

"You talking to yourself?" Marla appeared beside her, chuckling, along with Grace.

"Oh!" Suzanne said. "Hi, ladies. You're on your way to visit Aunt Adele?"

"Just leaving," Marla said. "I saw your text last night. Sorry I didn't get back to you yet. It's been crazy."

"That's okay." Suzanne's eyes darted back to the reception desk. "You might have wondered why Penny isn't here today."

"Is she sick?" Grace asked.

"Sort of." Suzanne explained in whispered tones how Penny had admitted to the vandalism and writing the online reviews.

"Wow," said Marla. "That's amazing. Every time she sees you, she thinks you're her priest talking to her in a confessional."

"But why would she write those reviews?" Grace asked. "Why would she vandalize Main Street?"

"Penny said she lost everyone and everything that mattered—her job, her business, and Herbie." Suzanne shrugged. "When he started dating Mary Frances, it was too much for Penny to take. She reacted in the only way she knew how. Such a sad soul."

"That's incredible how you got her to tell you everything," said Grace, a look of admiration on her face.

"I think it's Rob's influence on me. I look at people in a different way because of him." Suzanne put her hand to her heart. Rob may have angered her with how he handled Kevin, but still, there was so much to love about him. Now, if only she could extend that love to his son too.

"You've got to talk to Sergeant Dan about Penny." Marla insisted in a loud whisper.

"I already have. He came here yesterday. Penny called him herself, actually. She confessed everything." Suzanne said. "He wants to meet with all PMBA members this evening. In fact, you should've gotten an email about it already."

Marla checked her phone and nodded. "Here it is. We'll be there," Marla said emphatically.

Suzanne had no doubt.

Marla put her phone back in her purse. "What a relief to have this resolved right before the arts festival."

"The arts festival!" Suzanne threw her hands in the air. "I have a zillion things to do before Saturday. Gotta run. See you tonight at PMBA." Suzanne gave both women a quick hug and scooted down the hall.

Suzanne came to a halt at her mother's door and peeked into the room. Next to the picture window, her mother sat reading a book. Rain poured outside, but the room was brightened by a cheery combination of bold colors on the curtains and walls.

"Hi, Mom." Suzanne stepped inside. She leaned over and kissed her mother on the forehead. "What are you reading?"

"A Bible commentary."

"You're reading a Bible commentary?" Suzanne's eyes widened. "I never even knew you read the Bible itself."

"Oh, Suzanne, there are a lot of things you don't know about me." Her mother's eyes twinkled.

"You don't say. Maybe there's something you want to confess?" Suzanne laughed. Perhaps she'd bring that out in her mother too.

"You and I have had our differences over the years, Suzanne." Her mother's mouth curled into a smile. "You were always the free spirit, the explorer, the one who would take on any challenge. The opposite of your sister Andrea. If I have a confession, it's that Andrea is very much like me, at least on the inside. That's why I always had a hard time supporting the things you did—like having a career in the airlines instead of staying home and raising your daughter, like I did with you and Andrea.

Suzanne dropped into the chair next to her mother. What other revelations might her mother offer?

"And when you started going to all those different churches in different cities, well, not a one of them was

Roman Catholic. I was devastated. But the more you talked about your experiences at those churches, I realized you needed to explore them and make a decision on your own. That's just the way you are. I had to accept that."

"I never knew you felt that way—about all those churches and everything else, for that matter. I'm sorry for being such a worry to you."

"That's okay. It comes with the territory when you're a mother. Lasts a lifetime." Her mother chuckled. "Anyway," she said, looking down at her book, "I realized from our discussions you knew more about God than I ever did. That's why I started reading the Bible on my own."

Her mother picked up a worn Bible from the table beside her. "I've been reading Matthew this past week, and when I came to the sixth chapter, where it talks about not storing up treasures on earth, well, it was like I could hear God telling me to get rid of that junk I've been saving all these years. None of it matters. I see that now. So, you and Andrea can do whatever you want with it. I'm letting it all go."

"That's amazing. And wonderful." Suzanne looked out the window, then back at her mother. "It's such a relief. I have to admit, I've been worried about what to do with all that stuff."

"I guess you shouldn't have been worrying. After all, God tells us not to worry." She tapped her Bible. "That's in Matthew too."

Chapter 43

RACHEL

THURSDAY

Rachel dreaded having to attend PMBA's meeting in the midst of such a terrible downpour. At least the weather forecast predicted the rain would end late tomorrow—just in time for the town to dry out before Saturday's arts festival.

She dashed from her house to her car, Stan's giant golf umbrella protecting her from a drenching.

"Oof." She fell into the driver's seat, then caught her breath before backing out of the driveway. Branches and debris littered the streets, and puddles of water from oncoming vehicles splashed hard against her windshield. She glanced at the St. Christopher medal dangling from her rearview mirror and said a quick prayer.

A few minutes before seven, the country club's lot was already jammed. She pulled into a distant parking spot and hurried to the meeting room, hoping she'd get there before the meeting began.

Rachel made her way to the front of the room, plopped onto the Secretary's designated chair, and pulled her steno pad and a pen from her tote bag.

Mary Frances glanced at her watch and then at Rachel. After a roll of her eyes, she picked up her gavel. "I call to order this special meeting of PMBA." Mary Frances rapped the gavel on the wooden lectern.

All talking stopped.

"I think by now you know Penny Frampton has admitted to posting those bad reviews about our businesses, as well as smashing my front window and spraying graffiti on Rachel's storefront."

Heads bobbed all around the room.

"Yeah, we all know she did it—but why?" Walt Celinski called out.

"This isn't a news conference, Walt. You'll have to interview Penny to find out her motives. Our purpose tonight is to hear Sergeant Dan's summary of our options and decide how to move forward." Mary Frances motioned the officer forward. "I yield the floor to Sergeant Dan."

He stepped to the lectern. "What we have here, folks, is an odd situation. As you know, last year Penny got herself into a ... *a predicament*. She faced the consequences of that, and over time, everything seemed to get back to normal. But now we have this, uh, *new predicament* where Penny took it upon herself to get revenge on some folks she felt had wronged her."

He cleared his throat. "I've already talked with those of you who were directly affected by Penny's actions, so you know why she targeted you." He looked at Walt. "They'll be good sources for your newspaper story, if they're willing to talk."

Then he looked around the room. "Even if you weren't directly affected, if this behavior had continued, every business owner here could have been negatively impacted—especially with the arts festival around the corner. That's why I wanted all of you here tonight, to get your input on how to proceed with regard to Penny. Specifically, do you want to file charges, or not?"

He lifted a hand from the lectern. "Feel free to give your opinion. Who wants to talk first?"

Inez pushed herself up from her chair. "The review Penny wrote about my precious little dolls was so hurtful it made me cry. I couldn't imagine who would say such nasty things about them." She sighed. "But now that I know it was Penny, I have a different perspective. She's a little ... off, shall we say? And as the saying goes, *hurt people hurt people*. Penny's not the only one who has issues. We've all got them. I'm willing to forgive and forget."

There was a light murmur of agreement, then Sharon, owner of Hair & Care, stood to speak. "Penny's review about my hair salon caught the attention of the State Board of Cosmetology. They sent someone out to inspect my place. Lucky for me, we passed, but if we hadn't, I could have been shut down." She glared at those seated around her. "I don't know what charges we can file against Penny, but I think we should get even." She looked at Sergeant Dan. "So, can you tell us our options? What kind of charges can we file?"

"Well," said Sergeant Dan, scratching his head, "those of you who got a bad online review, you could band together and sue Penny for slander. Otherwise, you could just ask her to delete the reviews. The graffiti at Food 'n Fuel, that's a summary charge. Penny would have to pay a fine for that. For smashing Mary Frances's window, that vandalism. It's a little more complex because you've already reported that to your insurance company, haven't you?" He turned to Mary Frances, sitting at attention in a chair next to the lectern.

She grimaced. "Actually, I haven't gotten around to that yet. I had my cousin who owns the glass company in Lyondale come over. He, uh, fixed it." Her voice dropped. "For free."

"Well, I guess you know you can't file an insurance claim for something that didn't cost you a *penny*, no pun intended." Sergeant Dan chuckled as Mary Frances averted her eyes.

Dr. Hess, the town's elderly dentist, stood and pounded his fist on the table with unexpected force. "I agree with Sharon. We should file charges."

"Penny didn't write any reviews on you, did she?" Sergeant Dan asked him.

"No, but one day she might have." Dr. Hess sat down and crossed his arms. Pushing eighty, he was losing patients left and right to the new state-of-the-art dental practice over in Dunham City. His wife still booked appointments in pencil.

"Dr. Hess is right! Let's file charges!" came a voice from the back of the room, and someone near the windows said "I agree!" Throughout the room, others mumbled in agreement, the noise drowning out the beating of the rain on the wall of windows.

Rachel shrugged and continued taking notes as others added comments both for and against Penny. The lack of forgiveness by some of them astounded her. In this little town, who would suspect so many people could harbor so much anger? *God, help us treat Penny like you treat us.*

"Anybody else want to chime in before we take a vote?" Mary Frances said from the lectern.

Rachel stood. She paused for effect, as she'd seen Suzanne do. Soon all eyes were on her. Glancing around the room she saw people she loved, people she cared for.

"Look," she said, "we've all known one another, including Penny, for many years. Maybe our entire lives. Think back over your life. What mistakes have you made? Maybe you've committed a misdemeanor or even a crime. I know when I go into that confessional, I always have something to tell the priest. If we're being honest with ourselves, we have to admit we've all done wrong to others."

She took a deep breath and looked at the faces in the audience. They seemed receptive to what she'd said. Even Sharon looked attentive.

Rachel released the breath and continued. "I think what we should do about Penny is pretty clear—first, forgive her and, second, get her some help. Like Inez said, Penny's got issues. We can all see that, right? Let's make sure she gets some therapy so she can work through whatever caused her to do what she did. Then, maybe she won't do anything like this ever again."

Rachel took her seat and jotted down her comments for the record. Lightning brightened the room, immediately followed by a loud clap of thunder. The storm was right on top of them.

Sharon the hairdresser piped up loud enough to be heard over the heavy rain. "Easy to say, Rachel, but there are no therapists in this area, and besides, Penny's broke. She couldn't afford to get therapy. I still think we ought to file some kind of charges against her. She can't get away with this kind of stuff again. What'll it be next year, a murder?"

"Now, Sharon, calm down." Sergeant Dan waved a dismissive hand at her. "Look," he said, as he crossed his burly arms and eyeballed the group. "In my line of work, we see all kinds of people in all kinds of messes. I know to you folks, what Penny did might seem pretty awful, but compared to what happens in other places around the country, we're pretty darned fortunate here in Port Mariette. Think about it—what do you hear about on the nightly news? Horrible stuff, right? Marla, you live in New York." He looked at her, almost accusingly. "Wouldn't you agree?"

"Well, sure. In any big city, there's a lot more crime," Marla said with a shrug.

Sergeant Dan continued. "Let's not minimize what Penny did, but then again, let's not overreact. How about a little perspective here, don't you all agree?"

Rachel put her pen down and stood up again. "I agree." She bobbed her head around to make sure everyone was paying attention. "This is small potatoes, folks. Please understand, I'm not saying it shouldn't be addressed—it should be. But how about a little forgiveness for one of your own?" She sat down again and crossed her arms.

Mary Frances allowed the audience time to think, then she stepped next to Sergeant Dan at the lectern and took charge again. "Okay, folks, how about we get this over with so we can go home and get a good night's sleep—if we can sleep through this thunderstorm, that is.

"As for me, I've decided I'm not going to file any charges for my broken window," Mary Frances said, "and I'm willing to forgive Penny on one condition—that she agrees to have therapy with a licensed psychologist for at least three months. Lots of therapists let you pay on a sliding scale. She'll have to find one whose scale goes down real far."

She looked at Rachel. "Since she damaged your business, too, are you willing to agree to the same condition?"

"Sure." Rachel gave a firm nod.

"All right, then. We've got a decision on the vandalism and the graffiti. Now, let's talk about the negative reviews.

For those of you who got one, if Penny agrees to remove them, would all of you be willing to let this go?" Mary Frances waited until the murmuring died down. "If you agree, raise your hand." She glanced around the room. "Remember, this vote is just for business owners who suffered a negative review from Penny." She scanned the room again. "It looks like everyone who got a bad review has raised their hand, but let's make sure. If you disagree, raise your hand now." Not a single hand surfaced, not even Sharon's.

"Okay, Sergeant Dan, you've heard our decision, and it has been duly recorded by PMBA's secretary, Rachel Baran." Mary Frances smacked the gavel to make it official.

Suzanne raised a finger. "One more thing. If Penny's going to agree to therapy, we need to make sure she can pay for it."

"Well, I already mentioned the sliding scale," said Mary Frances, impatience creeping into her voice. "Do you have a better idea?"

"I haven't cleared this with my husband yet." Suzanne squirmed. "But I'm pretty sure I can persuade him to do online therapy with Penny at a fee she can afford, even if it's only a few dollars."

Rachel stood to address the group yet again. "Some of you may not know Suzanne's husband, Dr. Rob Jackson. He's a board-certified psychologist and is highly regarded in his field. He's written books and gives speeches across the country. Penny would be really lucky to work with him." She chuckled. "If we're being honest, we could all probably benefit from a few sessions with Rob."

Mary Frances pounded her gavel to quiet the chuckles and chatter. "All right, then, let's add that recommendation to the minutes, Rachel. If there's no further business, I call this meeting to a close."

Rachel jotted a few words then folded her steno pad shut. She walked out of the room with Suzanne. "That was a great idea about Rob."

"You think so? I hope he agrees. I can't believe I offered his services for practically free without even asking him." Suzanne shook her head. "I hope he'll forgive me."

A flash of lightning lit up the sky as they exited the country club. Rachel flicked open her golf umbrella. "Oh, I think he'll forgive you. How could he stay angry at his new bride?" She grinned.

"I hope you're right." Suzanne opened her umbrella and stood still, staring at Rachel. "I have to tell you, Rachel, you were amazing tonight. What a polished public speaker! Such an effective communicator! I wish Penny had been here to hear you speak up for her."

"Aw, thanks, Suzanne. Coming from you, I really appreciate that. Well, drive safely." Rachel dashed toward her car as she herself wondered where all that courage to speak up had come from.

Chapter 44

MARLA

FRIDAY

Marla tied the laces of her golf shoes and hopped into the cart next to Mitch. "I guess we should stay on the path today. The course will be all mushy after last night's thunderstorm."

"Mushy? My, what a big word. Is that Manhattan vocabulary?" Mitch teased, as he pressed the accelerator.

Marla poked him in the arm as a reply.

"We have to play our nine holes fast, by the way." Mitch cast her a sideways glance.

"What's the rush? You have to put up tents for the arts festival? Or is it supposed to rain again soon?" Marla wiped her phone's screen open and tapped the weather app. "Looks like we should be good for a while."

"It's not because the weather. And I'm not putting up any tents, either. The forecast for tomorrow is sunny and dry, all day long."

"That'll be a miracle. Then why do we have to hurry?" She hadn't golfed since last summer, and even then, she usually doubled however many strokes Mitch had on any given hole. Rushing, at least for her, was not going to happen.

Mitch cleared his throat. "Herbie bet me you and I couldn't finish nine holes in less than two hours."

"Two hours? Last summer, we never finished nine holes anywhere near that. Why would you make a crazy bet like that?"

"Just for fun."

Marla harrumphed. "How much are you going to lose?"

"Not much." He stopped the cart at the first tee. "Don't worry. It's only for a beer at the country club." He jumped out. "But since I own it, I don't want to give away any profits from sales of libations."

"Libations?" Marla chuckled. "Now there's a word only you would come up with." Warren might dazzle Marla with his mighty mind, but Mitch had a way of making her smile over a single silly word.

Mitch took a practice swing then belted his ball far down the fairway. He put away his driver then plopped back into the cart and hit the accelerator hard. "Knowing how competitive you are, I figured we'd stand a chance if I told you about the bet. Herbie said he'd be at the bar in exactly two hours." He stopped at the ladies' tee. "What do you think, can we do it?"

"Game on!" Marla hopped out of the cart and raced to the tee box, doing her practice swings along the way to save seconds. She shoved a tee into the wet turf and swung hard. After topping her ball, it dribbled about thirty yards down the fairway.

"Looks like Herbie's going to get his free beer." Mitch faked a frown.

"Yeah, I guess so. Why don't we just concede and enjoy ourselves?" Marla dropped her driver into the golf bag.

"I like your thinking." Mitch texted something to Herbie, then they continued their game, with Mitch making par or better on every hole and Marla coming nowhere close to that.

By the fourth hole, they'd talked about an assortment of topics, then Mitch said, "I'm sorry if I insulted you after church on Sunday."

"You mean that comment about being a sinner?" She smirked. "Not to worry. I wasn't insulted."

"Any particular reason you showed up for church?" Mitch asked. "Or is that question too intrusive?"

With Mitch, she never minded questions. He wasn't looking to gossip. He asked because he cared. "Not intrusive at all." She looked at her hands while rolling a golf ball back and forth between them. "I went to church because I was trying to pray."

"Hmm. Makes sense."

"You know Grace was upset with me because I'd been critical of Jesse and some others too. Well, I have to confess, she even accused me of being critical of you, Mitch."

"Me? Why?" His eyes showed genuine surprise, and instantly, she regretted she'd said it. Now, she'd have to explain herself.

"She heard me talking on the phone with Warren about you and Kim. I thought you two were dating, you see. That's the impression Kim gave when she came to the spa the other day. I told Warren I didn't understand what you saw in her. I made some sarcastic comments about how her cleavage must be swaying your decision to remain single, or something along those lines."

"Is that so?" Mitch's face remained expressionless.

Have I said too much? The wrong thing?

"I'm sorry," Marla finally said. "Who you date is your business. I'm just trying to be up front with you. You've always been that way with me, and I apologize for being critical of you."

Mitch rubbed his chin a few times. "Now, it makes sense."

"What makes sense?"

"At church last Sunday, some folks I know asked me how things were going with Kim. By the way they talked, I realized they weren't asking about her golf lessons—they thought we were dating." He took his hand off the steering wheel. "As I've told you and everyone else, I was only giving her golf lessons, but obviously, she'd been telling a different story. When you asked me about her in the parking lot, well, let's just say I'd already heard enough about her."

"I see. So that's why you were a little abrupt with me?"

"I was? Sorry. I didn't mean to be. I just didn't want any more rumors starting." He smiled. "After all, Warren will be here for the arts festival, won't he?"

"Yes, he's flying in Saturday morning."

"You wouldn't want him to hear rumors about you spending time with another man in a church parking lot, would you?" Mitch joked as he flicked his fingers on her thigh.

Marla looked at his rugged hand, and her breath caught. That should not be happening to her, at least not with him. She stiffened.

Mitch put his hand back on the steering wheel. "He might get worried knowing he's left you all alone in a treacherous place like Port Mariette, a town where men say licentious things to you, like *you stand out like a swan in a coal mine.*"

A swan in a coal mine. That's what Mitch had said to her the first time they bumped into one another last summer at the Dairy Mart.

"Are you trying to compliment me?" Marla asked, not knowing what else to say.

"Trying? Heck no, I'm succeeding. *A swan in a coal mine* is a compliment. You're the most beautiful creature this town has ever seen. The kind of woman any man would be thrilled to have by his side." He looked her in the eye. "I hope Warren knows how lucky he is."

Chapter 45

SUZANNE

FRIDAY

Suzanne counted the boxes and bags she'd already filled for the next St. Cyp's rummage sale. Fourteen. At this rate, it would take weeks to clear the place. Andrea would have to finish the job and deliver everything to the church. As for Suzanne, she'd catch a flight home as soon as the arts festival was over.

Since Sunday, she'd been praying, trusting, and listening. Now it was time for obeying. The Lord had made it clear she belonged in Carmel with her husband, even if that meant adjusting to having Kevin around. Seriously, how bad could it be? If she needed a break, she could always slip away to her studio in the casita.

For now, though, she had a lot of loose ends to tie up before the festival tomorrow. She picked up her phone to make a call to one of the consignment artists and noticed she'd missed a call from Rob. She pressed his number.

He answered on the first ring. "Hey, babe."

That voice. Oh, how she loved it.

"Hi, honey," she purred. "Guess what? I packed fourteen boxes of my mother's stuff today."

"Good progress." Rob said it with a smile, she could tell. "It's tough deciding what to do with every single item." He paused. "So, how did it go at the PMBA meeting last night?"

Uh-oh. She had forgotten about the commitment she'd made on behalf of her husband. "There was a lot of discussion," Suzanne said, buying time. "But in the end, everyone agreed to let Penny off the hook, on one condition."

"That's surprising. They could have pressed for all kinds of punishment. I've never even met Penny, but based on everything you've told me about her, she sounds very troubled. I feel sorry for her."

"I do too." *Sorry enough to volunteer my own husband to help her.*

"So, what's the one condition?"

Suzanne hesitated. "She needs to go to therapy for at least three months."

"That sounds reasonable."

"I thought so too. But Penny probably can't afford it."

"True."

"I—I said you'd probably be willing to provide the therapy. Online. At a very low cost." Suzanne blurted it out and cringed as she waited for Rob's reaction.

"Is that so?" He let out a loud laugh. "You're a lucky girl. I just got a call for a big speaking engagement. I can afford to cut her a break on the hourly rate."

"That's wonderful." Suzanne sighed, relieved. "Thanks, honey. I'm sorry for offering your services without talking to you first. It just seemed like a way to make sure Penny would get the help she needed."

"So," he said in a teasing voice, "you still trust that I'm a good psychologist?"

"Of course, honey. I think you're the *best*."

"That's encouraging." He laughed again. "Well, I'll make sure she pays a few dollars a session, just so she has some skin in the game."

"Good idea. How about I let Sergeant Dan know so he can connect you with her?"

"Sounds good."

"Now, tell me about your big speaking engagement," Suzanne said, happy to move onto another topic.

"Next weekend, there's a major conference for psychologists. One of their speakers had to have emergency heart surgery, and they asked me to replace him. They've offered me a small fortune to do it. It's also a great opportunity to sell my books. Best of all, after this, I'll be able to command even more for my speaking fees."

"That's phenomenal!"

"Thanks, honey." Rob lowered his voice. "Look, I know you like surprises, but there's just one little glitch. The conference is in Geneva, so I'll have to leave you alone for a couple days."

Great. She'd fly home after all this waiting, only to spend time alone with Kevin while Rob trundled off to Europe. Maybe she should just stay in Port Mariette a while longer and finish packing up her mother's house.

But hadn't she promised God she'd obey?

She took a deep breath and let it out. "Well, I'll miss you while you're away. On the bright side, that'll give me a chance to get to know Kevin better."

"I'm not so sure about that."

"What do you mean?"

"I've got another surprise. But this is one you'll love." He chuckled. "Suki called Kevin yesterday. Whatever it was they'd been arguing about, she must have realized she was wrong. Kevin said she apologized to him for everything, even for taking his Amazon boxes. Can you believe it? I wish you'd been here to see the change in Kevin. He hung up the phone and started repacking. He's already on his way to Seattle."

"Kevin's already gone?"

Has anyone changed the sheets? was actually her next thought, but instead of saying that, she decided to be gracious.

"I'm so happy for him," she said. "And for you, too, Rob. I know all this drama has been hard on you. Even for someone as selfless as you are, being caught in the middle is no fun." She paused. "I do have one question, though. If Kevin needs help dealing with his issues, does he have someone he can go to in Seattle?"

"He promised to make an appointment, and I'll make sure he follows through. He and Suki agreed they should go to someone together. I can't be the one talking with them. I lose my professional perspective with my own family. Look at how I let Emily take out her frustrations on me. And we won't even talk about how I handled the situation with my ex-wife."

Something had changed in Rob. Something had changed in her too. Maybe the rough start to their marriage would turn out to be not so bad after all.

Chapter 46

RACHEL

FRIDAY

Rachel pulled the pierogies from the cooler, loaded the van, and headed to Signore's. Tony had said he'd send someone to pick up the order, but since the arts festival would prevent her from spending time with him tomorrow, she wanted to see him today, even if only to say hello.

She'd be spontaneous. Unexpected. Surprising. Even a little bold.

Arriving before the lunch rush, she parked the van behind the restaurant, propped the back door open with a rock, and carried the first pan inside.

"Tony's in his office if you wanna see him," said one of the cooks, pointing down a hallway with a butcher knife. Another cook took the pan from her. "I'll get the rest of those pans for you."

Rachel nodded her thanks, then plumped the hair of her wig as she made her way down the narrow hall. All the doors were closed but for one. Not sure if it was his office, she took a baby step to peer inside.

She spotted Tony in a corner, his back to her. He was not alone. A brunette was resting her head on his shoulder as he embraced her, one arm around her back and the other cupping her head. Rachel's stomach churned, just like it had when she found the note in Stan's shoebox. Her mouth dropped open but she didn't make a sound. What could she say?—*Pardon the interruption?* Besides, if Tony saw her now, she'd be even more humiliated.

She took a silent step backwards then bolted down the hall. *Who was that woman?*

A customer?

A food supplier?

No. Her heart knew who she was—his rehired restaurant manager. Tony had been just a little too happy when he told her Gia was getting a divorce and moving back to Pittsburgh.

Now it all made sense.

What a rat. All that was missing was a note in a shoebox.

She flew through the kitchen, jumped into the van, and barreled down the highway toward home, emotions roiling. How could she have been so foolish to fall for Tony? Look how he'd treated Suzanne in high school. Why should she be surprised?

Tears trailed down her cheeks. As her sobs grew more emotional, she pulled off the highway to collect herself. She parked in front of a string of shops, each one bleak and unremarkable, a suitable match for her mood.

Hunched over the wheel and pouring out her hurt, she blew her nose again and again, severely depleting a fresh box of tissues. In time, she forced herself to calm down by breathing deeply while staring vacantly at the grim little shop in front of her.

A hair salon.

She looked inside. Empty, except for a middle-aged woman slouched at the front desk, staring back at her.

What's she looking at? Rachel pulled down her visor and adjusted her wig in the mirror. She snapped the visor back in place and took few more deep breaths.

Quickly, she grabbed her purse and leaped out of the car. She yanked the door of the hair salon open and trooped inside, afraid she'd change her mind, afraid she wouldn't.

With a flourish, she pulled her wig off.

"My grandson attacked my hair," she said to the woman at the desk.

The woman shrugged. "It happens."

"Can you give me a pixie cut?" She'd cut Tony out of her life just like that.

The woman led her to a chair and snapped a plastic cape into place.

The crisp snipping of the scissors matched Rachel's attitude. Seething, she watched in the mirror as the stylist finished the job Caleb had started. Twenty minutes later, she was back in the van, and soon after that, she arrived in her driveway, still reeling from the events of the day.

She flipped open the visor mirror and turned her head this way and that. Her hair was shockingly short, but the cut did flatter her face. She should have shed her long hair years ago.

She jaunted into her house.

Upstairs, she threw on a black bell-sleeved dress, the one reserved for visitations and funeral masses. Due to the aging population of Port Mariette, the dress got more use than any other item in her closet, but fortunately it was still in fashion. At least she hoped it was.

Before leaving, she checked her phone for the weather forecast. Rain. What else is new? She scratched her fingers through her pixie while slipping herself a sly smile in the foyer mirror. Even better than a wig. This cut would look great in any weather, rain or shine. She grabbed her umbrella and got back in her car.

When Rachel was young, Lipton's had been her favorite house on Millionaire's Row. Its fancy triangle-patterned windows and the staircase that swirled up and down fascinated her. The adults were always busy talking. All alone, she'd take off her shoes and squish her toes on the plush maroon carpeting.

Now, though, she didn't even like to drive by the place. Too many memories. Last April, it was Stan's heart attack. Then in the fall, cancer took her brother-in-law, Bud. This past winter, her sister Terrie succumbed to emphysema.

But today, she had to be here, no question about it. The entire town would show up to mourn the loss of poor little Tiffany Sanders, nearly killed right on Main Street all those years ago. Although she survived, her brain and the rest of her body had been severely damaged. Her parents pushed her all over town in a wheelchair—to church, sports events, and restaurants. No matter where they went, everyone lavished the girl with love and attention.

Rachel parked at the end of the lot and dashed through the rain into Lipton's. She spotted her friend Sandy Roczinski reading a note on one of the dozens of floral arrangements.

Rachel sidled up to her. "Hi, Sandy."

"Rachel—your hair!" Sandy gave her a hug. "I love it."

"Thanks."

"You've had long hair all your life. Pretty brave to make a dramatic change like that. What made you do it?"

"I needed a change." Rachel left it at that.

"Well, you sure accomplished *that*." Sandy laughed. "Maybe the Florida heat helped you decide."

"Maybe." Rachel shrugged.

"You got back pretty fast—I gather your mom's doing well."

"She is. The doctor said she's free to do whatever she wants, as long as she doesn't lift anything with that arm for a while."

"Amazing how some people are hale and hearty like your mom—and others aren't." Sandy's eyes swept over the casket.

"Yeah." Rachel said, glancing around, hoping Frank wouldn't show up while she was there. "Life's so unpredictable."

"Ain't it the truth."

"Have you been to bingo lately?" For years, she and Sandy had played bingo every Friday in the parish hall at St. Cyp's. Stan would do the dishes for her then work the concession stand wherever their boys were playing. "I haven't been to bingo since Stan passed."

"I know." Sandy exaggerated a fake frown. "I miss you. It's not the same without you."

"Maybe I'll come again sometime soon." She'd need a new diversion now that she wouldn't be playing Canasta anymore.

"Ted and I always thought it was so sweet how Stan would send you off to bingo. Anytime Ted worked the concession stand with Stan, he'd come home with stories about how Stan had little Tiffany laughing all night long." Sandy lifted her chin toward the casket. "He really knew how to make her feel special."

"Yeah, that was Stan."

"Ted said Stan would hunker down next to her and hold her hand, give her a kiss on her forehead."

"I know, he'd tell me about it too. So touching."

"Imagine how hard it would be for her to live like that. He was so sweet to her, it's no wonder she had such a crush on him."

Rachel's eyes bounced back and forth between Sandy and the casket. "A crush?"

"Yeah, a crush. Stan called Tiffany his Friday night date, and her mother always said she had a crush on him."

Tiffany! Rachel nodded, as if she knew all this, then excused herself. She stumbled to the casket and knelt before it. Poor Tiffany must have thought she was a homewrecker. Oh, Tiffany, you loved my Stan too.

Rachel made the sign of the cross and looked up.

Lord, forgive me for my anger.

Stan, can you forgive me too?

She rushed home, ran upstairs, and reread the pink note. How could she have leapt to such a conclusion about Stan? She held the note to her chest, like a tiny shred of his past, then put it back into the shoebox. Maybe someday she'd throw it away.

But not today.

Chapter 47

MARLA

SATURDAY

Brilliant rays of sun fanned across the morning sky as Marla arrived at Main Street just before eight. The light brightened the pansies dangling from flower baskets on the lampposts and punched up the colors of the shops' freshly painted facades. Even the asphalt along Main Street, still shimmering from the last thunderstorm, seemed to come alive.

Only hours from now, the whole street would be bustling. Without concerns about vandalism, one-star reviews, and especially rain, everyone's efforts to draw crowds to the arts festival would surely pay off. And once visitors sampled the offerings along Main Street, they'd come back again and again. What a boon this event would be for all of Port Mariette.

At ten, the high school band would kick things off with a march down Main Street, then Marla would sing *The Star-Spangled Banner* at the park by the bank. She had arrived early to check the sound system and rehearse at the mic.

Can't be too careful about such matters, especially since Grace would be watching.

Marla glanced at her phone. A minute before eight. Suzanne had promised to meet her at the Food 'n Fuel end of Main Street, where one of Pete's vintage cars had been strategically placed near one of the new highway ramps to prevent traffic from entering the festival area.

She strolled over to the old T-Bird and peered inside the porthole window. Something tickled the inside of her nose. She sniffed. This wasn't the scent of an old car. She sniffed again. Oddly enough for the month of June, it smelled like a whiff of Christmas. Did Pete store Christmas stuff in the trunk?

Perplexed, she looked up, facing the inbound ramp.

She gasped.

Fallen evergreens blanketed nearly the entire the ramp. She dashed over for a closer look.

Five pines down. Tree trunks, branches, needles, and mud coated the area. How would traffic north of Port Mariette get into town for the arts festival?

Boom! The ground shook beneath her feet as the last tree toppled.

She pulled out her phone, called Sergeant Dan, and calmly explained the situation. She'd learned from living in New York, panicking never helped.

"I'll be right there." He said it fast and hung up without even saying goodbye.

Marla stationed herself where she could flag down business owners as they arrived. "Be careful where you park and watch out when you're walking."

Suzanne appeared in the line-up of cars and opened her window as she neared the scene. "Good grief! What happened?"

"Not sure. Park over there." Marla pointed to Food 'n Fuel's lot.

Mitch, right behind Suzanne in his pickup, zipped to the end of the ramp and jumped out, shaking his head. "I told those highway engineers when they put in that ramp, they should take out every darned one of those white pines." He put his hands on his hips and pursed his lips. "After all that rain, this was inevitable."

"Inevitable?" Marla repeated.

"What do you mean?" Suzanne arrived at the scene, looking near tears.

"The construction compromised the shallow roots," Mitch said. "I guess we should be thankful we only have one ramp lined with pines. The other ramps don't have any trees at all."

"But this ramp's the important one," Marla said. "Most of the visitors will be coming from the north, from the Pittsburgh area. What are you going to do about it?" If anyone knew a solution, it would be him.

"Me? You think I can clear a half-dozen pine trees in, what, two hours?" He kept his hands on his hips and spread his feet apart. "This is an all-day project."

"Not if you get enough helpers," Marla said. "How many do you need?" No way would a bunch of white pines stand in the way of this arts festival.

Mitch pressed his lips together. "Lemme think for a minute." He paced near the trees as Marla and Suzanne waited with hands on their hips.

"Round up everyone who's willing to help," Mitch finally said. "Men and women both. No kids. Too dangerous for them. I'll get all my chainsaws. If we can cut everything up and get it to the sides of the ramp, we can remove the debris later. We just need to make the ramp wide enough for vehicles to get through."

"You think we can pull it off?" Marla asked. Clearing this ramp in two hours would be a much bigger challenge than finishing nine holes—which they of course weren't able to do. They didn't even come close. But with the ramp, there were far greater consequences than a beer. Drivers from Pittsburgh would have to be rerouted for miles on country roads, and most of them would probably just turn around rather than endure a long detour.

Mitch stared at the ramp one more time. "We'll do our best."

He left to round up chainsaws while Marla and Suzanne recruited workers.

Sergeant Dan parked his police car at the top of the ramp with lights flashing to block traffic, allowing cleanup work to safely begin.

Mitch, Jesse, Pete, Herbie, and Walt spread out with chainsaws in hand. They noisily sliced off branches for Marla, Suzanne, Rachel, Grace, and Andrea to carry away. Then the men chopped the trunks into pieces and rolled them to the side of the ramp.

Penny showed up a while after they'd started, looking distressed. As she climbed up the ramp she hollered, "Don't blame me, it's not my fault!"

"Don't worry, we believe you." Suzanne waved her hand, dismissing the concern.

Marla handed Penny a broom. "How about sweeping pine needles to the side of the ramp?"

Compliant as a penitent criminal, Penny swept. She never stopped until the ramp was cleared.

Chapter 48

SUZANNE

SATURDAY

Now that the ramp had finally been cleared, Suzanne slipped over to Food 'n Fuel for some water and a restroom. Might be her only chance today.

She stopped in the ladies' room first and caught Rachel scrubbing her hands at the sink. Suzanne still couldn't get over the dramatic change in Rachel's hair. Or in Rachel herself, for that matter. At the PMBA meeting a couple nights ago, she'd spoken like a true leader. What would have happened to Penny if Rachel hadn't spoken up?

"How's everything going out there?" Suzanne glanced at Rachel's reflection in the mirror. What was it about hair that caused people to give it so much attention? Men obsessed over losing it, women wanted it to be full and shiny. So much time, energy, and money spent on it. Must be vanity. Otherwise, we'd all obsess over our hearts, our bones, our lungs, or some other more critical body part.

"So far, so good," said Rachel. "How about with all your artists?"

"They're all set. But me, I'm dying of thirst. I forgot to bring something to drink."

"C'mon, let's go get you something." They made their way to the front of the store.

"No charge," Rachel said, handing it to her. You deserve a lot more than this for all you've done getting this festival off the ground."

"Aw, thanks." Suzanne smiled. "You've worked hard too. Everyone has. Especially on the ramp this morning. That was crazy." She opened the bottle and held it up. "Here's to PMBA's amazing secretary, my fellow ramp worker, and her fabulous new haircut."

Rachel giggled. "Aw, thanks."

"I'm going to miss you," Suzanne said, sadness clouding her eyes, as the reality of living the rest of her life in California with Rob suddenly hit her with surprising force. "Marla too. And my mom. My sister. I'm—I'm going to miss *everyone*. Even Penny." She attempted a laugh but failed.

"You'll be back." Rachel smiled.

"I know. But only once in a while." At least, she hoped that would be true. Who knew what life with Rob would really be like? Already, she was having a hard time catching his curve balls.

She wished she had more time to talk with Rachel, but it was nearly ten, and visitors were milling around waiting for the parade to kick off the event.

Suzanne gave the side of her head a quick smack. She'd forgotten to set up her own table!

Chapter 49

RACHEL

SATURDAY

Rachel glanced at her red hands as she worked next to Pete organizing the Food 'n Fuel booth. Even having worn gloves while clearing pine branches, she was a scratchy mess all the way to her elbows. Good thing she wasn't one of those women who got their nails painted every week. This week, it would've been such a waste of money.

At least her hair looked good. If she'd still been wearing that wig, what a sweaty mess she'd be right now. She gave her head a shake. Seemed like not a hair had moved. Such a weird sensation after a lifetime of long locks. She felt kind of naked and daring. Were people staring at her—or were they waiting for her food booth to open?

"Your new haircut's getting a lot of looks," Pete said.

Rachel nodded. She didn't care to discuss it with him. She might slip and mention the wig or even worse, the story behind it.

"Short hair looks so different on you, but I like it."

She bent down to get some more paper napkins.

"What made you do it, Mom? I mean, it's a pretty radical change."

Would Pete never let up? "Sometimes a radical change is a good thing, especially when it forces you out of your comfort zone."

"Uh-oh. Speaking of radical change, here comes Frank." Pete pointed a fork straight ahead.

Rachel could feel the tension mounting as Frank neared. He hadn't spoken more than a few words to her since they got back from Florida.

"Love the new haircut," he said, his eyes smiling. He winked, letting her know he'd keep her secret.

"Thanks." For the compliment and for keeping the secret.

"I know you're not officially open yet, but how about a couple of those wings with honey sauce?"

Rachel stacked some on a platter and handed them to him. "On the house."

Frank grabbed a wad of napkins "Got a minute to take a walk with me?"

Rachel looked over at Pete, and he waved her away. "Go on, I can set up the rest."

Frank gnawed at a chicken wing as they walked. "Movers are coming next Monday. Just wanted to let you know."

"I'm going to miss you, Frank." She meant it.

"I'll miss you too." He put down the wing and licked his thumb. "Any chance you're having second thoughts?"

Of course she was. She'd walked away from Frank—a wonderful man who'd always treated her well—and fallen for that jerk Tony. Frank had never cheated, not even at Canasta. Frank promised her a fun future together in Florida. She'd live close to her mother and her kids would want to visit her. She wouldn't even have to work.

What was wrong with her? She'd be crazy to let Frank leave town alone.

Her cell phone pinged with a text. She checked it. Tony, again.

She'd ignore this one like she'd ignored the others. She wasn't willing to give him a chance to make excuses. He'd crushed Suzanne back in high school. Rachel should have known better than to get mixed up with him. In hindsight, it was so clear—Frank's abrupt decision to move to Florida caused her to fall prey to Tony's slippery ways.

"Anything important?" Frank asked, looking at her phone.

"Nope." She put it away. "You've got honey sauce on your chin."

He wiped it with a napkin.

She watched as Frank rubbed his face. He *is* a bit of a slob.

"Did I get it all?" he asked, turning his face toward her. He had apparently nicked himself shaving. A tiny piece of tissue stuck to his chin.

"Yeah, you did." She looked him over. He had a mighty big belly. Heart trouble on the horizon? He ate a lot of junk food, watched TV for hours. Burped when he drank beer. His house was such a mess. The lawn sprouted more weeds than grass, and none of it was cut often enough. Sat on his porch instead of getting exercise.

Seriously, was this a man she'd want to spend the rest of her life with?

"Frank," she said, "you know I've given us a lot of thought. A *lot*. I am going to miss you, and I want you to know that. But there's just something missing in our relationship. I wish it could be different, but I don't think we're meant for each other as a husband and wife, together for the rest of our lives. Know what I mean?"

He gave a slight nod, his eyes downcast. "I guess I do. It's hard to marry again this late in life. We're all set in our ways, and change gets harder as we age." He chuckled. "Maybe if I made you swoon, you'd feel differently, but I guess I don't make you swoon."

"Swoon?" Rachel giggled. "I don't know if swooning is possible at my age."

Frank stopped to toss his empty plate in a trashcan. "Well," he said with a sigh, "I'd better let you get back to work. I'll stop by your house next week to say goodbye before I leave. Maybe we can play a round of Canasta."

"I'll have raisin cookies waiting for you." Her heart felt heavy just thinking about him leaving for good.

Frank was soon out of sight, mixed into the crowd lined up to watch the parade.

Rachel stood alone at the trashcan for a long minute. Had she made the right decision?

Chapter 50

MARLA

SATURDAY

Dirt under her fingernails? Even though she had borrowed a pair of Mitch's leather work gloves? Certainly not a good advertisement for her own spa. She shoved both hands into her pockets.

For nearly two hours, she labored on that ramp, then hurried to the other end of Main Street to belt out *The Star-Spangled Banner*. On the final note, Mitch hollered out, "Encore!" and everyone applauded.

Grace couldn't clap because she was videotaping the performance, but she grabbed Marla as soon as she stepped away from the microphone. "Amazing! Amazing! You were amazing!" Grace kept repeating herself.

Marla didn't mind.

Arm in arm, the two women wove through the crowds. All around them, people were talking, laughing, and buying. Word had gotten around about the massive effort to clear the ramp, which animated the visitors and opened their wallets. As far as Marla could tell, sales ought to far exceed the expectations of every PMBA member.

They finally reached the spa's allotted space, where Latoya and Hannah had done a nice job arranging the massage chair and product table. Marla pumped some hand sanitizer on her hands and waved them around until they dried, then she dotted some cologne behind her ears. It would have to do.

Nearby, Jesse had set up a simple card table with nothing on it but a stack of business cards. After today, his landscaping and painting business was bound to take off.

She caught him casting sideways glances at Grace, who was doing the same to him.

Oh, to be in love like that.

Warren had agreed to fly in today, bowing to pressure from Marla. This arts festival was the culmination of a lot of work, and she wanted to share the experience with him.

She'd overwhelmed him with reasons to come, just as she'd been overwhelming him with what he considered petty problems. To her, though, the problems had been significant. Since arriving in Port Mariette, she'd been consumed with the town and everyone in it—mainly Grace, but plenty of others too. Relationships with people here felt so unlike her New York ones. She couldn't figure it out.

Soon, she and Warren would return to Manhattan. That's where she'd been raised, that's where Warren lived, that's where her condo was, and her foundation too. To keep her relationship with Grace on track, she'd have to continue bouncing back and forth between Manhattan and Port Mariette. Life would be bumpy, but now that Grace was finally opening up to her, she'd do whatever necessary to keep their communication flowing.

"I'm going to run over to Rachel's to get something to eat," Marla said to Grace. "What can I get you?"

"Nothing for me. I've got a few energy bars. Want one?"

"No thanks, I'm starving. I'll need more than nuts and flaxseed."

"Understood." Grace laughed.

Hands hidden in her pockets, Marla meandered over to Food 'n Fuel's booth at the end of the street. Normally, Marla would have settled on a turkey wrap, but today she felt hungry enough to eat one of those whole Italian hoagies. She stared at one of them for a few seconds.

They really are huge.

Maybe only a half.

"Buy you lunch?" Mitch said, beside her.

Tanned, with his sleeves rolled up and his arms scraped and muddied, Marla caught herself staring.

"I think you earned a meal," he said. "How about a turkey wrap?"

Last summer, that's what she ordered after every round of golf with him.

He pulled one of her hands from her pocket. "My, my, what a dirty girl you are. Not very Manhattan of you." He chuckled. "There's a restroom inside Food 'n Fuel if you want to clean up before eating."

"Thanks for the idea," Marla said, putting the hand back in her pocket, "but I'm sure there's a mirror in there, and I'd rather not see how bad I look right now."

Mitch leaned an inch closer. "No need for a mirror. I'll tell you how you look—terrific."

Marla's eyes widened and her mouth dropped open. After she caught her breath, she managed a thank-you.

Mitch paid for their food and pointed to a small bench. "How about we sit over there?" She followed and took a seat next to him. The bench was small and their bodies touched, reminding her of the times they'd spent so close together in a golf cart.

Mitch said a blessing, and they bit into their meals.

"I'm famished," Marla said. After all that work, she really was hungry, and apparently Mitch was too. They did nothing but eat for the next few minutes.

Finally, Mitch spoke up. "You're a good worker, Marla. I think I might want to hire you."

"I've got the muscles for it." She flexed an arm, and he squeezed it. They laughed, and she held his gaze for a moment.

"This town's going to miss you, Marla."

"I can send more grant money anytime it's needed."

"I'm not talking about your money. I'm talking about *you*. Grace needs you, your Aunt Adele needs you, PMBA needs you ...." His voice trailed off.

"I'll be back soon. I want to make sure Grace doesn't forget about me now that she's tied up with Jesse."

"When will you be back?"

"Not sure." She swallowed her last bite. "Well, thanks for the lunch, Mitch." She wadded up the wrapping paper with her napkin and shot it into a nearby garbage can.

"Good shot!" Warren called to her from a few feet away, dressed in full Gucci—and fully out of place in Port Mariette. But still, so handsome. He leaned down and brushed her forehead with a kiss. He looked her over and whispered, "Having a rough day?"

She ignored the comment.

Mitch stood and extended his hand. "Good to see you again, Warren." He discarded the rest of his sandwich and walked away.

Warren took Marla's hand and led her along Main Street. "Looks like a real nice event."

"Thanks."

Between stops at the tables, she told him about the fallen trees, and he took a few minutes to catch her up on matters back in New York. "Yeah, you missed some great parties," he said. "And the mail at the foundation is piling up. Deanna can't handle it all by herself, you know. She's just the administrator, not the decision-maker."

"I know." As they neared the spa's setup, she pulled him to a stop. "Look at Grace," she said. "Can you see how she's looking at Jesse?"

He chuckled. "She's got it bad."

"Oh, yeah. Look at Jesse's eyes. He's got it bad too." She laughed then lifted her chin to Warren, waiting for another reaction.

His face was serene but blank. Could he ever say anything romantic to her?

They walked hand in hand past a few more tables, then at the end of Main Street, Warren stopped.

"Well, I guess that's everything. I'll bet you've had enough of Port Mariette for a while, haven't you?" He gave her hand a squeeze. "Ready to go home now?"

Marla turned around. Even from a distance, she could still see Grace and Jesse. He was touching her arm and she was laughing at something he'd said. An ache went through Marla's chest. She was just getting to know Grace, and now she had to leave. Grace would fill her emptiness with Jesse, and Marla would never be able to forge the relationship she desperately wanted with her daughter.

Marla inhaled deeply then let it out. "I've got to stay here a while longer, Warren." She nodded, as if convincing herself.

"Grace needs me. And I need her."

Chapter 51

SUZANNE

SATURDAY

Suzanne couldn't believe she'd forgotten to set up her own materials. She hustled down the street toward the art shop just as the parade began. At least that would keep visitors at bay for a while, and it wouldn't take her long to set up an easel anyway.

Drawing these caricatures would add to the fun of the festival. Even better, they'd give her a chance to talk to people about the upcoming art classes. She'd already posted notices on all the storefronts, and Walt's newspaper contacts had helped promote the classes. Registration was starting to fill up, and in a matter of weeks, Creation on Main would have a new and much-needed income stream.

Suzanne hurried into the back room for her supplies. She dug in a drawer and grabbed a handful of pens then tucked the easel under her arm. She'd need a couple chairs, too, but they'd have to wait for a second trip.

"Where can I sign up for your art class?" boomed a friendly and familiar voice from the front room.

"Rob!" She let go of the easel, dropped the pens, and ran into his arms. Sudden tears filled her eyes. "You're here!" She stretched her arms around his neck and planted a long kiss on his lips, as all her worries about him instantly disappeared. "Why didn't you tell me you were coming?"

"And spoil the surprise?" Rob laughed in that sexy laugh she missed so much. "I know how much you love surprises."

"Only the good ones." She playfully tapped his nose.

"Okay—how's this for a good surprise?" He pulled printouts of two airline tickets from his pocket and waved them in front of her face.

"What?" She grabbed them and absorbed the contents, her eyes growing round as saucers.

"Ready for a honeymoon?" Rob grinned. "We leave for Europe the end of next week. I'll give my speech in Geneva, and once we get that out of the way, we'll rent a car, tour Switzerland and France, maybe even Italy for a while—whatever your heart desires. So, what do you think, sweetheart?"

She lifted her head and kissed him again. "I couldn't have planned it better myself." She placed her hands on his cheeks and said, "Just the two of us, right?"

"Right, just us two." He wrapped his arms around her and held her tight. "I'm so sorry for putting you through all this."

She looked deep into his eyes. "We both learned a lot from this experience. I made mistakes too. I forgive you—but can you forgive me?"

"Nothing to forgive. But thanks for saying that." He gave her another tender kiss then looked around the shop. "I'll make it up to you—starting right now. What can I do to help you here?"

"Glad you asked!" Laughing, she took his hand and led him to the back room. "For starters, can you carry these chairs out?"

Chapter 52

RACHEL

SATURDAY

Hot summer sun beat down on the arts festival, bringing the temperature well into the eighties as morning melted into afternoon. With no rain to ruin the occasion, the crowd continued to swell, and the Food 'n Fuel booth was one of the busiest spots on the street.

Even with three employees helping out, Rachel and Pete struggled to keep up with demand, especially for their fresh-squeezed lemonade and chicken wings. This past week, she had filled both coolers to the brim, but based on the size of this crowd, it looked like they might still run out of a few items.

All day long, she'd fielded comments on her new hairstyle. She was thankful she no longer had to wear that blasted wig. Maybe someday she'd tell her boys what had happened—but not for a very long time, like after all the grandchildren had graduated. Until then, she'd be free to babysit them, and that's all that mattered—especially now that her life would feel so empty.

She'd never entered into a discussion with other women about needing a man in her life, although she'd heard many of them say they felt that way. Married to Stan all those years, she really didn't know any other way of living until he died. It took her a while to realize how deeply she felt that void. That's why when Frank came into her life, their companionship felt so comfortable. He filled that void, and life was pleasant.

With Tony, though, things had been different. He was the man she *needed*. The man she *wanted*.

If it had been Tony instead of Frank who'd asked her to marry him, she would have said yes without hesitation.

If it had been Tony instead of Frank who had asked her to move to Florida, she would have packed her bags.

Tony, not Frank, was the one who made her swoon.

Too bad he made that brunette swoon too.

"Can we have four pierogies?" Kim Kryzwicki's grating voice caught Rachel off guard.

"Oh! Sure." She filled a plate and handed it to her.

Donny Blue, the sound man, paid. "Keep the change." All of fifteen cents.

Maybe Kim was looking for a man to fill that void too.

Down the street, Rachel could see a small crowd gathered at the spa's long table. Grace sat at the far end, where she and Jesse kept leaning toward one another and laughing. Might be another wedding in the wings.

Marla stood like Vanna White at the other end of the table, engaging with visitors. She was made for that. The men wanted to flirt with her, and the women wanted to look like her. Hannah rang up the sales and Latoya kept everyone laughing while providing quick chair massages.

Warren had breezed by Rachel's booth a while ago. Waving goodbye, he said he had to catch an early flight back to New York. Seemed like it was hardly worth his coming. But maybe that's what people with lots of money do, fly around. Or, as the politicians say, fly over places like Port Mariette.

Across the street, Mitch sat on a bench, his arms stretched out on the back of it and one leg crossed over the other, looking like he was waiting for someone. He'd been there a while, with his eyes fixed on something or someone farther down the street. Maybe he was watching people getting chair massages. That Latoya was a hoot, a real crowd gatherer.

It wasn't like Mitch to sit still. Maybe he was tired from all that ramp work, or was coming down with that flu going around last week.

Sergeant Dan whizzed by Rachel's booth, obviously fully recovered from his case of the flu. He waved frantically at an access van driver and ushered him into Food 'n Fuel's handicap parking space. The driver opened the door and helped some women with wheelchairs and walkers get out of the van. Then Marla's aunt and Suzanne's mother exited, arm in arm and laughing.

Penny rushed over to greet them all.

Rachel could hear her describing how she swept pine needles off the ramp.

Rob and Suzanne strolled by, hand in hand. They stopped to talk with Sergeant Dan. Suzanne introduced the men, then the sergeant called Penny over. Rachel couldn't hear the conversation, but any member of PMBA could guess what they were discussing. Penny bobbed her head a few times as she shook Rob's hand and took his business card, then she left to rejoin the women from Sunset Hills.

Pete dropped a ladleful of red sauce. "Aargh!" It had splashed all over the place. "Lindsey just texted me. She'll be here in a minute."

"I'll clean that up. When she gets here, take a break. Give her a little tour of the festival."

Lindsey showed up with her hair bouncing in a wavy ponytail. "Hi, honey," she said to Pete.

"Hi, honey," he said back, his grin as wide as a watermelon.

Rachel gave Pete a push. "Go. Take a break." She smiled as they walked down the street, looking at each other instead of the artwork.

Andrea stopped by to get some food. "Isn't that wonderful about the honeymoon?"

"What honeymoon?"

Andrea explained about Suzanne and Rob's travel plans, which made Rachel think about Frank. She could have been leaving soon for a honeymoon too.

Sandy and Ted Roczinski were next in line, wanting a whole Italian hoagie and some chips.

As Rachel loaded their plates, Sandy said, "How about coming to bingo this Friday?"

"Sure. Why not?" Rachel struggled to smile. Was it *bingo* she'd created space for? Heaven help her if that's all she had to look forward to.

The line of customers seemed endless, and the quick pace helped keep her mind off herself, her void, and her newly created space.

Pete and Lindsey finally returned. He gave Lindsey a gentle peck. "See you tomorrow." She smiled at him and waved goodbye to Rachel.

Pete went inside Food 'n Fuel then returned with more food.

"You washed your hands, didn't you?"

"Mom, you can't be serious. You think I don't know food safety regulations yet?" He laughed.

"Can't be too careful, especially with being outside."

"Sometimes you're a little *too* careful, Mom. You gotta live a little." He winked at her.

Was he referring to Frank or something else? She'd have to pin him down on that.

She squatted to get more paper plates from a box underneath a table. When she got up, her knees creaked a little. Maybe Pete was right—she did need to live a little now, while she still could.

As she arranged the plates at the end of the counter, the next person in line caught her eye.

"Tony! What on earth are you doing here?" Rachel blurted it out, realizing afterwards how silly she sounded.

Tony spread his hands out on both sides. "Uh, maybe I'm here for an arts festival?"

"Oh, of course." Rachel averted her eyes.

"You got your hair cut." He continued to examine her head. "You've had long hair all your life. How come now?"

"I needed a change."

"Well, that's a change for sure."

"You don't like it."

"I didn't say that."

"Didn't need to."

"Well, you gotta admit, it'll take a little getting used to. After all, you've had long hair forever." He paused, as if realizing he needed to say something nice. "But you look as pretty as always."

He hates it. Good. Glad he hates it.

"You weren't answering my texts or calls."

"I've been busy."

The line at the booth had shortened. "Why don't you take a break, Mom?" Pete said. "Give Tony a personal tour of the festival." He waved her away. "Go on, we can handle it without you for a while."

What excuse could she give? She untied her apron and threw it under the counter. May as well get this conversation over with.

They moved away from the booth and she pointed to the ramp. Like a bored tour guide, she explained the early morning clean-up efforts. "It still looks pretty messy over there, but at least it's passable. If we all hadn't gotten here so early, more than half of our visitors would have been cut off."

They turned and walked down Main Street. "I know you've been busy," Tony said. "But why didn't you get back to me? It's not like you to go silent. I was worried about you." He stopped walking and looked into her eyes. "You're acting a little strange. Are you okay?"

"Like I said, I'm fine. Nothing's wrong with me." She kept moving.

"I guess you're just stressed. This is a big event. Looks like everything's going well, though. Glad you're not having a problem." He reached to put his arm around her.

She backed away. "It's *you*, Tony, who has the problem."

"Huh?"

"Can't seem to stick with the same woman, can you?"

"What the heck are you talking about?" Confusion reigned in his eyes.

"I saw you in your office with that brunette."

"Brunette?" He pulled his chin back. "When was that?"

"Yesterday, when I dropped off the pierogies."

He shook his head. "That was Gia, the manager I rehired." He kept shaking his head. "You must have come into my office when she was crying on my shoulder."

"You had your arms around her."

"She was having a meltdown, Rachel. I needed to calm her down so she wouldn't quit on me."

"Quit? She just started working for you again."

"Yeah, but she was talking crazy. She said she wanted to move back south, she'd made a mistake moving back to Pittsburgh, she thinks she's going through early menopause, blah, blah, blah, like I really want to hear all that personal stuff."

"Oh!" Rachel lay a hand over her heart. What an idiot she was. "Well, if she's that unstable, maybe it'd better for you if she did quit."

"But then I wouldn't be able to turn Signore's over to my son until I hired someone else, and it's nearly impossible to hire experienced restaurant managers. Gia may not be perfect, but at least I know how to manage her moods."

Rachel looked down. "Oh. I guess I let my imagination get carried away." Like it was a note on pink paper.

He lifted Rachel's chin with the tips of his fingers. "And if Gia quits, then I wouldn't have any time to spend with you. With your sexy new short haircut which I love." He tipped his head to the side. "What made you do that, by the way?"

"Temporary insanity?" Rachel shrugged.

"Understandable," Tony said. "This arts festival turned into a much bigger deal than I ever expected." He took her hand and they sauntered from table to table, chatting about the works of art. Midway down the street, he stopped at the lone empty storefront. "Future home of Sweet Treats!" He extended his arm with flair.

"You're really going to do it?"

Tony grinned as they walked over to the storefront. "It's official. I signed a lease with Herbie about an hour ago." His grin got wider. "And I'm going to talk with Suzanne next."

"Suzanne? Why?" Her stomach churned. Was this going to be another game he played?

"You said she'll be putting her mother's house up for sale soon. Once I'm done with Signore's, I don't want to have a daily commute for my candy business. I want to have time for ... other things." He pulled her close and wrapped his arms around her. "Like my sweet angel."

Rachel threw her arms around his neck and looked deep into his dark brown eyes.

"Time is short," he said. "Let's spend it well."

"Together." They said it in unison and laughed the way people who are falling in love laugh.

He kissed her long and hard, and to Rachel, it seemed the entire town went silent watching them.

But she didn't care. She kissed him back.

About the Author

Chris Posti's debut novel, *Falling Apart, Falling for You* (Elk Lake Publishing, 2022), won multiple awards, including the Christian Market Book Award for Contemporary Novel of the Year, as well as Finalist/Third Place Selah Award Winner for Contemporary Women's Fiction, Finalist in Next Generation Indie Book Awards, Finalist in The Author Zone (TAZ) Awards, and Honorable Mention in Angel Book Awards.

Chris is a member of three writing organizations—American Christian Fiction Writers (ACFW), Women's Fiction Writers Association (WFWA), and Pennwriters. She lives with her husband in a suburb south of Pittsburgh, PA. If she's not writing, she's probably playing with her grandsons, creating something artsy, or helping to organize her next high school reunion.

DEAR READERS—

Thank you for reading *Maybe Now, Maybe Never*. I hope you related to these women coming to grips with the many unexpected changes in their lives. Even more so, I hope their stories encouraged and inspired you.

I welcome your questions and comments, and if you are part of a book club or an organization seeking speakers, I'd be delighted to speak to your group in person or online about any aspect of fiction and nonfiction writing. My email is chris@chrisposti.com and I'd love to hear from you.

You can sign up for my (very rare) newsletters on my website, chrisposti.com. If you sign up, I'll send you something surprising!

PS—If you enjoyed the book, would you please take two minutes to write a brief review on Amazon? It would mean so much. Thank you!

QUESTIONS FOR DISCUSSION

1. Have you ever worn a wig, gotten a facelift or a tummy tuck, or done anything significant to alter your appearance? How did it affect you and others? Would you do it again? What did you learn from the experience?
1. Marla admits she has backslidden in her faith. She is surely not the only one who has! What are some signs you or others may have backslidden? What helps you or others get back on track?
2. Rachel has a habit of leaping to (wrong) conclusions about people. Why do you suppose a person might have such a habit? How might one overcome it?
3. In the end, Marla decides to stay longer in Port Mariette so she can strengthen her relationship with Grace, her daughter by birth. Do you think Marla made a wise decision?
4. Suzanne's husband Rob has a caretaker personality. Benefits? Downsides? Do you ever feel like you take care of everyone else but no one is there for you?

5. Aunt Adele lives in an assisted living home but manages to stay youthful in her behavior, her conversations, and her physical body. How do you imagine she achieved this?

6. If someone presented you with tickets for a European vacation just one week from today, would you have reacted as Suzanne did? Why was she thrilled instead of dismayed?

7. Only a little more than a year after her husband's sudden passing, Rachel has already formed what appears to be a relationship that will endure with Tony from her high school days. Do you think she is relying too much on past memories? Or perhaps she's looking through rose-colored glasses? How can widows and widowers decide they are ready to have a new relationship? Is companionship a better alternative than remarrying later in life?

8. Grace shocked Marla when she confessed to being lonely. Who in your circle of family and friends might be lonelier than you've realized? How can you find out if someone is lonely, and what might you do for or with them? If it's you who feels lonely, how can you reach out to others?

9. Rachel knows her commandments—do you? Can you recite them? If you have to look them up, you might notice the Catholic version of the Ten Commandments, established by St. Augustine, is slightly different from the Protestant version, and even within denominations, there are some variations.

Falling Apart, Falling for You

Made in the USA
Monee, IL
22 January 2024